A Green Journey

Other books by Jon Hassler

THE LOVE HUNTER
SIMON'S NIGHT
STAGGERFORD

A Green Journey

JON HASSLER

William Morrow and Company, Inc. · New York

Portions of this novel appeared originally in
McCall's Magazine as "The Holy War of Agatha McGee"
in July, 1978 and "The Holiday Vigil of Agatha McGee"
in January, 1979.

Library of Congress Cataloging in Publication Data

Hassler, Jon.
A green journey.

I. Title.
PS3558.A726G7   1985   813'.54   84-91152
ISBN 0-688-03982-0

Printed in the United States of America

First Edition

1 2 3 4 5 6 7 8 9 10

BOOK DESIGN BY LINEY LI

To my mother
Ellen Callinan Hassler

And to the memory of my father
Leo B. Hassler
1896–1984

The author is grateful to
the John Simon Guggenheim Foundation for the
generous award of a fellowship in
connection with this work.

Things throw light on things,
And all the stones have wings.

—Theodore Roethke

A Green Journey

1

ON THE NIGHT BEFORE CHRISTMAS, a snowy night with wind in the forecast, Janet Raft arrived at Agatha McGee's house on River Street.

Janet's father helped her out of the car, carried her suitcase up onto the front porch and took off his cap before he rang the doorbell. Facing Miss McGee always made him nervous. Thirty years ago Miss McGee had been his sixth-grade teacher at St. Isidore's Elementary, and he remembered how cross she used to become when he dotted his e's or failed to memorize his catechism or forgot the square root of something. He remembered, too, the summer he returned home to Staggerford from the Army and Miss McGee hired him to paint her house and how worked up she got when he dribbled paint. He dribbled quite a lot of it. "Look here, Francis," she kept saying—everybody else in town called him Frank—"you've got paint on my window glass and paint on my stone foundation. Why, you've even got paint on my geraniums." And now after all these years of falling short of Miss McGee's expectations, he was presenting her with his daughter Janet—seventeen, unmarried and nine months pregnant.

Agatha McGee opened the door. She was a slight, white-haired woman in her middle sixties. The smile she wore this Christmas Eve was two parts festive and one part grim.

"Come in, Janet, and please hang your coat in the closet over there. Come in, Francis, and set her suitcase over there at the foot of the stairs. Goodness, aren't either of you wearing anything on your heads? It's a night for catching cold, Janet, and a cold is the last thing you want in your condition. Now turn around and start right home, Francis, you've got twenty miles

13

to drive and the radio says practically every road in Minnesota will soon be drifting shut."

Mr. Raft did as he was told, but on his way out the door Agatha called him back.

"Aren't you going to kiss your daughter good-bye?"

He stepped into the living room once more, gave Janet a peck on the forehead, then paused for further instruction.

"That's fine, Francis, now be off with you. I'll keep you posted by phone."

"We haven't got a phone, but the neighbors do. Janet knows the number."

"Very good, and Merry Christmas to you and the girls."

"Same to you." He put on his cap and fled across the porch and down the steps and into the swirling night.

Agatha closed the door and regarded Janet, who had hung up her coat and was standing awkwardly beside her suitcase. She wore maternity jeans and a summery, short-sleeved maternity top. Her brown hair curled at her shoulders, and her brown eyes were cast down. She folded her hands over her middle as though to hide the great part of her that protruded into the room. She was feeling as uneasy as her father had felt, for she, too, having gone through the sixth grade under the command of Miss McGee, would have preferred staying in someone else's house. But when Dr. Maitland had asked Janet if she had friends in town, she couldn't think of any. "Well, your time is near and there's bad weather coming and I can't have you stranded in the country," the doctor had said. "I'm sure Miss McGee will take you in. She speaks of you as one of her most promising students." There had been a hint of regret or resignation in the doctor's voice; promise unfulfilled—that might have been the implication. "Her house is only a block and a half from the hospital," he had added.

Now, installed in that house, Janet said, without raising her eyes, "Hello, Miss McGee."

"Please look me in the eye and say that, Janet."

She did so. It had been a long time since she had looked this closely at her old teacher, whose eyebrows were the color her hair used to be: gingery. She looked slighter than ever these days, her shoulders narrower, her face paler, her eyes sharper.

She wore a simple yet rich-looking lavender dress with a stand-up collar and tiny cameo earrings. This was no classroom outfit; she was dressed this way, Janet assumed, for midnight Mass.

"Hello, Miss McGee."

"Oh, that's ever so much better. You see, this is no time for hangdog expressions. This is a time for strength. You're about to give birth in a blizzard, and the poor baby's father is a thousand miles away and God knows if he'll come home and marry you, and furthermore if you insist on keeping the baby you've got years of great responsibility ahead of you. So promise you'll refrain from self-pity. Promise you'll be strong."

Janet gathered her strength. "I promise." She smiled a small, bright smile.

"Wonderful. Now I'm happy you've arrived safe and sound. You're a bit late, you know. I was afraid you were stuck in a ditch."

"We opened presents before I came, and I guess it took longer than we planned. I'll show you my presents. They're in my suitcase."

The suitcase was heavy, and Janet shared the weight with Agatha as they climbed the stairs to the room Agatha let out to lodgers from time to time. They set the suitcase on the bed, and Janet opened it and drew out her gifts—a hankie, a bracelet and a paperback book from her three younger sisters. "And wait till you see this—it's from Dad and my Aunt Marge and Uncle Bert." She carefully unfolded a lacy white baptismal dress. "For the baby."

Agatha took the dress and shook out the folds. She held it at arm's length. "My, how exquisite. How beautiful."

"Dad and my Aunt Marge said I should ask you to be the baby's godmother."

"Oh? But that must be your decision, Janet, not your father's or your aunt's."

"But I agree with them. I'm having it baptized Stephanie if it's a girl and Stephen if it's a boy. Stephanie was my mother's name."

"And the baby's father? Have you consulted him about this?"

"Oh, yes, Eddie says it's fine with him." This was a lie. The thought of Eddie Lofgren caused her cheeks to color slightly as she gazed past Miss McGee and recalled that parched week last spring when Eddie turned up at the Lofgren farm down the road from her own and took her on dates to the movies. Eddie had been born and raised three hundred miles south of here, in Omaha, but Janet knew him from the several summers when he had come to spend a month or so with his cousins on the farm. Last spring he had turned up wearing an Air Force uniform. It was late March. Janet's father and all the other farmers were talking of nothing but the dry season—the winds were blowing the fields away—but Janet was untouched by all that fret, for she was busy learning sex from Eddie, though not enough about its precautionary aspects. She loved sex. She loved Eddie. For two weeks Eddie loved her, he said. Then he was gone, to an air base in Greenland, and Janet was pregnant. Her father was enraged. He swore he'd take his shotgun after that blackhearted young bastard in the pansy-blue uniform, never mind if he was in Greenland or Timbuktu, but Janet argued against vengeance, and so did her aunt and uncle. Being with child had caused Janet neither panic nor grief, only an occasional day of vague sadness. It was her destiny, she knew, to have a husband and children, and if the order was reversed, so what? She was determined to be a doting mother. Anyhow, fatherless babies were not a rarity among her friends and relatives. Aunt Marge, in fact, had given birth twice before she had married. Time passed, and her father's anger cooled. Now, with the birth imminent, it disappeared.

Agatha draped the baptismal dress respectfully over her arm. "Tomorrow I'll press out the wrinkles."

"*Will* you be godmother, Miss McGee? We'd all be so honored."

"Yes, indeed. And *I'm* the one who is honored."

Later, after coffee and the weather news on television, they set off for midnight Mass together in Agatha's clean, old Plymouth. Between the parking lot and church Agatha, watching Janet's ungainly waddle through the deepening snow, felt her sympathy turn to pity. She linked her arm in Janet's and said, "You know, keeping the baby isn't your only alternative. There are agencies that see to finding good homes for babies."

"That's what Dr. Maitland keeps telling me. And the social worker, too. But there's no way I'd give up this baby, Miss McGee. I'll get along just fine. Even without Eddie—I mean, even if Eddie doesn't get home for a long time. Aunt Marge lives close by, and she's had four babies of her own."

"As you wish." Agatha wasn't surprised by the girl's resolution. Running through the Raft clan, along with the several paternity puzzles, was a tradition of stubbornness.

St. Isidore's was packed to the walls. Janet and Agatha were ushered into the choir loft, where they sat on the last two folding chairs. The organ boomed, the choir stood up to sing, and out onto the altar streamed twelve acolytes, a cloud of incense and the pastor, Father Finn. It was a fine ceremony, to Agatha's way of thinking. In the old days, you never judged Catholic ritual—a Mass was a Mass. But nowadays, churchgoing could be a horrifying surprise—guitars on the altar, female acolytes, charismatics babbling in tongues. Lucky for St. Isidore's, thought Agatha, that Father Finn remained the pastor year after year; he approved of change when Rome gave him no choice (Mass in English, Communion in the hand), but when left on his own he was too stable, according to Agatha and half her fellow parishioners, to depart from tradition. Or too dull-witted, according to the other half. And lucky for the diocese of Berrington as a whole that Bishop Swayles stayed in charge long past retirement age. Such a dear old reactionary, Bishop Swayles. Surely his replacement, when the dreaded time came, would be some progressive hotshot like the current bishop of Duluth, who last month had officiated at a polka Mass in his cathedral. Now, sitting beside Janet, Agatha whispered her thanks to God that tonight everything at St. Isidore's was so lovely and orthodox.

During the "Gloria," a teenage couple climbed into the loft, holding hands and whispering. They stood near Janet's chair and spent most of the Mass in a modified embrace, gazing into one another's eyes. The boy was in constant motion—his foot tapping, his shoulders revolving as though he heard a fast piece of music in his head. The girl chewed gum.

How sacrilegious, thought Agatha, but how enviable they must look to Janet.

How dreamy, thought Janet, but how sacrilegious they must look to Miss McGee.

"That's Janet Raft," whispered the girl. "Look how big she is, and she's not married."

The boyfriend craned his neck for a better view of Janet, then whispered, "What a bummer."

During the rest of the ceremony Agatha asked God to forgive Janet (after all, a sin was a sin) and to bless the baby with good health and to keep all the Rafts, little and big, in His care.

When they returned home in the wee hours, Agatha sat down to another Christmas Mass, this one on television, the Pope in charge, and Janet plodded up the stairs to bed. She stopped on the landing and said, "Wouldn't it be nice if my baby was born on Christmas Day?"

"That would be a blessed event indeed, the birthday of our Savior."

"But I don't feel anything yet."

"Well, the twenty-sixth would be nice, too. That's the Feast of St. Stephen."

Lying in bed, Janet heard a hymn to the Virgin Mary drifting faintly upstairs from the television. She thought about virginity, Miss McGee's in particular. She wondered why the woman had never married. She wondered if ever in her whole life any man had kissed her. Surely not, she decided, falling asleep.

About kisses, Janet was correct: Agatha had never been kissed, at least not with ardor. The reason Agatha had never married was that when she was young and had the opportunities she hadn't felt the need, and later, feeling the need, she had no opportunities. Her best opportunity had been a young man named Preston Warner, who would have kissed Agatha with ardor in 1938 if she had permitted him to. "But I can't marry a farmer," she had told him at the annual Grange picnic the summer she was twenty-five, and along with Preston Warner she rejected a house, a barn, a herd of Guernseys and a hundred acres of fertile soil. "I was born to teach, not to churn," she had said, not realizing that he was her last chance, though it's doubtful that realizing it would have changed her mind. She loved classrooms. Barns made her sneeze.

2

THE BABY ARRIVED neither on the twenty-fifth nor on the twenty-sixth. Nor on the twenty-seventh (John the Apostle) nor on the twenty-eighth (the Holy Innocents). On the twenty-ninth (Becket of Canterbury) Janet felt a pain, but it was gas.

The Christmas blizzard had never materialized. The entire week remained dark and dispiriting. By the thirtieth of December Janet's strength had begun to wear down. Instead of helping Agatha around the house as she had been doing, she gave herself up to fatigue and self-pity. She ached all over. In the late afternoon she sat in the dark living room and absently turned her sleepy eyes to the window, following the occasional car passing along River Street, its tires squeaking on the packed snow.

"At least turn on the light in there and pretend you're reading," Agatha called from the kitchen. "I can't stand the sight of dejection in my front room."

Janet switched on a lamp and picked up the *Staggerford Weekly*. She absently scanned a page or two. Then she struggled out of her chair and lumbered into the kitchen.

"Look, Miss McGee—all these gifts for the first baby of the New Year! There's just loads and loads of great stuff, and I *know* my baby will be the one. I just *know* it!"

She spread the newspaper on the kitchen table, and Agatha leaned over her shoulder to read. This was the annual New Year promotion by the Staggerford merchants, and pictured in a full-page display were the many gifts to be showered on the New Year baby—a brass-wheeled bassinet and four dozen disposable diapers, a rattle, a rocking horse, booties and much more.

"How grand." Agatha calculated the value of the merchandise. "It must come to nearly two hundred dollars. But don't build yourself up for disappointment, Janet. Babies will be born when they will be born."

"Mine will be born on New Year's Day. I just *know* it!"

Janet tore the page from the paper, and during the evening and throughout the next day she wore it to tatters by continually unfolding it, reading it, folding it and returning it to the pocket of her maternity dress.

"Janet, those are mere earthly possessions," Agatha cautioned. "You mustn't become too fond of them."

"But they're exactly the things a mother *needs*," said Janet, unfolding the page once again.

True, thought Agatha, and who was more needy than Janet?

Janet returned to the living room and saw her father and two of her sisters approaching the house. They came in, spoke politely to Agatha and stood on three sides of Janet, puzzling over her lack of labor pains. Francis Raft, following a few moments of silence, turned to Agatha and suggested they all go out to dinner at the Jiffystop Lunchroom. Agatha declined but urged them to take Janet; it would pep her up.

As the front door closed behind the Rafts, Agatha heard the back door burst open and a voice call to her through the kitchen.

"Agatha, I heard all about it from Bertha and Addie, you've had that pregnant Raft girl here for a week. I got home on the noon bus. I tell you, Agatha, eight days in Berrington is my limit. They don't have the same channels we do."

Lillian Kite came into the living room carrying her plastic bag of knitting. She was Agatha's neighbor from across the alley, a large, loose-jawed woman wearing tonight her pink, quilted, ankle-length coat and her dead husband's large deerskin mittens. She had white hair, a red complexion and a desperate need to know everything that had transpired in Staggerford while she was gone. She had spent the holidays with her daughter Imogene, a librarian employed by the city of Berrington.

"Addie says she's good and big. I just love a good, big pregnancy, and to think I've had one right out my back door and I had to be gone all the while. Bertha wonders how you can let a Raft in your house for a single night, let alone a whole week." Bertha and Addie, widows down the block, belonged to Lillian's network of newsgatherers. "She said it was a Raft that went berserk back in the forties, remember, and beat up that man in the carnival."

"That isn't the Raft I've taken in."

"And there was a Raft used to work for Lyle at the state park, I think it was Janet's father—isn't his name Frank?—and more than once he came to work with a hangover, Lyle used to say."

"Nor is *he* the one I took in. Come into the kitchen, Lillian. If you haven't started supper, you can eat with me."

"I was thinking of heating up a chop."

"Heat it up tomorrow. I have a slice of ham big enough for the two of us, and some nice butter beans."

"Why not?" Lillian threw off her mittens and coat and sat down at the kitchen table. From her bag she drew out her knitting-in-progress, something tubular and very long in blue and green, together with needles and a ball of yarn. "Isn't it a shame the way we let our cooking go, Agatha? We never cook up a decent meal the way we used to in the old days. Lyle's appetite was wonderful right up until the end."

"Speak for yourself. It's a myth that I ever cooked a decent meal." Agatha cranked open a can of butter beans. "What's that you're knitting?"

"A cap."

"But it's five feet long."

"A stocking cap."

"Won't it drag on the ground?"

"It winds around like a scarf. You see them in Berrington."

Agatha set her ham to frying and her beans to boiling. She stood at the stove, watching Lillian knit.

"Would you like a glass of wine?"

"I'd die for a glass of wine. Imogene had me drinking crazy juices the whole time. She's into health foods."

"How is Imogene?"

"Fine. Bossy. Says I watch too much TV."

Agatha opened a bottle of the plum wine she had made last summer, using wild plums she had picked on the banks of the Badbattle River.

"Bertha says the baby's a week overdue. I was two weeks overdue with Imogene. I've always thought it's good for the baby's brain if it's overdue. It's like holding them back a year in kindergarten."

Agatha sat down and they devoted their attention to the deep red wine for a minute, Agatha sipping, Lillian smacking her lips.

"You were overdue yourself, Agatha. I remember your mother telling my mother when we were girls. Most of the smart people I know were overdue, and that's why I think the brain is formed mostly during the last week or so of pregnancy." More swallowing, more smacking. "I came on time."

Agatha closed her eyes, nodding.

"There's no better example than my Imogene, she's been smart as a whip since day one, and day one was fourteen days late."

"True," said Agatha. She remembered Imogene as a girl, very brainy, a humorless bookworm from age five, and to this day strikingly unattractive in a graceless, gangly way. Imogene had got her degree in library science and until last year had been in charge of the Staggerford Public Library. Now she was working in Berrington for twice the money. Some thought her main reason for moving was to look for a man, but Agatha didn't think that. Agatha knew a lifelong spinster when she saw one, and Imogene, at forty, had all the marks. Self-sufficiency was one, self-absorption was another; not to mention imperiousness.

Agatha set the table, served the meal. As they ate, Lillian relayed additional information from Addie and Bertha: a heart attack, a car accident, two funerals and a broken hip. Then it was back to Imogene:

"You ought to see the Berrington Public Library, Agatha, it's bigger than a supermarket. You wonder where Imogene finds the time to read all those books."

Agatha was brought up short by this remark, realizing that here was another way in which Lillian's view of life was askew. Because she was a stranger to books while her bookish daughter was such a compendium of abstruse knowledge, Lillian misunderstood the work of librarians. She thought librarians understood all the books they checked out—their curative powers, their side effects—the way doctors knew the drugs they prescribed.

Lillian resumed her news report—a chimney fire, a litter of kittens, a pilfered newspaper dispenser in front of the Hub Cafe. Agatha only half listened. Lillian, Agatha's dear, tiresome neighbor since girlhood, had been a widow now for several years. Throughout his career Lillian's husband, Lyle, a state park ranger, had spent more time in his state park than was required of him, and it wasn't hard for Agatha to figure out why—Lillian was powerfully boring. It had long ago become clear to Agatha that she and Lillian were friends not because they held interests or experiences in common but because for nearly seven decades their back doors had been facing one another across an alley. At least once a week, usually on Saturday mornings, Lillian and Agatha met to share a pot of coffee and whatever they knew of their neighbors, and that was exactly as much of Lillian as Agatha could stand. She knew, of course, that a mind as frivolous as Lillian's was not without its virtues. The woman was honest, simplehearted and enviably placid. Nevertheless, it was a mind spongy with sentiment and empty of logic, and the light it gave off was so dim that it sometimes made Agatha shudder the way she used to when she was six and afraid of the dark.

After the meal, after helping Agatha clear the table, Lillian put on her coat, stuffed her five-foot cap and needles and ball of yarn into her bag and drew on her mittens.

"Will you come and watch television with me, Agatha?" It was a standing invitation.

"No, thanks, I have schoolwork." It was a standing excuse.

Lillian went to the door and opened it. A cold draft came in from the back porch and swept across the kitchen floor. "I should have worn something on my head, they say twenty below tonight."

"You have a cap in your bag."

"Oh, so I do." Lillian took out the cap and pulled it down over her ears. A knitting needle embedded in the stitches lay across her brow, and a length of blue yarn ran down between her eyes to the bag in her hand.

Agatha turned away.

"Oh, I almost forgot, Addie says the Raft baby's father is that cousin of the Lofgrens from Omaha. They were seen around together nine months ago."

Agatha shrugged.

"Did Janet mention him at all?"

"Yes, she dropped his name a time or two and implied he'd return and do right by her, but that was only for my benefit. She's seen the last of him, I'm sure. He's in Greenland, fixing airplanes."

"Dear, oh, dear, who will she find for a husband, being a mother and a Raft besides?"

Lillian went out calling goodnight, her cap hanging down to her heels.

3

As THOUGH BY AN ACT OF WILL, Janet's pains began shortly before midnight on New Year's Eve. By 1:00 A.M., Agatha was
guiding her over and around the hazards of the dark street—
patches of ice on the sidewalk, drunks emerging from house
parties—and into the hospital. By 2:00 A.M. the pains were very
frequent, and Dr. Maitland was summoned from home. By
three the pains had subsided. The doctor took a nap. At four,
the pains meant business, and the doctor followed Janet and
two nurses into the delivery room. All this time Agatha kept
watch, first in the labor room with Janet, then in the waiting
room with Daniel Buckingham, Jr., whose wife was also about
to give birth.

Daniel Buckingham, Jr., was a pudgy man of thirty-five with
liquor on his breath and a diamond in his necktie. His family
owned Buckingham Furniture. "Have you someone in sur-
gery?" he asked. He sat deep in a soft chair with his hands in
his pockets.

"A friend in delivery," said Agatha. "Janet Raft from the
country. Perhaps you know the family."

"Ah, yes, the Rafts. We hired one as a clerk one time. Not
the most reliable. And this one is unmarried, I'll bet."

Agatha nodded curtly.

Daniel Buckingham, Jr., burped. He said, "It's a shame the
way people like that reproduce themselves." In his hazy vision
he did not recognize Agatha's squint of anger. He mistook the
narrowing of her eyes for sleepiness, and he persisted. He said,
"Scum of the earth."

She sprang off her chair. Her eyes were small as sparks, but
brighter.

"In the sight of God, this baby of Janet Raft's is as sacred

25

and noble as any Buckingham that ever walked the face of the earth!" She proclaimed this with her finger in the air, and when she had spoken she was too angry to sit down. She strode out into the corridor and was met by a nurse with good news— Janet's baby was an eight-pound boy with a lot of hair: the first birth of the New Year.

Down the hall came Janet on a wheeled cart. Stephen was pink and wrinkled and sleeping at her breast. Janet's smile was groggy. "Stephen is the New Year baby," she mumbled.

"So he is," said Agatha. "How providential."

She went home, and after phoning Mr. Raft's neighbors in the country, dropped into bed. When she returned to the hospital at noon, there were two babies behind the glass, lying on their stomachs and looking somewhat cross-eyed at one another. Daniel Buckingham III was bald and smaller than Stephen Raft and three hours younger.

Daniel Buckingham III was announced as the New Year baby. The story appeared on the front page of the *Weekly*, published the day Janet left the hospital. Standing at the check-out desk with Agatha holding Stephen and her father signing welfare forms, Janet saw the headline: *Booty Belongs to Buckingham.* Since the birth of Stephen, Janet had given the New Year gifts scarcely a thought. Her heart, in this first flush of maternal joy, contained little room for what Agatha had called "mere earthly possessions," so it was with very little resentment that she showed the newspaper to Agatha, who was outraged.

"Horrors! They've made a mistake. I know whom to see about this. We'll go directly to Buckingham Furniture."

"I'd rather not," said Janet. "I'd rather get right home with Stephen."

"This won't take long," said Agatha. They bundled up the baby, stepped out into the bitter January wind and got into the Rafts' cold, rust-eaten car. Downtown Francis Raft double-parked, as Agatha told him to, in front of the furniture store, and the three of them went inside with the baby. Agatha asked for Daniel Buckingham, Jr., and they were led through a maze of chairs and sofas to the manager's office.

Daniel Buckingham, Jr., sober, was a bit wary. Unlike half

the people in this town, he had not been a student of Agatha's (he had attended public elementary), but her power was well known to him. He stepped out of his office and looked from Janet (who now held the baby) to her father, and then in order to melt the icy gleam in Agatha's eye he decided to use the folksy approach. He removed his glasses, put on a smile and said, "Good morning, Agatha." As soon as he uttered her first name he regretted it. He had heard her called Agatha by certain other people who had somehow earned the privilege, but on his own tongue it sounded clumsy. Agatha, to stress his error, replied, "Good morning, Junior."

He removed his smile and replaced his glasses.

"I want you to meet Francis Raft and his daughter Janet. And here in this blanket"—she folded it back to reveal a pink cheek and a brown eye—"is my godson, Stephen Raft, who was born on New Year's Day, approximately three hours ahead of your own son, to whom the New Year's gifts were mistakenly given."

Daniel Buckingham bit his lip, remembering his rash words in the waiting room.

Francis Raft made himself at home in a deep Naugahyde recliner. Janet handed him the baby.

Agatha continued, "It was a serious oversight, Mr. Buckingham, but the remedy is simple. You are an officer of the Chamber of Commerce; simply pick up your phone and tell the merchants to gather together a duplicate set of gifts and deliver them to Mr. Raft's car, which is waiting outside your store with the motor running."

"But, Miss McGee—"

"And tell them to hurry, Mr. Buckingham. We are double-parked."

"But let me explain. We know all about this baby, and it's not the *official* New Year baby. Look . . . the Chamber of Commerce has been honoring the New Year Baby for many years, and it has never been our policy to award gifts for—in plain words—an illegitimate birth."

Janet edged around behind Agatha and implored in a shy whisper, "Please, I'd rather just go home and forget the whole thing."

"Mr. Buckingham, I have never heard of anything so deceitful. Show me the stipulation in the newspaper that says the baby of an unwed mother is not qualified for these gifts."

"It's an unwritten policy, Miss McGee. The Chamber has always felt that unwed mothers don't want the publicity."

"We're not asking for the publicity, we're asking for the merchandise."

"But you see, the merchants expect the publicity when the gifts are awarded. They are promised a front-page article."

"Which they already have—in today's paper. Now please get on the phone and tell your colleagues they're guilty of the worst kind of discrimination, namely, prejudice against the poor and helpless. By disqualifying Stephen Raft, they have violated his civil rights. I'm sure the American Civil Liberties Union would take a special interest in a case like this."

"But, Miss McGee—"

Stephen began to cry.

"And tell them to hurry over here with the gifts. The Rafts are twenty miles from home, and it's nearly time for the baby's next feeding."

Daniel Buckingham turned and looked into his office. He frowned at his phone.

Janet pleaded softly, "Let's forget it, Miss McGee. I don't really need the gifts. Aunt Marge has diapers and things."

"What's got into you, Janet? Don't you realize these gifts are rightfully yours?"

"But they're only earthly possessions," Janet reminded her.

"Not anymore. Now they're incriminating evidence."

Daniel Buckingham turned back to Agatha. "I really don't think I have the power to do what you ask. Ray Keegan of Staggerford Drug is your man. He's president of the Chamber this year."

"By all means call Raymond Keegan. He's a well-meaning man. His spelling was atrocious as a boy, but he always meant well. Tell him it's his four dozen disposable diapers we're interested in."

Stephen, shrieking, punched his way out of his blanket, and Francis gave him back to Janet.

Daniel Buckingham sat at his desk, dialed his phone and

asked for Ray. Then he hung up and looked at Miss McGee with relief. "Ray's not in."

Stephen screamed and coughed and kicked.

"I can see that this is going to require more time than we can spare, Mr. Buckingham, so what we'll do is take your store's brass-wheeled bassinet now and return in a few days for the rest of the gifts."

"Now, wait a minute—that bassinet is a fifty-seven-dollar item. Surely you don't expect one of those."

"Think how awkward it will be for you when I tell everyone at the next Sodality meeting and at the next PTA meeting, to say nothing of my neighbors and friends, how all that merchandise went wrongfully to your very own son. It will look like crass favoritism, Mr. Buckingham, and people will think twice before doing business with you."

He made a sour face.

"Furthermore, the Sodality has been put in charge of refurnishing St. Isidore's rectory. It would be so much easier for us to buy the furniture here than go to the city for it."

He scratched his nose and murmured, "I believe we have one more bassinet in stock. I'll have a clerk take it out to your car."

"And when you speak to the merchants, tell them not to pull any fast ones. We have last week's ad with which to verify what they give us. Good-bye, Mr. Buckingham."

"Mind you, I'm not making any promises. I can't speak for the entire Chamber, you know. All I can do is my best."

"Your best is all we ask." Agatha had turned and was leading the Rafts to the door. She called back, "As I tell my twelve-year-olds, Mr. Buckingham, you can save yourself a peck of trouble by doing things right the first time."

As Francis Raft and the clerk folded the collapsible legs of the bassinet and loaded it into the back seat, Janet and Agatha stood at the car, their backs to the wind, and set a tentative date for Stephen's christening.

Then Francis got in behind the wheel and Janet said, "Come on, Miss McGee, we'll give you a ride home."

"No, thank you, I could use the exercise."

"Well, how can I thank you? School starts Monday, and you've given up your entire vacation for me."

"Keep your baby warm and clean, Janet, and hold him in your arms as much as possible. Now get along with you and be a good mother."

As they drove away, Janet waved and her father tipped his cap.

Watching them go, Agatha said a silent prayer that Janet might be equal to the challenges ahead of her; then she turned and went into the Hub Cafe. She sat at the table in the front window and ordered coffee and a cookie. She watched the people pass along the street. She watched the streetlights come on in the early twilight. She sipped her coffee slowly, savoring her first moments of peace since Christmas Eve. She turned her mind to her schoolwork, the lesson plans she would have to devise and the great many papers she would have to correct before classes resumed on Monday. Normally she found schoolwork absorbing, but this afternoon it struck her as vaguely tiresome. The first thing she had to correct was a spelling test—how paltry compared to helping a new life into the world. She felt hollow. She felt as if some part of herself had been removed and carried away in the Rafts' rust-eaten car, some vital organ such as her heart. She knew enough about being alone to realize that this feeling was deeper and broader than loneliness. More than once she had taken lodgers into her house and felt lonely after they left. But loneliness was always dispelled in the classroom; students were her solace. Today, however, schoolwork seemed trivial.

By force of will she overcame this somber state. She blamed it on fatigue. She paid for her coffee and cookie, left a twenty-cent tip and set off for home. Passing the brightly lit window of Buckingham Furniture, she smiled to think how ironic it was that her interest in the New Year gifts had intensified as Janet's had diminished. Then she stopped, arrested by a new suspicion of foul play. She turned and went into the store.

Daniel Buckingham saw her coming. He strode forward, wearing a tentative smile. Was it too much to suppose she had come to thank him?

"Thank you, Daniel, for your efforts on behalf of justice."

He beamed. "You're welcome, Agatha." Her first name sounded right this time.

"And now, Daniel, exactly how many authentic New Year babies has the Chamber cheated in the past?"

His smile faded. He looked away. "I've heard it said that we overlooked two."

"And the Chamber knows who they are?"

"Well, of course there are hospital records, but, Agatha, they're probably in their teens by now. What would they want with rattles and booties and things like that?"

"You're right, Daniel. Cash will be fine."

She pulled the door shut and continued on her way, against the wind.

4

In her front room Agatha pulled a chair up to the ornate walnut library table that for several decades had stood in her father's law office on Main Street. She opened her lesson plan book and imagined the next nine-week period, the term of Greek mythology, long division, northern European geography and other such material requiring endless drilling and testing. As she paged through her textbook titled *Economic Geography for Young Readers,* she wished she had something more interesting to do with her evening. She was unable to call up much enthusiasm for North Sea oil or the flax of Norway. In fact, the textbook itself seemed to have faded or been bleached in the year since she looked at it last; she could have sworn the pictures of Scandinavia had been in full color, but here they lay before her in black and white.

She reconsidered Lillian's standing invitation, but television, even in color, was numbing, as was Lillian. She thought of Addie and Bertha. No, they were both addicted to seven-card rummy. Then she thought of her mail. She hadn't checked her mailbox when she came home. She went out onto the front porch and found three letters—the monthly electric bill, a late Christmas card missent to Montana and a gray envelope from Ireland that, as always, gave her heart a little kick. She returned to her study table and laid the letters in a row before her. Though she usually tore into the Irish letter first, tonight she decided to save it till last and let her excitement build.

She opened the electric bill for December. Goodness, what an expense to have another person in the house. Alone, she was in the habit of burning one light at a time. Janet left lights on all over the place.

She opened the Christmas card. It came from Catherine Allen, a former student who was now a nun teaching sixth grade in Illinois. Her Christmas message each year struck Agatha as oddly calculating for a nun. This one was no exception:

> Greetings from the nunnery, where I've concluded that the best thing about being a Dominican is the way the order takes care of you when you retire, which I will do ten years from next spring, and I can hardly wait, sixth graders being such brats.

Agatha thought back: Could Catherine Allen be in her mid-fifties already? Yes, she had been in Agatha's first class. Agatha had been twenty-two that year, her students twelve. Well, best of luck to her—retirement wasn't easy. Agatha had already tried it. Last spring she had retired as an act of protest against the changes in St. Isidore's curriculum, from which religion had been eroding for a long time. After a couple of years on the verge of jumping ship, what finally pushed her over the side was a memo from the principal's office announcing two outrageous innovations: the venerable and immutable "Baltimore Catechism" was to be scrapped, and students would no longer be required to attend daily Mass.

"I cannot remain here and be party to the secularization of St. Isidore's," she had said, handing her letter of resignation to Sister Judith, the principal. "Had I wished to teach in a public school, which this is fast becoming, I'd have done so from the start and made three times the money."

Her retirement lasted two weeks. It was hard to pinpoint her primary reason for going back to work. It might have been the coaxing of Father Finn, who insisted that the parish school could not long survive without her. It might have been her frightening confrontation with idleness; she visited the Staggerford Golden Age Center and found a dozen women and two men amusing themselves with paper dolls. Or it might have been her discovery that retirement provided a very weak position from which to attack the forces of secularization; there was no better observation post than the classroom.

So this past fall she had returned to her job. With her own money she bought a fresh supply of "Baltimore Catechisms"

and handed them out to her nineteen sixth graders. They recited from it each morning for twenty minutes, upon returning to the classroom from Mass. She planned to teach four more
years and retire for good at sixty-eight. At sixty-eight her small
pension from St. Isidore's would be slightly less small. Also at
sixty-eight she had an annuity coming due.

She studied the front of Catherine Allen's Christmas card
for a minute—a cross-eyed Santa drinking a cocktail with his
coat off—and then she threw it into her wastebasket.

She slit open the gray envelope from Ireland, and a snapshot fell out. It was a color photo of a tall man of approximately her own age standing in front of a village pub, together
with another tall man and a tall woman. The name O'HAN-
NON was lettered over the door. All three faces were squinting harshly at the camera. She unfolded the letter.

Dear Miss McGee,

Many thanks for the fine likeness of you before the lilac
bush. Here you have not only a look at me, as you re-
quested, but a look at my brother and sister as well. That's
the door to the family enterprise behind us. Matt is bar-
man and Marion is barmaid and I'm paying them a call
one afternoon in the middle of last summer. That's me on
your right. My old mother would not be put on display
that day despite the sunshine, but stayed rocking by the
fire in the kitchen. She's eighty-five and stiff in the joints
and scarcely goes out the door from one week to the next.
Both Matt and Marion, like me, are unmarried—a singu-
lar Irish tradition, if you'll pardon the pun. The pub sup-
ports the three of them comfortably but without frills.

I was born upstairs in the front room. You can make
out the sill of the window. The picture was taken by the
Guinness driver who was making his rounds that afternoon with his truck of beer.

The pub provided me with a good upbringing. The men
on their stools sipping their pints were an interesting bit
of humanity. You might say they were the collective father I was deprived of, my own having died when I was

small. For his death (though they never laid hands on him) I blame the British, who imposed a curfew on the town every night during the Troubles of '16 and allowed nobody outdoors no matter how pressing the reason. One such night my father was stricken with horrible stomach pains, food poisoning as it turned out (from what, we never knew), and the stupid, detestable British soldiers, not recognizing a life-and-death matter when it stared them in the face, didn't allow Paddy or Mother to run for the doctor. He died at dawn in the most awful agony, God rest him.

And you, Miss McGee, did you have both parents to a good age?

Rain here today, bit of sun yesterday.

At Sunday Mass our choir sang Palestrina. Heavenly.

With sincerest regards,

James O'Hannon

Agatha searched in the drawer of her table and found a bottle of glue. She drew Catherine Allen's card out of the wastebasket and pasted the photo over the drawing of Santa Claus. She stood the card at the base of her table lamp. She studied the photo for a long time. James was handsome. He had a long face with hollows under his cheekbones. His thick hair was unruly and white. Were the deep wrinkles in his brow permanent, or was it the sun making him squint? On his lips she saw the hint of a smile, a trace of good humor. She reached back into her drawer for a sheet of her gray stationery edged in white. She uncapped her fountain pen and wrote.

Dear Mr. O'Hannon,

I am grateful for the snapshot. I see something of a cousin of mine in your sister's face. I think it's the short upper lip and the small eyes and dark hair. You and your brother appear to be close in age, but apparently he's the older if it was he who tried reaching the doctor the night your father died. What a dreadful time it must have been for all of you. I am adding your father to the list of the dead I pray for, and your mother to my list of the living. Goodness, over fifty years a widow—the perseverance.

Both of my own dear parents lived to be old, thank you for inquiring. We were close all my life. I was something of an only child, for my brother was much older than I and died of the influenza of '18. I was born when my parents were in their late thirties and I think they never quite got over their delight in my existence. My father was an attorney, the first to open a law office here in Staggerford. He served several terms in the legislature in St. Paul. My mother was of the O'Malley family that settled in this area in 1890 and made themselves a name and a fortune in dry goods, and then lost most of it (the fortune, not the name) in the Depression. My father died at seventy-eight, my mother at seventy-nine, so I was orphaned, you might say, at forty.

The temperature has been dropping all day and it's below zero this evening. All is ghostly white out my window—moonlight falling on the icy street and the frozen river beyond it.

A stupid new wrinkle at Mass last Sunday. Impious handshaking.

Yours very truly,

Agatha McGee

This exchange of letters between Ireland and Minnesota had begun the previous spring when it seemed to Agatha that not only St. Isidore's but also the entire Church of Rome teetered on the brink of chaos. Religious turmoil horrified her. All her life she had been more inflexible than the Church—or steadfast. Every time Rome announced some new accommodation to a century that was already two thirds gone, Agatha felt betrayed. Her heart had been broken countless times since Vatican II, for it was not too much to say that Agatha loved the Church of her girlhood above everything else in the world. The Church had been her primary conveyance through life. At the age of three she had begun learning prayers and piety and scrupulous behavior from her parents. At seven she had made her First Confession and First Communion. At twelve she had pledged herself in Confirmation to the front-line defense of the faith. Defending the faith was easy in those days because the Church, having picked up nineteen centuries of momentum, was traveling steadily along a straight track with all the signals clear. True, it sometimes came to a junction where a few of Agatha's friends and relatives got off (a cousin apostacized during the stern reign of Pius XII, and two friends from her girlhood fell away during the liberalizing reign of John XXIII), but nearly everyone else she knew stayed comfortably in place. Now, however, the Church was moving through a confusing maze of switches. Droves of the faithful disembarked and wandered away, lost. It seemed to Agatha that even the bishops got lost, judging by how often they called meetings to haggle. And judging by their barbaric disregard for holy tradition. The pain in Agatha's breast was acute each time they announced that more rites and prayers and saints (all of them antique, to be sure, but still serviceable) were to be dumped. She thought she would die when Latin (dead for centuries yet incorrupt) was buried.

Accordingly, Agatha had taken out a subscription to an international newspaper called *The Fortress,* an outspoken weekly that restored hope in the hearts of readers who believed as she did. What they all believed was this: Only by remaining constant in its laws could the Church continue to offer perfection as a goal for humanity to strive for. Only by preserving the old rituals could the Church continue to hold out beauty and vision as possibilities in a world of blind, violent disorder. It was in the letters column of *The Fortress* one day last April that Agatha was introduced to James O'Hannon:

Dear Editor,

Your readers will be happy to know that there is at least one corner of the world largely unaffected by the turmoil in the Church. We've switched to saying Mass in English, granted, but little else has changed. Our bishops, unlike

their American counterparts, seem not attracted to nov-
elties. They trust instead the tried and true.

>With sincerest regards,
>
>James O'Hannon
>Ballybegs
>County Kildare
>Ireland

"They trust instead the tried and true." This sentence was
so much like the line of a poem, so much like the metrical verse
Agatha preferred to the fractured lines that passed for modern poetry, that it tumbled around in her head for weeks after
she read it. It prompted her, finally, to write to Ballybegs,
trusting the town to be small enough and the man prominent
enough for her letter to find him.

Dear Mr. O'Hannon,

   How reassuring to know of the stability of Irish Catholicism. Pray God it endures. Our bishops scorn the tried
and true. They love instead whatever's new.

>Yours very truly,
>
>Agatha McGee
>Staggerford, Minnesota 56470
>U.S.A.

He wrote back immediately, amused by her rhyme, he said,
and curious to know about the state of worship in her parish.
She responded at length, getting several layers of liturgical
complaint off her chest. He wrote a second time, taking up her
case, advising her to stand back a little from the heat. "Let the
Church work out its own destiny, Miss McGee. Love it, be
faithful, but don't let yourself be thrown off balance at every
twist and turn."

His tone in this letter struck her as high-handed and his advice not at all sensible. She, a woman of action, stand back from

the heat? Hardly. She'd make a mighty poor bystander, and she had a good mind to tell him so, but on second, third and fourth reading she found his letter so full of warm sincerity that she replied without polemic. And without delay. And when his third letter arrived she was amazed to find herself tearing it open at the mailbox instead of carrying it in to her desk and carefully slitting it open with the ivory blade handed down from her grandmother, as she had done with every other letter of her life.

Dear Miss McGee. Dear Mr. O'Hannon. Beginning with their exchange of photographs in midwinter, hard on the heels of the birth of Stephen, the tone of their letters changed. By April—their first anniversary as correspondents—their preoccupation with religion was gradually dropping away and they were writing of other things. Equipped, both of them, with long, clear memories, they began to review random incidents from their near and distant past. They told of their childhood, their schooling, their friends and neighbors. Being keen observers of their fellow townsmen, they formed the habit of including one or two prose portraits in each letter. From Ballybegs: the old woman newsagent, the deranged nun at Presentation Convent, the tippling bus driver. From Staggerford: the four widows on Agatha's block, the Raft family, the staff of St. Isidore's. And from both sides of the Atlantic, students—for James too, it turned out, was a teacher. April turned into May, May into summer. They wrote more often. They wrote at greater length. *Dear Agatha. Dear James.*

No one occupied more space in Agatha's letters than the Rafts.

Dear James,

Stephen is teething. Doesn't five months seem early for teething? My, how nearly perfect is my ignorance of babies and the way they grow. And how complete is the delight I take in this one. Janet and Stephen drop in on me nearly every week when she comes to town to the market. I call on them about once a month, timing each visit so as to arrive when the Raft house is slightly less hectic than normal, which is to say when Janet's hyperactive younger sisters aren't likely to have friends in. It's a house much too small for a man and his four daughters and baby grandson. LeeAnn, a truck-stop waitress, is seventeen, a year younger than Janet and a high school dropout. Karen, fifteen, is a freshman and her father's best help around the farm now that Janet is devoting full time to her baby. Sally was in my sixth grade this past year, as bright as Janet was at that age, I think, but not as eager to learn.

My neighbor Lillian Kite asked me the other day if I wasn't getting beneath myself visiting the Rafts, if there aren't limits to Christian charity, as she puts it. What Lillian doesn't understand is that my relationship with the Rafts has nothing to do with Christian charity. I go and see them because there is a liveliness in their house lacking in my own, and because they are all so nice to me and because Janet is the latest in that series of girls I told you about, my hardscrabble girls. And, oh, yes, because I do not find it unpleasant to hold Stephen on my lap. . . .

Hardscrabble girls. That was Agatha's term for the daughters of improvident or missing parents who lived on the stony farms in the forest north of town, farms consisting of small fields cleared a generation ago by grandfathers who didn't understand that the acidic soil so good for jackpine and thistle was bad for corn and grain. The hardscrabble grandmothers, Agatha's contemporaries, invariably bore eight or ten children by the time they were thirty-five, and bore seamed faces and gullied necks thereafter, while Agatha herself, having grown up slightly pampered in the largest, most comfortable house on River Street, went away to earn her four-year degree at a Franciscan college and returned home to the teaching job that was to be her entire career. The next generation of hardscrabble mothers bore half as many children as the grandmothers and somehow managed to age more slowly, but they looked out at their limited world with the same pale, weathered eyes of the grandmothers, eyes sadly reconciled to want. And now in the third generation, along came Janet, who had been spared those eyes, thank God. "There's nothing reconciled about Janet," Agatha wrote to James. "One look at her and you know she'll never fit into that sad, passive mold of her forebears. Nor will Stephen. But how I wish the two of them could move out of that crowded house. How I pray she'll find a good husband."

To this day the hardscrabble farms were being doggedly cultivated by fathers and stepfathers with sense enough to know they would seldom produce profitable crops, yet without vision enough to move away. "Move where, Miss McGee?" they would say whenever Agatha suggested they seek a better life elsewhere. "To Berrington," she would tell them. "They're always hiring at the paper factory."

She said this to Janet's father one day in late summer. She was out driving the roads north of town in her old, highly polished Plymouth. It was a hot, breezy day in August and she was looking for wild chokecherries. She came driving up over a rise and there was Francis Raft standing in a parched field of hay. She knew instinctively what he was thinking. In a good year he might cut three crops of hay from this field, but this was another bone-dry summer and he was wondering if he could get even a second cutting before fall.

Agatha pulled over and stopped. Francis Raft came shambling out of his field and down through the rocky ditch and up to the car. He put his head in at her window. "Hi, Miss McGee, you should have called ahead. We'd've had the coffeepot on."

"No, this isn't a social call, Francis. I'm picking chokecherries." She leaned away from the long, dirty bill of his John Deere cap. "How are you? How is Stephen?"

"I'm fine. Stephen's fine. He turned eight months, you know."

"I know. On the first. And how are the girls?"

"The girls are fine. LeeAnn's kind of wild. That age, you know."

"She's still seeing that truck driver?"

"Safe to say she is, one truck driver or another. Got herself a weakness for truck drivers, working like she does at the Jiffystop Lunchroom."

"And Janet?"

"Janet's fine. Seems like life's been a little easier around here since Janet had Stephen. Getting welfare money of her own, I mean. But all the same, it's tough trying to feed six mouths, my own included, on a sixty-acre hay crop when it never rains. You can understand that, can't you, Miss McGee?"

"I can. I do."

"Now, as far as chokecherries . . ."

Francis Raft straightened up and peered around him at the horizon of trees on all sides. He was a lanky man with over-sized hands and a weathered face the color of rust. His sweaty, checkered shirt was gauzy thin at the elbows and shoulder blades. Throughout his life he had been one of the unluckiest men Agatha had ever known. She remembered the sixth-grade recess when he broke his ankle playing kickball. She recalled that as a senior in high school he contracted a strange fever that lasted seven weeks and prevented him from graduating, but it didn't prevent him from being drafted into the Army, where he picked up malaria. His choice of a wife was a hard-scrabble neighbor with weak lungs. She died giving him his fourth daughter.

"I know a secret clump of chokecherries that's way back from the road. It's on a ways. I'll show you." He got into the car and directed her along dusty roads three miles north, a mile east and another mile north. She stopped where he told her to, and they got out. Carrying her two galvanized pails, she followed him along a path through the pine woods to what had once been a homestead in a clearing. A small house had collapsed into its shallow cellar. Each outbuilding was a mound of gray boards jutting up out of the weeds. A few pieces of atrophied farm machinery stood up to their axles in waving grass. The vanished occupants had obviously been in the habit of making wine or jam and then throwing the pulp and pits out into the yard, for standing within a fruit stone's throw of what had been the back door was a semicircle of fruit trees—juneberry, plum, chokecherry. Agatha saw that the juneberries had already been harvested by birds and bears and the plums were still too green for picking, but the chokecherries were deep burgundy and hanging in thick clusters, ready to drop.

"Answer me this, Francis: Is the chokecherry a tree, or a

bush?" Standing in the shade of her straw sunhat and holding a pail in each hand, she was studying the spindly trunks, the thin, angular branches. She was enjoying the play of the hot breeze through her sky-blue blouse, through her blue-rinsed hair. She loved summer above all seasons. From September to May she was never quite warm enough.

"It's a tree," said Francis, smiling at the words *Answer me this.* They took him back to grade six.

"But it stands no higher than lilac. What makes it a tree?"

"Waaaal, there's some would call it a bush, I suppose, but I call it a tree." Francis lifted his John Deere cap and smeared his hairline sweat with the back of his hand. "If I'm ever in doubt about how much credit to give a thing, I always give it more, to be on the safe side."

"Yes, that was always your way, wasn't it?" *Always too easygoing, always soft in your judgments*—she left this part unspoken.

"And you, Miss McGee, you always give it less, ain't I right?"

"Oh, do I, Francis?" More than once in the recent past Francis had surprised her with straight talk like this. Before Stephen was born, before she had been drawn into the Raft family as a kind of godmother to them all, this man had been less candid with her, more reverential.

"Sure you do, that's your way. Always been your way. I saw it when you had me in school, and I saw it again when you had the girls and I saw it again when you started coming out to the farm. Any borderline case always gets less from you, rather than more. It's what made us all work so hard in your room." He stepped into the chokecherry growth, parted some leaves and cupped a cluster of the fruit in his bony, calloused hand.

"Was that bad?" she asked. "Would you have had it any other way?"

"Waaaal." He shook his head. "Not for my sake." Then he nodded. "But maybe for yours."

"And what does that mean?"

He took one of the pails from her and stripped the berries into it. They drummed on the metal like fat raindrops. "What I mean, standards and all are good, but it's got to be hard on the person who's setting them up." Picking further, he slipped behind a screen of branches. "What I mean, what's the fun in life for the person who's so strict all the time? It's got to be hard never letting your hair down. Always being up to snuff yourself and expecting everybody else to be always up to snuff. When do you let your hair down, Miss McGee?" You didn't ask her a question like this face to face; that's why he was all but concealed by leaves.

"I make chokecherry wine, Francis, and on cold winter nights I sometimes take enough to make me a little tipsy, if that's what you're asking."

He gave a joyful whoop. "You tipsy! Now, that's a picture. That's what I like to hear. Everybody needs a little jolliness in their life, ain't I right?"

"And I've taken trips." She stepped forward and began filling her pail. "I've flown to Phoenix at Christmas with a group of teachers. I've flown to Washington, D.C., seven times with students. Last summer I drove to Ames." She fell silent, wondering why she was standing here among farmyard ruins justifying herself to Francis Raft. Or rather to these bushes, for Francis had now completely disappeared behind a snapping of twigs. And bushes they were, certainly, not trees.

She raised her voice to its most self-assured tone: "As for my high standards, it's my nature, Francis. It's much easier to live your life according to your nature than to go against it."

But she wasn't nearly so confident as she sounded. A year had passed since her aborted retirement, a year during which she had often asked herself if it was her nature after all to be the woman she had been. Had she truly followed her destiny? And if she had, why wasn't her career leaving her more content as it came to its close?

They filled both pails in less than an hour. Driving him back to his farm, Agatha asked Francis if he ever despaired of making a comfortable living on his sandy plot of ground.

"You mean do I ever think of giving up the farm? No sirree, it's my life."

"But your garden is behind again this year, and your hay is sparse and going to seed. How do you bear this life, never knowing if your harvest will support you from one year to the next?"

"How do I bear it?" He put his hand out the window, cupping and sifting the air as though it were soil. "Nothing unbearable about it, in my view. One of my neighbors down the road, he talks about picking up and moving away. This life ain't fit for a dog, he says. But me, I'm just one of your natural-born jackpine savages, I guess. I do my share of complaining, but give me a sixty-acre hayfield and enough pine trees around me to keep things private and I'm happy as a tick on a fat sheep. It's my way of life, see? When my hay crop is good, it's like winning a bet. When it's bad, it's welfare and food stamps. It was different in my old man's day. When my old man was farming this land, it was more of a life-and-death deal than it is now. It seemed like he never knew a day's peace of mind in his life. He died of nerves, you remember. Just plain worried himself to death. But now with welfare and food stamps, farming this sandy piece ain't no life-and-death deal. It's do my best and hope to make it on my own, and go on the county if I don't. It's like you say, we each of us have our own natures and it's no sense going against them."

Oh, to be so reconciled. Agatha came to a stop beside his field.

"Nice seeing you again, Miss McGee." He got out. "Come again when you got time for coffee."

"I will. I'll bring you a bottle of last year's wine. It was a good batch."

"I'd be much obliged." He waved and went down into the rocky ditch.

She leaned out the window. "Francis, the reason I brought it up about your farm, I heard they were hiring at the Berrington paper plant."

Turning around, he took off his cap and gently swatted the thought away from him. "Naw, that ain't for me."

"Eight dollars an hour, I'm told."

"Naw, I'm much obliged, Miss McGee, but this here's where my roots are." He pointed to the flat rock he was standing on.

5

MANY HOURS OF SLEEP were lost in the Raft house before Stephen's last tooth came in. Then there was croup followed by a siege of eczema. After that it was clear sailing. When he was one he took four steps between the couch and chair in the front room; the next day he took ten or twelve stumbling steps out the screen door and fell off the front porch into a cluster of squawking chickens. The Raft sisters ran to his rescue. They turned him over in their arms looking for bruises and feeling for broken bones. All was well. His weeping subsided to whimpering. The chickens settled back into their soft, sleepy clucking.

When he was two he began saying "Papa," meaning Grandpa, and "Kirkie," meaning tractor. When he was two and a half he looked up from his applesauce one noon and said, quoting his Aunt LeeAnn on the subject of a recent boyfriend, "Arnold's such a pukehead."

At three, quoting all three of his aunts, he began teasing his mother with the phrase "Randy the dandy," for this was the winter Janet fell in love with Randy Meers.

Randy was the son of Carl and Louise Meers, who lived in one of the fashionable new houses on the west end of Staggerford. There were seven such houses, and they were called the Hemlock Addition. Carl Meers was a realtor; Staggerford Realty was his firm. Louise Meers was the senior and dominant member of the Staggerford City Council. Randy was their only child.

Janet and Randy had entered first grade together at St. Isidore's, but in all their years as classmates they probably hadn't exchanged twenty words—they belonged to separate circles, the country circle and the town circle. In junior high Randy had been admired from a distance by Janet's small circle of timid girlfriends. They adored his curly blond hair, his dark eyebrows, his mysterious eyes.

In high school Randy distinguished himself as a tenor for three years but dropped out of chorus when he was a senior because the director required them to sing such boring pieces. Janet made her mark as the only mother in the graduating class of ninety-eight students, in which she ranked third and Randy ranked twelfth.

After high school Randy's parents sent him off to college in the East, where he joined a fraternity, sang in the men's chorus and flunked out after seven months. Next, they sent him to college in the West, where he contracted mononucleosis and again flunked out. Then he was sent to a trade school in Minneapolis to learn radio announcing, but this occasioned his romance with Cheryl Burdick, a former schoolmate from Staggerford.

Cheryl Burdick was employed by the city of Minneapolis as a flagperson on its street-repair crew. She was a short, mouthy redhead who knew how to cook. Within a week of discovering one another, Randy moved into Cheryl's two-room apartment over a store that sold waterbeds and quit going to radio-announcing class. At the end of fall term they broke up. Cheryl joined the Army and went off to boot camp. Randy returned home.

Randy's father hit the ceiling. His return on two and a half years of tuition, room and board was a son with eleven college credits. He could have invested in a goddamn buttonhook factory and done better than that, he said to his wife the day he handed down his ultimatum: Randy had twenty-four hours to make up his mind whether he wanted to become an associate of his father's in Staggerford Realty or become night cook at the Burger Skillet out on Highway Four, which the Meerses had an interest in. In a rare flush of optimism, Randy decided to learn the real-estate game—zoning, interest, earnest money, points—and amount to something.

"The first sensible choice you've made in your life," said his father. He added Randy's name to his office stationery.

"Marvelous, marvelous," said Randy's mother. She helped him pick out two suits and half a dozen neckties.

For some time before this, Janet Raft had been spending her Saturday nights at the Brass Fox, a log-cabin nightspot on the shore of a small lake about five miles east of Staggerford. The Brass Fox was all things to all revelers. One weekend it might be the site of the annual public school faculty dinner and dance, and the next weekend the target of the sheriff's drug raid. Six nights a week the music was produced by a muffled-sounding jukebox that gave off a gloomy purple light, but on Saturdays the Beaver Dam Trio came in and played country-western live. The flashy woman who played the piano was married to the older man who played the drums and she was having an affair with the younger man who played the guitar and sang; everybody knew about this triangle, including the drummer, who was too stoned to care. For Janet and two of her sisters and their friends, the Brass Fox was society. Around nine on Saturday nights Janet, Karen and LeeAnn would arrive in their father's flatbed truck, having left Stephen at home with Sally, who was too young for the Brass Fox. They drank beer, ate hamburgers and danced. At about one in the morning Janet and Karen would drive home without LeeAnn, who would be delivered later by some boy. In the course of time Karen took to driving home alone, Janet having paired off with Randy Meers.

Randy liked music. He was a good dancer. Sometimes the Beaver Dam Trio let him sing a song into the mike. Sometimes between sets he and Janet would walk down to the ice-covered lake and stand under the pines and talk. Sometimes they went to Randy's car to talk and kiss. One night in April when the moon was bright enough to show the way, they set off down a logging road that led deep into the woods, and they made love on a blanket to the thrumming of a million frogs. The following week they spent all of Saturday night in Randy's bed at home, his parents having flown to a realtors' convention in Dallas. This was the night he told Janet he loved her and wanted to marry her. He said he was tired of being single and ready to settle down.

"Oh, Randy, Randy," said Janet, holding his face tightly to her breasts and feeling that her heart would surely burst with joy. "Oh, yes, yes, Randy."

The Meers's house on the hilly end of Hemlock Street had a walk-out basement, which was converted into an apartment for the newlyweds, and by the middle of June Janet found herself living for the first time in her life under the same roof with a washer, a drier, a bathtub, a color TV and a deep freeze, to say nothing of two parents-in-law and a husband with a flagging spirit. Though optimistic by nature, Janet found this arrangement inferior to the paradise she had imagined, largely because of the circumspect Mrs. Meers upstairs, who though always civil was never quite warm. At least not warm to Janet. She was fairly warm toward Stephen, and that made up for a lot. Janet had known women like this before, but never at such close range—stiff women whose affection you had to qualify for without being sure of the requirements. It seemed to Janet, the more she studied her, that Mrs. Meers had two things in life she prized above all else, and most of what she did and said was directed at strengthening her grip on those things. One, of course, was Randy—it was for fear of losing Randy that she had consented to the marriage. The other thing was prestige.

Or, as Janet's father called it, uppitiness. "You married into uppitiness," he would sometimes say to her without a trace of humor in his face but probably meaning to be funny. "I think it's swell you keep coming back to see your old man after you married into uppitiness." He would be holding the screen door of the farmhouse open for the two of them as he said it, and then he would chuckle as he bent over and lifted Stephen up so that his head touched the low ceiling of the front room. Then as man and boy exchanged a wet kiss, Janet heard her father's chuckle turn into a purr of pleasure—a soft, throaty noise she had never known him to make before Stephen was born.

In the autumn of their first year of marriage, Janet got a job and Randy got the blues. Her job, which she acquired through Agatha's intercession, was in the principal's office at St. Isidore's, where she worked as receptionist and secretary. She was highly regarded by the school staff. As receptionist she was altogether pleasant and helpful, and as typist she was improving. Moreover, she was mechanically inclined. St. Isidore's janitor had a talent for sweeping but not for fixing, so it was

Janet the teachers called upon when the ditto machine leaked fluid or the bulb blew out in the film projector. Having grown up helping her father repair his makeshift farm machinery, she had a natural way with tools. She understood hinges and drains and fuse boxes. The day the school became filled with a faint unhealthy smell, it was Janet who traced it to, and repaired, the exhaust fan in the furnace room. On the first day of snow in November the janitor couldn't remember how to start the gasoline-powered snowblower, and the sidewalks around the school remained uncleared until Janet went out and showed him how to adjust the carburetor.

But while Janet soared, Randy sank. Janet called it his down mood. Randy's mother called it his brown study. Randy's father called it his goddamn lazy streak. On days when Randy was depressed, he was late for everything. He got up late and went to bed late. He was late for work and late getting home for supper. Janet tried to overlook his down moods. Her sister LeeAnn had had moods like this when she was fifteen and had outgrown them. So what if Randy had a touchy temperament? Was that any reason to regret getting a husband and a father for Stephen from one of Staggerford's best families? Besides, there was a lot about Randy to love. He was gentle. He was smart. He was handsome. When he was in the mood for sex, which wasn't quite as often as Janet wished, he could be such a turn-on. His eyes were wonderfully mysterious.

Now and then, alone in the principal's office with little to do, Janet would turn Randy over in her mind and try to pinpoint the cause of his depressions. Was she at fault? Were his parents? No, his gloomy periods seemed to come and go without any relation to events outside his head. It was a problem of attitude, mostly his attitude toward work. How unlucky, thought Janet, that an apprentice realtor should lose his belief in property.

"Janet, what does it mean to own property? What does it really mean?" He was in the habit of asking this when he came home in the evening.

"It means you can live on it." Janet was frying hamburgers on her deluxe gas range the first time he asked. There was a load of clothes tumbling in the drier off the kitchen. In the living room Stephen was falling asleep in front of the color TV.

"But a lot of people don't live on the property they own, Janet. What does it really mean for them to have title to that property when the property isn't making any difference to them and they aren't making any difference to the property? Fields and forests, I mean. That land exists the way it is no matter who owns it. It's just there. Why is the whole surface of the earth divided up among owners? On the fourth day or whenever God made the earth, did he say, 'Go forth and make real estate out of all the dry land'? Janet, I'd really like to know what you think about this."

Such talk amused Janet at first, but then it got tiresome, his finding absurdity in every commonplace thing. Nor was Janet the only one who was irked. At the office Randy gave his father fits by asking what difference taxes and interest rates made in the larger context of life. One noon hour, when his father and his secretary were gone from the office, Randy answered the phone and said to a prospective buyer inquiring about the terms of a mortgage, "Really, Mr. Robertson, are we going to care all that much about mortgages when we come to die?"

Nevertheless, encouraged by Janet and driven by his father, Randy made sporadic attempts to sell property, but his manner with clients was chilly one day, apologetic the next. He was known to lose prospective buyers halfway through the showing of a house. "Now, I guess this is the dining room," he said one day as he wandered into what was obviously a bedroom far removed from the kitchen, and then turning to the man and woman who had met him at the front door by appointment, he found that they had slipped back outside and were getting into their car.

Granted, this wasn't a good year to be selling houses (interest rates up, employment down), but Randy couldn't sell Grade A milk to a goddamn creamery in the best of times, as Randy's father explained to Randy's mother in December when he fired him and arranged for him to be night cook at the Burger Skillet out on Highway Four.

In January, Randy lost the Burger Skillet job, not because he couldn't keep up with the slow night trade, but because he couldn't see what difference hamburgers made in the larger context of life. From Burger Skillet he went to the Jiffystop Station and pumped gas for three-fifty an hour, a very discouraging salary considering what the Arabs were getting for a barrel of oil. From Jiffystop he went, in March, to Spring-Flo Water Softeners, where things began looking up. Janet and Mr. and Mrs. Meers, taking note of Randy's improved state of mind, grew hopeful again.

The sales office of Spring-Flo Water Softeners, a new enterprise in Staggerford, occupied a dusty storefront on Main Street. Before Randy signed on, it had been a two-person operation. An oily-haired young man named Archie was sales manager. He wore a big diamond on his little finger. The broken bow of his glasses was held together by Scotch tape. The Spring-Flo bookkeeper-secretary was an anemic young woman named Polly, whose primary form of communication was the wink. Her wink meant okay. Having examined his application form and finding it in order, she winked happily at Randy. As he was leaving the office after his interview, he caught her winking approvingly at Archie. Her false black lashes were the dominant feature of her plain, pallid face, which made her wink seem very portentous. She could stop men in their tracks by winking at them as they walked past the office window.

Archie spoke with a Kansas twang, and what he spoke of, continually and ecstatically, were suds and sales quotas. Randy, charged with Archie's enthusiasm, sold seven softeners in his first three weeks on the job. Each time he brought in a new order, Polly winked joyfully, and Archie reminded him that twenty sales in ten weeks would qualify him for a weekend for two in Las Vegas. That may have been Archie's mistake. Las Vegas in the larger context of life? Randy's skepticism returned, settling over his ambition like a blanket of snow. He grew very bored with the suds demonstration Archie had taught him to perform in the kitchen for the lady of the house, illustrating how Spring-Flo water produced a gallon of suds while natural tap water produced only a pint. He adjusted his opening remarks so that fewer and fewer ladies of houses invited him into their kitchens. Whereas in March he had averaged eleven demonstrations a day, by May he was down to two. Most days he knocked off early and drove out to the Brass Fox, where he shot pool all afternoon with the daytime regulars, most of whom were men living on unemployment benefits or pensions, most of them older than Randy, all of them happier.

As the warm rains of spring opened the lilacs and turned the lawns green, Randy went home to supper each evening in a blue funk. He kept *TV Guide* open beside his plate and studied it like a map, planning his course through an evening of TV.

Janet was amazed at the control TV exerted over Randy; it moved him the way no flesh-and-blood person ever could. Watching *M*A*S*H* reruns, he could be moved to tears or to his falsetto laugh. He was sometimes lifted so happily out of his six-o'clock funk that after Stephen was put to bed he would turn to Janet with his eyes no longer impassive but gleaming with lust. She loved that look and all it led to.

To Janet's regret, sex was one facet of her marriage that she couldn't bring up with Miss McGee. Miss McGee took a dim view of Randy, forcing Janet continually to defend him, and it would have helped if she could bring sex into it, not to dwell on it but to point out that good sex at the right time cured so many ills. Miss McGee was wise and kind and strong and almost everything else people claimed she was, but she didn't know the first thing about sex. Janet sadly recalled the morning of her wedding when she couldn't put up with Miss McGee's disapproving silence any longer. She was being married from Agatha's house, and as they were about to leave for church, Janet asked her outright why she was holding back her wholehearted support, and Miss McGee had said something vague like, "Oh, I don't know, Janet, weddings always make me pensive," and Janet had pressed her to be frank, saying, "Tell me, what does any other man have that Randy doesn't have?" and Agatha without a moment's hesitation shot back, "Common sense and pep." At that, Janet wept like a baby in her arms. But only for a minute. She washed her face and got married and never looked back.

6

THE FIRST YEAR of Janet's marriage was Agatha's forty-sixth and final year of teaching. A bittersweet year. Looking back through her gradebooks, Agatha found that she had improved the minds of over twelve hundred twelve-year-olds, and that was certainly nice to know, but what did she have to show for it but gradebooks? Her past seemed a span of innocuous days. And her nights? Her most dramatic recurring dream in recent nights was one in which she had difficulty opening a jar of peanut butter.

"Was it wise of me after all," she wrote to James, "to have confined my career to one small classroom in one small town? Wouldn't I be coming away from my life's work with a higher heart if I hadn't been washing the same blackboard for forty-six years?"

She had put the question to Janet, explaining that her work had been more of a joy in years past than it was now, and Janet had said, "You peaked early, huh?" There was something of Agatha in the way Janet delivered succinct remarks like this. Janet was no longer the timid girl, abashed and pregnant, who had showed up at Agatha's door four years ago. The spunk Agatha had detected in her at twelve was coming out now at twenty-one. It wasn't exactly Agatha's brand of spunk, however. Janet was slower to criticize. "She has a heart like her father's," Agatha wrote to James, "warm and large. But too lacking in discrimination for her own good. If she weren't so soft in her judgments, she wouldn't have married the man she did."

Each Friday after work Janet picked Stephen up at nursery school and stopped at Agatha's house on the way home. Agatha enjoyed this weekly visit; it allowed her to act motherly and godmotherly. What Janet enjoyed was the pride she felt at being

55

welcomed into Agatha's stately house; it was sort of cramped and humiliating living in the Meers's basement. While Janet and Agatha discussed St. Isidore's, Stephen, after his cookie, went straight to the toy chest Agatha kept for him in the living room and amused himself with a platoon of tiny lead soldiers last played with by her brother in 1902. Stephen was nearly four. He had pale blue eyes, a chubby, ruddy face. His normal expression was serious, which made his slow smile, when it appeared, irresistibly engaging, suggesting deep pleasure beyond his years. The smile wasn't directed at the godmother as often as she wished. In her forty-six years of disciplining children she had perfected the meaningful frown to the point of using it when she didn't mean to, and the little boy found her rather forbidding, though not so forbidding as his Grandmother Meers, who was forever going at his fingernails with a brush that hurt.

Having no nieces or nephews, she urged him to call her Aunt Agatha, but he couldn't help using the name his mother and stepfather always used. "Why is everyone so formal with me?" she wrote to James. "I've been universally known as Miss McGee, it seems, since before the time of Columbus."

During these Friday visits whenever Agatha touched lightly on Randy, she saw Janet rise quickly, sometimes hotly, to his defense. She had to admire the girl's loyalty, but why had she chosen a husband who was extending his adolescence into its second decade? It saddened her to think of all the daughters of weak fathers she had known who hadn't been satisfied until they became the wives of weak husbands. Even in the sixth grade Randy had been a little eccentric. Agatha recalled his pure, strong singing voice and his knack for mathematics. She recalled his secretive ways. She remembered that his palms were always sweaty. He had no close friends. He was easily distracted by daydreams. His eyes were the most expressionless Agatha had ever known in a child of twelve. And now at twenty-one he was still secretive and friendless and his face was as unreadable as ever. He was attentive to his mother, and Agatha always admired that in a young man, but he didn't get along well with his father. And he lacked ambition. And last June when Agatha shook his hand at the wedding reception, his palm was still clammy.

Having expected the worst of this marriage, Agatha wasn't surprised at the pitiful phone conversation she overheard in school one day. She heard only Janet's half of it, but it wasn't hard to imagine what Randy was saying on the other end as Janet strove to cheer him up. Between the school office and Agatha's classroom was a locked door of frosted glass through which traffic never passed but voices did if you listened carefully. It was by listening carefully one noon hour while her students were at lunch that Agatha came to understand how deep were the caverns of Randy's gloom.

Janet began: "Hi, hon, how are things?"

Not so hot, apparently, judging by what she said next: "Oh, come on, Randy, none of that. I know it isn't easy selling water softeners, but no job is all roses."

There was a long pause, at the end of which Janet sighed audibly through the frosted glass, and Agatha, grading a pile of oversized papers (four-color maps of the Midwest), gave up trying not to listen. Given a chance to eavesdrop, Agatha usually took it despite her ethical sense, because what you overheard was invariably more interesting than what you were told.

"Randy, stop that kind of talk. Archie doesn't mean anything personal when he says those things. Just remember he's your boss and it's his *job* to say things like that. He's got to say whatever's good for business, right? Look at *my* job. Sometimes Sister Judy or one of the teachers will tell me I'm doing something wrong or not fast enough and I know they don't mean it as a personal insult. They mean it to help me and to keep the school running smooth—

"Randy, please stop being so *down* all the time. We'll get by, I've got a check coming Friday. We can use a little of it for Stephen's wagon and fifteen dollars toward groceries and still have enough left for the car payment—

"No, please don't ask your mother for any more money. It's not her responsibility to bail us out every time we get behind. It's our lives, Randy. We'll do fine on our *own*—

"Don't tell me you didn't follow up on that lead Archie gave

you. Randy, you can't quit seeing your leads. . . . Yes, I know
I'm quoting Archie and you're tired of hearing it, but Archie
wouldn't be sales manager if he didn't know his business. . . .
Randy, don't talk that way about Archie. What if he heard you?
. . . Well, where *are* you calling from? . . . The Brass Fox?
Oh, Randy, it's only noon."

Another audible sigh. Then, more brightly: "Tell you what:
Why don't you come to school and let me take you to lunch in
the cafeteria? I promise I won't say a word about softeners.
. . . That's better, hon, keep your hopes up and you'll do great.
See you in a few minutes."

Agatha heard her hang up, then dial.

"Polly, it's Janet. . . . Yeah, I know all about his attitude,
that's why I'm calling. Is Archie there? Thanks."

After a few seconds: "Archie, Janet . . . Yeah, I know, Archie, that's why I'm calling. I just wanted to say he'll be fine.
He's a little worried now about paying bills, but he'll get over
it. . . . Oh, now, Archie, don't let him upset you like that. He
has these times when he's down but he always gets fine again.
Just be patient and talk to him, Archie, that's what I do. . . .
Not *yell*, Archie! Just talk. Tell him his troubles aren't all that
big and life does have meaning. . . .

"No, that's not true, he is *not* a detriment to Spring-Flo. Didn't
he bring in two doubtfuls last month, and didn't one of them
buy a five-year supply of softener salt?"

A long pause, Janet murmuring as she listened, then: "All
right, if that's your last word, I understand. . . . Yep, I know
business is business. He brings in a new order before the end
of the week or he's out. He'll do it, too. I promise he'll do it if
I have to buy the softener myself."

Janet hung up and pushed her swivel chair away from her
desk. Agatha saw her silhouette through the glass, saw her lean
far back, her head lolling, her chin pointed at the ceiling, her
long hair hanging. She saw her stretch her arms straight up
and flex her fingers. She heard her sigh once again. Agatha
was at a loss. Despite her lifelong skill at matching solutions to
problems, she couldn't envision happiness for Janet as long as
she was married to Randy. It was nearly enough to make you
condone unmarried cohabitation, perish the thought. If they

were merely living together, Janet could leave him. But the strange thing was, Janet didn't want to leave him. She loved him, so she claimed.

"Well, here I am." Randy's shadow darkened the frosted glass. "What are you doing, exercising?"

Janet giggled. She remained as she was, head back, arms up. "Come here, you hunk."

Randy leaned over and the silhouettes merged, Janet's arms closing around his neck. His head bobbed—four smacking little kisses, then a longer one. Then he straightened up. "Hungry?"

"Starved." Her laugh was low and throaty. "In more ways than one."

They left the office.

With a dozen maps ungraded, Agatha sat staring at the frosted glass. Their silhouettes lingered in her mind. So did the sound of their kisses. She rose and went to the window and looked out over the busy playground. Children running, pulling, sliding, calling, spinning. If you traced all these children back to their beginnings, you came to kisses. She was immediately astonished at having entertained such an earthy thought. She returned to her desk and stared blankly at Mary Simpson's messy map of the Midwest while the kisses sounded in her head, four short and one long, like Morse code. She pushed the maps aside. She opened her purse and took out James O'Hannon's latest letter, which she hadn't had the courage to read a second time, so jolting was his cry of loneliness:

> I've had only three true friends in my adult life, Agatha. When I was a young man teaching in Knockbridge there was an old schoolmaster named Hagarty who was a delight to talk books with, but I left Knockbridge after four years and went to Gleen, and anyhow Hagarty was in decline by that time, getting old and more drawn into himself. A different man at the end of my time in Knockbridge, he was, than at the beginning. Forgetful.
>
> Then after I was in Gleen for two or three years I began to hit it off with a shopkeeper named Johnson, a fat, ironic man who told uproarious stories, but Johnson was

a Protestant and there was wedged between us the disapproval of my fellow Catholics. They never came out and said anything, mind you, but it was always present in the air of that secretive, bigoted town on the border of Ulster—a suspicion concerning any Catholic who took up with a Prod unless conversion was the motive—and when it became clear that Johnson's conversion was not my motive, they began spreading it around that my conversion was Johnson's motive. Way off the mark, they were, Johnson being the next thing to an agnostic, holding his Protestant faith by the thinnest of threads. Then, seeing conversion was not the story, they began changing their tune. It started going around that Johnson and I were homosexuals. Gleen was ugly and I was glad to leave it.

Here in Ballybegs I was for several years the close friend of a fisherman named Langtry. He used to take me fishing. He was jolly, high-spirited company. Too convivial to be a success at the fishing. At the slightest sign of foul weather he'd not go out on the water but remain in the town all day visiting in and out of pubs. Being unmarried, we took our meals together quite often. Oh, it was a great friendship while it lasted, but now we've grown apart, he being in his cups half the time and squiring an old dame up the coast the other half and I being less willing to go out in boats the older I get.

Are you ever lonely, Agatha, living alone?

She thought it brazen of him to ask. His previous letters had been more discreet than this. She returned it to her purse and took a fresh sheet of paper out of her desk drawer. She wrote *Dear James*. She went on to say nothing directly about his friendlessness or her loneliness. If she replied with the whole truth—why wouldn't she feel lonely at times?—he might be encouraged to do more probing and destroy one of the qualities she most enjoyed about this correspondence: giving or withholding at will. Wasn't that the great advantage of living one's life alone, the control?

She did, however, reply to his question indirectly by broaching a topic she'd been mulling over for some days. What would he think of her coming to Ireland for a few days at the end of the school year?

His return letter mystified her. Ample time had elapsed for her letter to reach him, yet he made no mention of her proposed visit.

She wrote again, saying she would arrive at the Gresham Hotel in Dublin on Friday, the twenty-sixth of May, probably in the late afternoon.

7

THE TRIP HAD BEEN Lillian Kite's idea at first, or rather Imogene's. On the day Garvey Travel, Inc., of Berrington blanketed central Minnesota with a brochure promoting ten days in Ireland, Imogene studied it from front to back, including the fine print concerning allowances for missing luggage, and decided that Ireland would be good for her mother.

Imogene was in the business of enriching people's minds, her own being the standard to shoot for, and every so often she tried to enrich her mother's. Ten years ago she had sent her mother on a seven-day train trip to St. Anne's Shrine in Quebec, from which she returned enriched; not that Lillian was much impressed with the shrine or with Quebec City, but she was full of new information gathered from her seatmates on the train. A woman from Wisconsin spent four hundred miles listing the wrongs perpetrated upon her by her first three husbands. A woman from Albany, New York, who had twice shaken the hand of Nelson Rockefeller, showed her how to knit a five-color afghan.

Four years ago Imogene had bought her mother a seat on a chartered bus to Iowa, where Pope John Paul II was flown in to say Mass in a meadow. She missed seeing the Pope because by the time his helicopter touched down and the ceremony began she was so exhausted that she stayed on the bus to sleep. (She had had to leave home at 3:30 A.M.) But the trip wasn't entirely a waste of time; besides witnessing a fatal, six-car accident on the interstate, she got acquainted with a woman from Des Moines who gave her a recipe for pickled sunfish.

It was twilight of a muddy March day when Lillian tracked grime into Agatha's kitchen, calling, "Look at this flier, Agatha, it's ten days in Ireland at the end of May. Imogene says you and I should go." She drew the Garvey Travel brochure from her knitting bag and thrust it at Agatha. "A trip to mark my seventieth birthday," she says, "and a trip to mark your retirement."

Agatha glanced at the brochure and handed it back. "Why not take Imogene instead?" She did not tell Lillian that this same brochure had turned up in her own mailbox four days ago, and after a moment's excitement at the thought of flying to Ireland and meeting James O'Hannon, she realized that the tour leader was to be the new bishop of Berrington, a man she abhorred, and she had torn the brochure in half and thrown it away.

"Imogene's vacation isn't till later in the summer. She says you're the one to go with me, Agatha, being Irish and all." Lillian slipped off her jacket and sat down at the kitchen table. She patted her hair in place, then peered into her knitting bag. "It's only fourteen hundred dollars, air and land portion both."

Agatha plugged in her coffeemaker. She picked the brochure off the table and studied again the color photos. "Did you ever see anything printed in such horrid taste, Lillian? Look at Bishop Baker's face superimposed smack in the middle of the Cliffs of Moher." This was on the cover. The man was smiling broadly, exposing irregular teeth.

"Imogene says he's cute. He comes into her library and takes out books in person." Lillian unloaded her knitting onto the table, the sleeves and back of a mustard sweater. "She says Bishop Swayles never read books, that's what made him such a stick-in-the-mud."

"Tell Imogene not to blaspheme, Bishop Swayles was a saint." Agatha unfolded the brochure. "Look at this trick photography here on page two. If the man's going to go around with his collar off, why doesn't he at least put on a tie?" With his hand extended and his sport shirt open at the neck, Bishop Baker was stepping forward out of the Book of Kells, obscuring St. Mark. He was a chunky man whose massive brow and receding hairline gave an intellectual aspect to his round, happy face. A deceiving aspect, thought Agatha. "Lillian, I think it's dreadful the way Bishop Baker goes around impersonating someone with brains." Agatha regretted these words the moment she uttered them, fearing she had committed the sin of calumny; but luckily Lillian, engrossed in a dropped stitch, hadn't been listening.

Agatha's sadness last summer at the death of old Bishop Swayles had been doubled by the appointment of Bishop Baker as his successor. In the aging hierarchy of the Catholic Church, Bishop Richard Baker, at fifty, was a kind of whiz kid. You kept seeing his picture in the secular press all the time. Any evening he might appear on page three of the *Berrington Daily* running in a marathon or blowing a trumpet in a jazz band or playing tennis with some Democrat. Writing his column in the diocesan paper (in a graceful prose style Agatha had to admire in spite of herself), he displayed certain passions she deplored. Pro football and unilateral disarmament, for example. Progressive theology and Bix Beiderbecke. He urged his flock to call him Dick.

In his early weeks as bishop he had visited all the parishes in his jurisdiction, saying Mass and delivering folksy homilies. At St. Isidore's he had exhibited an aw-shucks manner that Lillian and practically everyone else found sweetly disarming but that repelled Agatha. She suspected that it was feigned and concealed a will as strong as her own, a will bent on loosing barbarism on the diocese. Once again her letters to James O'Hannon began to fill up with Church affairs. Every time the bishop put a new, hellish, heartbreaking plan into effect, Agatha sent a tattling letter to Ireland. Short of teaching nuns, the bishop closed six parochial schools; not St. Isidore's, thanks be to God. Then, short of priests, he put six nuns in charge of three small parishes; again not St. Isidore's, double thanks be to God. Currently he was remodeling the cathedral in Berrington or, in Agatha's view, gutting it; she had seen pictures in the paper. Not to mention the rumor going around that he was not opposed to liturgical dance—men and women in tights cavorting in the sanctuary.

Lillian's needles were clicking at high speed. "Agatha, we've never gone on a trip together."

This was no accident.

Agatha said, "I drove you to Bishop Swayles' funeral."

"I mean a real trip. I've always said you should have gone with me to see the Pope."

"But you didn't see the Pope. You stayed on the bus, you said."

"I didn't need to actually see him. Just knowing the two of us were in Iowa together, him and I, made me feel holy. I slept the sleep of the blessed on that bus."

Agatha served coffee and white cake. Lillian added twelve rows to a mustard sleeve. She repeated her plea but Agatha said no, her conscience wouldn't allow her to support anything Bishop Baker was involved in.

"Oh, go on, Agatha, you're too strict with yourself. You'd enjoy the bishop, Imogene says."

"I'll enjoy his ten-day absence from the diocese."

But the following Friday, visiting with Janet, Agatha changed her mind.

When Janet and Randy were married the previous June, Mr. and Mrs. Meers had offered them a trip abroad as their wedding gift. The trip had been put off because summer was the high season in real estate and Randy stood a good chance of making a sale (though not good enough, as it turned out), and it was further delayed during the fall and winter because of Janet's job at St. Isidore's. But now, with the appearance of the Garvey Travel brochure in March, the four Meerses, senior and junior, agreed that the time had come to plan the honeymoon. Mr. and Mrs. Meers had been to Ireland themselves and remembered it fondly. Mr. Meers remembered the beautiful racehorses he had lost so much money on and the smooth, dark stout he had drunk so much of. Mrs. Meers remembered the lovely feather ticks in the guesthouses and the good prices for wool sweaters in the West. Mr. Meers was almost certain that Randy, who was taking forever to grow up, would never learn to enjoy such fine things as stout and horseracing, and Mrs. Meers doubted if her new daughter-in-law, with nothing in her background but a fatherless son and forty acres of hay, had any regard for feather ticks and Connemara knits, but travel was said to be broadening and just by chance Randy and Janet might be improvable.

Furthermore, the Meerses had relatives in Ireland. A cousin of Mrs. Meers had married an Irish newspaperman named Fermoyle, who was now an editor high on the staff of the *Irish Times*. The Fermoyles lived on a well-to-do road in the Blackrock section of Dublin; they had a daughter Randy's age who was attending Trinity College. Mrs. Meers wrote to her cousin, who replied in haste saying yes, indeed, she and her husband and daughter would be overjoyed to have the young couple over for a stay. She urged them to pay for the air portion of the tour only and leave the sightseeing to the Fermoyles.

So it was arranged. In late May Stephen would live for ten days with his Grandfather and Grandmother Meers, who had become fond of the boy, each in a distinctive way. Mr. Meers treated Stephen, in the best sense, like a dog. Arriving home from work, Mr. Meers would call for the boy to come running and he would pat him on the head and feed him one of the wrapped pieces of toffee he carried in his pocket in case a real-estate client showed up with kids. After dinner he liked the feel of Stephen snuggling up to him on the couch as he read or watched television. The kid was good-natured and not too squirmy. His wife treated Stephen like one of her civic-improvement projects. As the perennial chair of the city council she had taken the lead in upgrading the quality of life in Staggerford—new sewers, new lighting along Main Street, a new zoning system—and now she saw it as her duty to upgrade the quality of Stephen's life. Stephen was four and perfectly impressionable. In ten days she could get a good start on teaching him polite talk and table manners, and she could buy him the darling vested blue suit she had seen in the boys' department of Staggerford Clothiers.

Behind Agatha's back the school staff was gearing up for her retirement—the reception, the dinner, the speeches—and Janet was assigned the task of determining whether she might enjoy, as her retirement gift, Garvey's tour of Ireland. She brought it up during her Friday visit.

"No, Janet, I already turned Lillian down. She'd be such a

troublesome companion on a trip abroad, and so would the bishop."

"Then why not sign up for the air portion only? That's what Randy and I are doing."

Agatha was about to say no when she was visited by a vision of James O'Hannon walking with her beside a large body of water. For the past two weeks cascading water had been showing up repeatedly in her dreams and she had awakened each morning with a deep yearning for something she couldn't identify, a longing so lush that it must have been rooted for years under the surface of her daily life. But a longing for what? She had tried to give it a name. Adventure? A challenge? Those words were close, but adventure was a man's word, and challenge was a speechwriter's cliché. Was there no term for a woman's desire to feel herself passing through undiscovered country for a change? Was there no term for the urgent wish to be swept off the flat expanse where she had spent her adult years and to be set down among waterfalls? Because of her recurring dream this yearning, though it had no name, was now associated in her mind with foam and spray and the whole range of sounds that water makes.

"The three of us could leave the group at Shannon and go to Dublin on our own," Janet was saying. "You could go sightseeing with us and the Fermoyles, or whatever you wanted. You could go to Dublin Castle and look up your family tree. Sister Judy says that's what Irish Americans usually do. I might do it myself. The grandma I didn't know was named Flynn."

The large body of water was the ocean. Agatha felt James take her hand as they stood in the wind and looked out at the whitecaps. She heard the waves breaking on the rocky shore. James was bending to say something in her ear.

"Yes, Janet, I believe I'll go."

While Agatha waited for James to acknowledge her travel plans, a second letter arrived from the Blackrock section of Dublin, this one addressed specifically to Janet. It was from the Fermoyle daughter, Evelyn. She wrote to say how eagerly she looked forward to meeting Randy's bride. She remembered Randy from her childhood when she had lived in the States for a year, and she could see from the wedding snapshot that he was still blond and good-looking. Was he still so serious? She hoped Janet could break away from him long enough when they were over so Evelyn could take her around to a couple of posh dress shops on Grafton Street. Surely she'd want to take home an Irish jacket or skirt. And she knew of a smashing new place for lunch—just the two of them?

Janet, who had grown up in a farmhouse with slanting floors and a leaky roof, was excited and intimidated at the prospect of lunching in a European capital, to say nothing of walking into a posh dress shop. Would her lack of savvy embarrass Evelyn? Would Randy object to her spending money on an Irish jacket or skirt? Why should he? It was her money. Hers was the steady income in this marriage, not his.

In April Janet, by tampering with her travel plans, caused all the arrangements to fall apart.

The trouble began with Stephen. With tears in his eyes, Stephen told his mother he didn't want to live for ten days with Grandfather and Grandmother Meers. Grandmother Meers was too strict. Whenever he spent a day with her, she watched him every minute. She watched him play, she watched him eat. She invited other old ladies over to the house, and the other old ladies watched him play and watched him eat. At this, Janet realized how completely Stephen shared her own feelings about Mrs. Meers, and she found this endearing. She realized as well exactly how much she was going to miss Stephen. She decided that Stephen should go along to Ireland.

Whereupon Randy backed out. Randy was miffed. Not a day went by (he told her) when Janet didn't favor Stephen over himself, and what kind of a goofy honeymoon was it going to be anyhow, with the kid along? Not that he had anything against the kid, he was a decent enough kid, but let's be reasonable.

Janet thought it over for a night and a day and gave in. When Randy got home from Spring-Flo in the evening, she admitted that her idea had been a bad one. Because she had been a mother for a lot longer than she had been a wife, nearly three years longer, she sometimes doted on Stephen and slighted Randy (she admitted), but she did so without thinking, never on purpose, and to prove she loved Randy very much, she had decided to leave Stephen at home after all. She had arranged for Stephen to stay the first few days with Grandfather and Grandmother Meers and the last few days with Grandpa Raft on the farm.

But it was too late to appease Randy. He had sold only one Spring-Flo softener in the past three weeks, and he was feeling glum and hopeless. He didn't believe the airplane would get as far as Ireland, and if it did, he didn't see how he could possibly have a good time there, and if he had a good time, how could he return to his meaningless life in Staggerford?

At school the next day Janet's eyes were pink from crying. "We're not going," she told Agatha. "Of all the rotten things— we're not going."

"Who's not going where?"

"To Ireland. Randy says we're not going. He says the plane is going to crash on the way over. When he gets in his down moods he says things like that and actually believes them."

"What right does he have to say you're not going?"

"Well, he's saying it." Janet stamped her foot.

"Listen, Janet, he can say *he's* not going, but he can't say *you're* not going."

This made sense to Janet. And as long as Randy was staying home, why not take Stephen along on Randy's ticket?

This made sense to Agatha. She, Janet, Stephen and Lillian would form the Staggerford delegation to Ireland. They would leave Lillian with the group at Shannon and rejoin her there ten days later for the flight home.

But it didn't make sense to Stephen. To Stephen the farm was paradise. He was more than willing to endure a few days in the Meers household if it earned him a few days on the farm. Everything was happily haphazard on the farm: play, meals, bedtime. Last time he stayed there overnight his Grandpa Raft had made him a slingshot and let him steer the tractor. His Aunt Sally and Aunt Karen had taken him fishing in the river. Aunt LeeAnn and her boyfriend had taken him for a spin in a dump truck. So it was no wonder that when his mother told him he was going to Ireland after all, he responded by lying on his back and kicking the floor with his heels and then, later, by crying himself to sleep. Janet relented. She'd go alone.

So in the end Garvey Travel signed up three travelers from Staggerford. Lillian Kite would travel with the group, Janet Meers would stay with the Fermoyles and Agatha McGee would meet the man in her life.

8

TWO WEEKS BEFORE HER DEPARTURE, a second man entered her life: Bishop Richard Baker.

It was at Mass on the first Sunday in May that Father Finn climbed into the pulpit and said, "I have here a letter from His Excellency the bishop," and Agatha steeled herself for bad news.

"'After much prayer and meditation,'" Father Finn began to read, "'I have decided to change our system of Confirmation. . . .'" Here the elderly priest paused to cough and blow his nose. He had been in this parish for many years and was not eager to read on, not with Agatha, who had prepared the seventh graders for Confirmation, sitting defiantly in her customary pew. This year there were seventeen candidates for Confirmation. Throughout the winter and spring Agatha had held special classes for them, drilling them in their catechism, assigning them brief readings from the Bible, regaling them with the lives of saints and telling them all she knew (which struck them as precious little) about the world, the flesh and the devil.

Father Finn returned his handkerchief to his sleeve and continued, "'Beginning immediately, I intend to stop visiting the parishes of this diocese for Confirmation. All joy and spontaneity have gone out of this wonderful, meaningful sacrament. It has become a rote exercise. From now on I will confirm the souls entrusted to me only when those souls come to me as individuals and ask to be confirmed. They may do this at any time. They may even be adults before the Holy Spirit moves them. Any time is the acceptable time, as long as they come to me and ask. Affectionately, your servant, Richard Baker, bishop of Berrington.'"

The letter was followed by a sermon, but Agatha, awash in a tide of anguish, heard none of it. After Mass, she followed Father Finn into the sacristy and told him the bishop was mentally disturbed. "Has he forgotten that we expect him here next Sunday evening? The date was approved by the Chancery months ago. You must go to Berrington immediately, Father, and talk some sense into him. You must tell him how we feel as a parish."

Father Finn, divesting, looked pained. He was a small, gentle man, and without his microphone he had a small, weak voice. He was a priest of middling intelligence serving a parish of middling spiritual and financial resources and determined to keep to the middle of the road. "And how *do* we feel as a parish, Agatha? Don't you see that our orthodox opinions, yours and mine, aren't everybody's cup of tea anymore? Fully half this parish is happy with change, and I am their pastor as well as yours."

She gave him her level look. "Were you ordained a priest or a politician?"

"Now, Agatha."

"Admit it. You're not going to challenge the bishop on this."

"A priest doesn't tell his bishop what to do."

"Very well, then, it's up to me."

That afternoon Agatha wrote the bishop a letter. If Confirmation (she wrote) were a purely temporal matter, like taking out a loan, then she could understand delaying the decision until adulthood, but this was a spiritual matter of immeasurable importance, and who was more in need of the Holy Spirit in these treacherous times than twelve-year-olds? Confirmation was a week away. Her students were eager to become soldiers of Christ. They had been fitted for new suits and dresses. Their sponsors had been alerted. The Sodality had cleaned the church, even the basement. Sincerely, Agatha McGee.

Return mail brought the bishop's reply. How gratifying to know that the laity were taking an interest in Church policy. How fortunate for the Church that people as venerable as Miss McGee remained alert to the concerns of her parish. Affectionately, your servant, Richard Baker, bishop of Berrington.

Worked up, Agatha read the letter to Father Finn over the

phone. "He's evading the issue, Father. He makes no mention in his letter of next Sunday at St. Isidore's."

"Then I think we can assume he's not coming."

"And I resent being called venerable. It makes me sound like a building with pillars."

"You are highly esteemed around the diocese, Agatha."

"Esteemed is just as bad."

"It comes from your lifetime of dedication to St. Isidore's. And from a lifetime of speaking your mind."

She wondered if this was a compliment. "Are you saying I'm a crank?"

"Far from it. You are known as a strict follower of your conscience. But so is the bishop, you see. You must admit that he too has a right to follow his conscience."

"But his is in error."

"Don't be too sure. He prays for guidance."

"So do I."

The priest paused. "Then why do you suppose your viewpoints are so far apart?"

"Obviously his prayers aren't being answered. I'm going to Berrington on Saturday, Father. You might call ahead and tell him I'm coming."

"Impossible. The bishop takes no appointments on Saturdays. He golfs in the morning and he hears confessions in the afternoon and he says Mass in the evening."

"He hears confessions at the cathedral?"

"Yes, for two hours every Saturday. He doesn't need to—he has two assistants to hear confessions—but he insists. He really is a conscientious man."

"What time does he hear?"

"From two to four, I think."

"That fits my schedule just fine."

When Agatha arrived at the cathedral in her shiny old Plymouth, confessions had already begun. She stood inside the heavy main door and gave her eyes a minute to adjust to the stained-glass gloaming. Then she stepped over to a man kneeling near the back and asked him where the bishop was hearing. He pointed to a confessional where a number of people stood in two lines, one leading to the dark, curtained enclosure where the penitent could be anonymous, and the other leading to a chair facing the confessor. She chose the anonymous side, that line being shorter and the face-to-face method being progressive. Waiting her turn, she averted her eyes from the remodeled high altar devoid of statues and ornamentation, plain as a Quaker meetinghouse—a desecration.

Her turn came. She knelt in the dark enclosure. Bishop Baker opened the small aperture between his compartment and hers. She whispered, "Bless me, Your Excellency, for I have sinned." She saw his head in profile, his hand raised in blessing. She continued, "Since my last confession, which was two weeks ago, I have been troubled by the sins of anger and despair."

"Ah, yes," the bishop mumbled, "the age-old demons, anger and despair." He bent his ear to the screen and nodded sympathetically. "Tell me, what is the cause?"

"A certain person, Your Excellency. A man."

"I see. Now, it is sometimes possible to rearrange our lives so as to avoid such a person. To ignore him."

"Not in this case, I'm afraid." Her voice was no longer a whisper. "This man is my superior, though he calls himself my servant, and I have been conditioned to follow his orders, unwise as they are."

The bishop drew back slightly from the screen, from the emotion in her voice, its forthrightness, its power. He said, "But certainly if he's an occasion of sin for you, he must be avoided."

"Don't you understand there are certain people who occupy such important positions in our lives that we can't avoid them?"

"Yes, I suppose. Who is this, if I may ask?"

"You."

"Pardon me?" He leaned close.

"You, Your Excellency. You are the cause of my anger. You drive me to despair."

"Me?" He leaned away.

"You are withholding the sacrament of Confirmation from the young people of St. Isidore's in Staggerford." Her righteous resonance carried through the curtains, so that some of those waiting their turn covered their ears while others listened intently. "You are denying them the gifts of the Holy

Spirit, which in case you've forgotten, are seven in number: wisdom, understanding, counsel, fortitude, knowledge, piety and fear of the Lord. We're expecting you tomorrow evening at seven."

The bishop drew himself erect in his chair. Though they had never met, he knew this must be the legendary old lady of St. Isidore's. He said, "I must tell you I've never been so certain of a decision in my life. With Confirmation I see no need for haste. The Apostles were grown men when the Spirit came to them in tongues of flame. I will confirm your aspirants when they come to me as individuals and declare themselves ready. Now please try to understand."

She sighed, said nothing.

"Have you anything else to confess?" he asked softly.

"No."

"Then I absolve you in the name of the Father and of the Son and of the Holy Spirit. Go in peace." He slid the panel shut.

"Wait, I'm not finished," she said, but she could tell by the murmur that the bishop was already listening to the penitent on the other side. She waited, and when he opened her panel once again and raised his hand in blessing, she said, "It is I again, Your Excellency. I wish to know where and when an aspirant might be confirmed."

"At my house. At any time. Just call ahead."

"Very good."

"Yes, very good. Good-bye, Miss McGee." He shut the panel.

She knelt for a moment in disbelief (how did he know her name?), and then she left the church. She went next door to the bishop's residence, a limestone mansion webbed with cracking mortar and greening ivy. The door was opened by a woman about Miss McGee's age. She had a dust mop in her hand and something chewy in her mouth. She said, "Yes?"

"I wish to know the bishop's plans for tomorrow evening. Is his secretary in? Or one of his assistants?"

"Nobody here right now but me." The woman shifted her food from one cheek to the other. "But I can tell you if it's Sunday night it's bridge."

"Bridge?"

"Every Sunday night, him and his friends."

Agatha thanked her.

A few of Agatha's seventeen students belonged to families whose progressive sympathies kept them home, but a dozen of them, together with their parents and sponsors and here and there a grandparent, gathered at Agatha's house at seven o'clock on Sunday evening. Father Finn had been invited but sent his regrets. When the group was complete, Agatha phoned Berrington to double-check.

"Yes, the bishop's having friends in," said the housekeeper. "Who is this, please?"

Agatha hung up and set in motion to Berrington a caravan of thirteen cars and a pickup truck. She rode in the lead car with Mr. and Mrs. Fielding, their son Roger and Roger's sponsor, Harry Eggleston.

It was a blustery evening—first rain and then sun and then rain and sun together. When they arrived at the cathedral and parked along the street in front of the bishop's residence, small hailstones lay melting in the grass.

According to plan, Roger Fielding and his parents and his sponsors were the first to leave their car and accompany Agatha to the front door. Though Roger Fielding was small and looked younger than his twelve years, Agatha had chosen him for his fluency and spunk. As he stood on the bishop's doorstep he pressed down his hair and buttoned his new blue blazer and rehearsed his lines aloud. His parents stood on the step below and behind him, Mr. Fielding fidgeting and whistling and Mrs. Fielding praying silently. Behind them Agatha stood shoulder to shoulder with Harry Eggleston, a garrulous bachelor of about fifty, a neighbor and friend of the Fieldings. He kept glancing at Agatha and grinning. He was enjoying this adventure immensely.

Again it was the housekeeper who opened the door. Tonight she was eating a carrot.

"I wish to see His Excellency," said Roger.

She peered at him sternly. "The bishop is occupied."

"But I'm here to be confirmed. I'm sure he'll see me if you tell him I'm here to be confirmed."

The housekeeper looked from one face to another. She looked beyond the Fieldings and said to Agatha, "Is this a joke?"

Agatha shook her head. She had decided to say not a word during this entire mission for fear of inadvertently violating some new rule of the bishop's. Besides, Roger knew what to say.

"I have memorized the entire catechism in order to be confirmed. I am ready to become a soldier of Christ."

There was a sudden shower of rain, and the housekeeper stepped back to let them all into the front hall. "Wait here," she said, and she went through an archway into an adjacent room. It was a long room, the walls hung with gilt-framed portraits of long-dead prelates. At the far end, before a crackling fireplace, the bishop sat at a card table with three other men. They were absorbed in their cards. Agatha took Roger by the elbow and placed him prominently in the archway. She placed the grinning Harry Eggleston behind Roger's right shoulder. She asked Mr. and Mrs. Fielding to stand behind Harry. The housekeeper interrupted the game; the four men looked up from their cards, the bishop with his back to the archway. On his left sat a young man in an open-necked shirt, and on his right a fat, florid man whose jowls wobbled as he moved his head. The bishop's partner was a small gray man with thick glasses and a gray goatee. The bishop turned in his chair, and all four men regarded the boy standing in the archway. The bishop rose and approached the boy, carrying his cards with him. He wore a purple shirt of limp velour and looked shorter than Agatha expected a bishop to be.

The bishop was puzzled. He extended his arm to shake the boy's hand. Roger, schooled, went to one knee, kissed his ring and implored, "Your Excellency, I wish to be confirmed."

"Confirmed?" Bishop Baker raised the boy to his feet. "I must say you've chosen an inopportune time." He glanced at his hand of cards.

"Any time is the acceptable time, as long as one comes to you and asks. I quote from your letter of May the fourth."

The bishop examined the boy's face for signs of insolence but discovered none. He looked at Harry Eggleston, who chuckled, and at the fretting parents. His eyes fell on Agatha, and although they had never been introduced, he knew her instantly. All was clear to him. He smiled at her. It was the smile of someone bested in a game. And her smile, while she tried to keep it respectful, was triumphant.

He said, "What's your name, son?"

"Roger, Your Excellency."

"Well, Roger, come with me. Bring your people along. Never let it be said I'm not a man of my word." He led the boy down the long room to the card table. His parents and Harry Eggleston followed. Everyone, including the housekeeper, shook hands.

The bishop called to Agatha, who had remained in the hall. "Won't you join us, Miss McGee?"

She shook her head. She wanted to be near the door to direct traffic.

He turned to his housekeeper and asked her to fetch his holy oil.

"And your miter and staff?" she asked sarcastically.

"No, Mrs. Curry, those won't be necessary."

She left the room by another door and returned in a moment with a tiny vial. The bishop put a drop of chrism on his thumb and asked Roger to kneel before him. "What name are you taking, my son?"

"Edward," said Roger.

The bishop told Harry Eggleston to place his hand on the boy's right shoulder. Harry did so, turning back to wink at Agatha.

The young man at the card table looked amused; he was Father Lansky, the bishop's assistant. The fat man gave off snorts of impatience. The small man with the goatee sat with his mouth open, awed.

Bishop Baker laid his hand on Roger's hair and touched his oily thumb to Roger's forehead, saying, "I sign thee, Edward, with the sign of the cross and I confirm thee with the chrism of salvation." Then he gave the boy a light tap on the cheek and told him to rise. He shook his hand warmly and said, "So there you are, my son, a soldier of Christ."

"Thank you, Your Excellency. Aren't you going to ask me any questions?"

"Such as?"

"Catechism questions."

"You know the answers, do you?"

"Yes."

"Then that's my only question." He shook hands with the Fieldings again. "A fine boy you have here."

The Fieldings bowed and retreated from the room. Harry Eggleston moved around behind the fat man and examined his cards. The Bishop threw Agatha a farewell smile and sat down.

"I bid one heart," said the fat man.

"God," said Harry Eggleston, "I wouldn't bid hearts with a hand like that."

The fat man's temples turned scarlet.

Agatha opened the front door to let the Fieldings out and the Krugers in. Charlotte Kruger was a girl of such pure, striking beauty that even the fat man was magnetized by her blue eyes and straw-colored hair as she led her parents and her sponsor up to the bishop's right shoulder and said, "I wish to be confirmed."

"What? Another one?" Bishop Baker got up and cast a desperate glance at Agatha in the archway. "All right, my dear, what name are you taking?"

"Mary."

"Fine. Please kneel. Mrs. Curry, where is my chrism?"

He confirmed her. He helped her to her feet. Excusing himself to his friends, he accompanied the Krugers to the hallway, where he intended to concede victory to Agatha and bid her good-bye, but before he could speak to her she was opening the door for the next group—Sammy O'Connor and his parents and three of his grandparents.

"More?" said the bishop.

"Just ten more, counting Sammy here," said Agatha, breaking her silence.

The Bishop leaned out the doorway and saw the thirteen cars and the pickup. He saw dozens of people strolling about the grounds, stretching their legs and taking the cool air between showers of rain. He drew back inside and put his hand on his breast where Agatha thought his pectoral cross should be hanging on a golden chain, and said, "Lead them all into the church, Miss McGee. Father Lansky and I will come over and give you some proper ritual." He said this with neither magnanimity nor malice. He said it with wonder. Then he turned to Mrs. Curry and asked if she could rustle up a few snacks for after the ceremony.

The fat man, hearing this, threw down his cards and left the house by a rear door. Harry Eggleston took his place and invited Sammy O'Connor's father to sit in the bishop's chair.

"What do you say we switch to seven-card poker?" said Harry.

"Fine with me," said Father Lansky, the young man opposite, "but not now. It looks like we're about to adjourn to the church."

In the sanctuary of the cathedral (not so austere in candlelight as in daylight) the Bishop confirmed the twelve (not excluding Roger and Charlotte, for the second time) with enough pomp to satisfy even Agatha. There were lengthy prayers, an extemporaneous homily and incense. There were no catechism questions. The closing hymn was one that everybody knew, "Holy God," and they made it reverberate off the vaulted ceiling.

Then back to the house. Wearing his cassock and cross, Bishop Baker worked his way through the crowd, shaking forty or fifty hands and saying, "My house is your house, welcome, welcome." He steered himself in the direction of Agatha, who stood in a corner with Sammy O'Connor and Roger Fielding. He congratulated the boys. He congratulated Agatha. "I'm all admiration," he said. "If only more people had your spiritual zeal."

"If only more bishops," she said.

His laugh was exuberant. "Please be first in line for refreshments."

She took the arm he offered and they stepped up to the table laid with snacks and drinks; Mrs. Curry had done well.

Agatha heaped her plate with coldcuts, crackers and sweets.

"Miss McGee, I'm hoping this is the beginning of a friendship between us." He popped a Korn Kurl into his mouth.

"Oh?" She was arrested with an olive partway to her lips. Friendship? Didn't he understand that this was only the initial engagement in a lengthy war?

"C. H. Garvey tells me that you and a young woman friend are flying with us to Ireland."

"So we are."

"He says you're leaving the group at Shannon Airport and going to Dublin on your own."

"I'm told there's a train direct."

"There is, but I'm renting myself a car for that very same trip, and I'd be more than happy to drive you both to Dublin."

"You're leaving the group? You're its leader."

"No, Garvey's the leader. I shouldn't have let him use my name. I'll be with the group only during their four days in Dublin. I have Church business to tend to. I thought I was doing Garvey a favor, and I guess I was, but it turns out to be a deception really."

Agatha chewed the olive, frowning.

"Please come along. I'll be glad to have company on the road, and you'll find it so much more convenient than the train."

"I've always been fond of the train."

"I'll drop you at whatever doorstep in Dublin you say."

This was hard to decline. So was the moral duty to accept a peace offering. "Janet and I are staying at separate addresses. Could you deliver her as well?"

"Of course." He gave her the smile from the front page of the brochure. Up close it was warm, unfeigned.

She nodded. "All right, Your Excellency."

"Call me Dick."

"Not on your life. I wasn't brought up to call bishops by their nicknames."

"Richard then? Anything but Your Excellency."

She tried out Richard in a whisper, facing away from him. It sounded scarcely more episcopal than Dick. "No, I'll call you Bishop."

Under his chuckle was a sigh. What a tough case she was.

They were separated at the table by a pack of hungry twelve-year-olds. The bishop covered his plate with carrot sticks and cookies and went to stand by the wall beside Father Lansky, who was stirring his drink with a pretzel.

"A nice way to meet our people from out of town, wouldn't you say, Bill?"

"Yep, nice party."

"I'm thinking we should start a series of get-togethers like this."

"But not on our bridge night." Father Lansky looked longingly at the card table at the end of the room from which their friend with the goatee had disappeared. Three men and a woman from Staggerford made a foursome of whist.

Nibbling a cookie, the bishop kept his eye on Agatha across the room. His proposing to drive her across the Midlands of Ireland was more than a peace offering; it was part of his plan to phase out St. Isidore's school. Already more than half the parish was clamoring for its demise because it drained the parish bank account every year. Salaries for teachers were shooting up. State regulations were becoming ridiculously stringent— lunchroom refrigerators of a certain cubic footage, cooking fans of a certain rpm, a thermostat in each classroom, new lighting. There was no way a parish of twelve hundred souls could keep up with all that. Bishop Baker had already closed six schools, had met with six degrees of opposition and had learned that the best way to overcome a strong pro-school faction was to identify its leaders and win them over to his side. Or failing that, at least convince them that his reasons for closure arose from logic and not from the devil. His first target was Agatha. He must try to win her confidence, disarm her. It was clear to him now that he could function much more easily as bishop if she were on his side instead of opposing him at every turn.

And if he won her over, would she not be of immense help to him in the long term? Was it too much to hope that Agatha would become the ally he needed among the laity in Staggerford, a kind of vice regent not of the clergy? He relied on laypeople in various locations to keep him up to date on his see and to promulgate his plans. Consulting with his priests was all well and good for apprising him of parish statistics (births and burials, budgets and baptisms), but it took the laity to give you the big picture, the sense of a parish's social groups, its friendships and animosities, its lines of force. In his ten months as bishop he had established the necessary contacts in most of his parishes, but Staggerford remained unexplored territory. He was acquainted with the Meerses and a few other couples there, but only well enough to know he wasn't eager to know them any better. His prime candidate now was Agatha McGee. She had lived there all her life. She had taught at St. Isidore's for forty-six years. She had outlived five bishops of Berrington. What a fund of lore she must be. What a hell of a bishop she'd make.

9

THE PASSENGERS ON the night flight from Minneapolis to Shannon were excited and noisy and were keeping Agatha awake. Those who weren't chattering and rustling newspapers as though it were midday were overreacting to the movie that had been flickering on the screen since Newfoundland, something about visitors from outer space. Agatha kept seeing through her closed eyelids eerie flashes of orange and purple light and she kept hearing gasps from those sitting nearby.

"Look, she's leaving him," blurted Lillian Kite. "She's taking their son and moving out. Couldn't you just cry when wives pick up and leave like that?" Lillian removed her right earphone to let in Agatha's response.

Agatha spoke without opening her eyes. "It's only a movie, Lillian."

"And what a movie! Look, he's standing there in the street watching her drive away."

Agatha looked: A suburban street. Neighbors in their yards witnessing the breakup. Husband slouching back into his house. Blackout. Husband weeks later, haggard, whiskered.

"What's his problem, Lillian? Why doesn't he shave?"

"He's got space creatures on his mind that are trying to make contact with Earth, using a little melody, and his wife doesn't understand. The melody goes dee dee dee *dee* dee, like that."

"I can't say I blame her."

"But she'll come around to his way of thinking, just watch now."

Agatha watched Lillian watching. Lillian's complexion was high pink—two bloody Marys at JFK. Her white hair was disheveled. Red plastic tubes ran from her ears to the socket in the armrest. On her lap she held a ball of yarn and a lurid

87

tabloid open to a page of divorcing movie stars.

Turning to the window on her right, Agatha examined her face reflected against the black universe. She tightened an earring and ran a finger along her jaw. She could be looking a lot worse, she decided, considering she had suffered through two takeoffs and one landing and it was past her bedtime. She had risen at five this morning. At eight o'clock she and Janet and Lillian had left Staggerford by bus. At noon they had met the larger touring party at the Twin Cities airport. At two they had boarded a 727 and flown to New York, where at seven-thirty they had boarded this DC-10. God only knew what time it was now. Lillian had already set her watch ahead to Irish time, which was a small hour of the morning, while Agatha, afraid of being presumptuous, had decided to wait to see if she touched down alive before letting go of Minnesota time, which was not yet midnight. Could God himself say what time it was outside this dark porthole? Did time even exist at thirty-nine thousand feet?

"Oh, it's so sad," said Lillian, her eyes filling. "Is there anything in the world sadder than love going haywire?"

Agatha opened her purse and took out her compact. "I thought it was sad last winter when the grain elevator caught fire and burned to the ground." She switched on her overhead light.

"No, love going haywire, Agatha—that's worst of all. Think of the *really* sad things in Staggerford in the past fifty years, and what are they but affairs of the heart? Think of the time Charles Finletter and Henry Taggert had their fistfight on the hospital steps, both of them claiming to be the father of Mrs. Taggert's premature baby."

Agatha smiled. "That was too funny to be sad."

"Funny?" Lillian was offended. "It was sad, Agatha, just plain sad! And remember how sad it was when Frankie Porter fell in love with that woman who lived next door to the Porters on Vine Street? What was her name? She was married to a salesman and they didn't live there very long. Frankie's wife came home that one afternoon and found them having a picnic on the grass between their houses, Frankie and the salesman's wife. That was very sad when you think about it."

Powdering her face, Agatha thought about it and chuckled, surprised by her own levity, for hadn't she taken these scandals as seriously as Lillian when they were new? Why did they now seem so comic? Was it the giddy altitude of this airplane? Or was she light-headed at the prospect of coming face to face with James O'Hannon, who had written, finally, and said he would call for her at the hotel on her first evening in Dublin? Scattered through this letter were phrases she found curiously stilted. "Pleased by this opportunity to make your acquaintance in person." "Anticipation of the highest order." In fact, the whole letter was strangely formal. She blamed it on his excitement, for why wouldn't he be as nervous and excited as she? She prayed he'd be as eager.

"Agatha, you have a very odd sense of humor. Think of the grief that picnic between the houses caused. And remember the time Mr. Chalmers was having his affair with Mrs. Hanson, and one night when he was over at her house he let her use his car to drive downtown to buy beer, and she parked a block away from the liquor store so nobody would notice, and when she went to drive home she put it in the wrong gear and crashed through the plate glass of the five and dime?"

Agatha covered her eyes, bouncing with mirth.

"Oh, Agatha!" Giving up, Lillian raised her eyes to the movie.

Closing her compact and peering ahead down the aisle, Agatha saw Bishop Baker emerge from behind the curtain separating the common herd from first class, where he had been sitting with C. H. Garvey. The bishop was wearing a checkered sport shirt. She watched him advance down the aisle, beaming at his flock, stopping here and there to dispense a sprinkle of chatter. As he drew near, Agatha switched off her light, turned her face to the window and pretended to sleep. After a minute she heard him address Lillian in a spirited voice.

"Ah, Mrs. Kite, isn't this fun? How's the movie? How was your dinner? I see Miss McGee is asleep. When she wakes up, please tell her it's not too late to change her mind if she wishes to stay with the group."

Lillian said, "I will, Your Excellency," her voice raised in joyful deference.

"None of that formality, Mrs. Kite. Call me Dick."

"Yes, Your Excellency." A giggle. "Dick."

"C. H. Garvey is worried that she and Janet will miss a lot if they go off on their own. 'The Essence of the Emerald Isle,' he says, 'with Special Attention to Its Catholic Heritage.' "

Agatha recognized the quote from the travel brochure. It was a wonder the way bishops learned to talk in capital letters like that. Also the way they dwelt on money. Had he come back here to row twenty-nine of economy class to shake her and Janet loose of an additional seven hundred dollars apiece? To think she and Janet would be riding in the same car with this man all the way from Shannon to Dublin. A daunting prospect.

"Happy landing, Mrs. Kite, I'll see you later."

Next Agatha heard him speaking to Janet, who sat behind her, but she couldn't make out the words.

"Your first flight, Janet?" Somehow he knew it was—Janet looked so wide-eyed and untraveled.

"No, I was up once in a small plane at the fair."

"Your first extended flight then."

"Yeah, except the jerk I was up with knew I was scared and wouldn't come down and *wouldn't* come down and it seemed *very* extended to me."

The bishop liked Janet's smile. She smiled with her eyes. They were striking eyes, dark brown and lively. The bishop was aware of Miss McGee's reputation as a surrogate mother to certain unfortunate girls, advising them and sometimes even taking them in to live with her; Janet was the latest in this series, so he had been told. He was given to understand that Janet had become at seventeen the unwed mother of a son, and last year at twenty she had married Randy Meers, son of Carl Meers, the man who made such splendid cash contributions to the Church out of the profits of Staggerford Realty. According to hearsay, it was an unfortunate marriage from the Meers point of view, a marriage doomed from the start, Janet's father being nothing but a dirt farmer and her mother being many years dead and Janet having no training beyond high school. And no work experience to speak of. And no style. And no promise. So it was said.

Accordingly the bishop had been prepared to meet a pitiful waif at the airport this noon. How delightful to meet instead this attractive young woman who by flashing her cheery smile at the bishop while she helped the two old women through the airport entrance turned all the hearsay to nonsense. What did the gossips mean, no style? Who could predict in the long run that it wasn't Janet who had made the poor match? If Randy Meers was such a hotshot husband, why wasn't he on this plane with his wife? A squabble? Illness? What was the story there? According to Garvey, Randy had signed up for the tour, then backed out.

The bishop had met Randy at a Knights of Columbus dinner in Staggerford last summer. He thought there was something odd about the boy even then. Boy? Yes, for although he was twenty-one, "boy" was precisely the word for Randy Meers. The bishop was guest speaker that night and had scarcely uttered his last sentence when Mr. and Mrs. Meers stood up and came forward through the crowd, pushing Randy recklessly ahead of them. They parked him nose to nose with the bishop— or rather nose to Adam's apple, Randy being tall—and Mr. Meers said, "Here's our boy, Bishop, home from college and working for me in real estate." Mr. Meers was large, bald and beaming. He looked distinguished. Had he buffed his scalp that it should gleam so fiercely under the fluorescent lights of the KC hall?

"The last time I met a bishop was when your predecessor baptized Randy," said Mrs. Meers. A handsome woman with a lot of gold at her throat and wrist, she was semidrunk this evening, her eyes unfocused.

Randy, taller and more handsome than either parent, said sourly, "Not baptized, Mother. Confirmed."

"Oh, how stupid of me." Mrs. Meers covered her eyes, pretending shame.

Mr. Meers said, "Bishop, whenever the Church needs real-estate advice, Randy and I are at your service. Kiss his ring, Randy."

"No, please, that's medieval." Bishop Baker restrained Randy, who had begun to go to his knee. He shook his hand instead. A soft, moist hand. His hair was blond and curly, his eyebrows

black. Something about his face struck the bishop as unformed. It was a long face with prominent features that would
someday be craggy but as yet were softened by a boyish mouth
that might have been a girl's. His full, mobile lips were more
expressive than his eyes. The eyes told you nothing. They were
black and beadlike and concealed whatever was going on behind them. Was this the face that launched a thousand gossips
who went about predicting divorce for a man who had married beneath him? Bishop Baker would like to take a few bets
on that, now that he had met Janet. He was tired of busy-
bodies telling him how real-life stories would end. Real-life
stories wrote themselves and often included some very surprising chapters.

The DC-10 was passing through turbulence of a minor sort,
and Bishop Baker swayed in the aisle as he said, "Just remember, Janet, if you and Miss McGee change your minds, you're
welcome to stay with the group."

"Oh, we'd never do that. We're going to be busy the whole
time. I'm seeing people in Dublin and Miss McGee's doing her
famly tree."

"All right then, fine." The bishop, reassured, moved on down
the aisle. He had brought it up only for Garvey's sake. Garvey
had phoned the Chancery a couple of days ago to say that enrollment for this tour was disappointingly small and had asked
the bishop to see what he could do—as though the bishop,
having lent Garvey his name as a favor, was responsible for
recruiting pilgrims to Eire. Tonight in first class Garvey had
brought it up again, had been harping on the figure of fourteen hundred dollars (two additional land portions) and the
difference it would make in his margin of profit. As if Garvey,
with his fourteen-room house on the Badbattle River and his
Chrysler Imperial, needed the money. No, let Garvey take the
tour bus across Ireland without Agatha McGee and Janet Meers.
Let the bishop have the pleasure of their company, particularly that of Agatha McGee, whose good opinion he was determined to win if he had to move heaven and earth to do so;
Agatha McGee, who at this very moment (he was quite sure)
was not really asleep but only pretending.

* * *

Facing the window, head drooping, hands limp in her lap, Agatha felt Lillian leaning close, smelled her toilet water. Her breath.

"Isn't the bishop just the sweetest man?"

Agatha shrugged.

"Will you stay with the group, Agatha? I wish you would."

"No, I'm sorry."

"Oh, you're such a spoilsport. You heard him, there'll be a place for you and Janet right up to the last minute. Just write a check for the other seven hundred and you'll see a lot more of Ireland than you can see by yourself."

"He's one to talk. He's not staying with the group."

"He'll be with us after three days. He's going to join up with us when our bus gets to Dublin on Sunday. Please."

Agatha turned and looked straight into Lillian's eyes. "I've told you over and over, Lillian, I'm tracing my family tree." She looked away. This being the first lie of her life, she was mortified at having had to repeat it so often. The truth—the secret truth—was James.

"But your family tree won't take you the whole ten days."

"It might."

"It would be more fun for me if you stayed with the group."

"These are all lovely people, Lillian. You'll have the time of your life. You'll make a lot of new friends." Not for anyone's sake would she give up this adventure, never mind if rumors of romance drifted back to the townspeople who had been watching her every action since she was seven years old, townspeople of all ages who admired Agatha's straight and narrow predictability without realizing the extent to which their scrutiny was its cause.

She had already sprung a few surprises. First was her refusal last week to join the Berrington County Retired Teachers Association with its insipid lectures on how to build birdhouses and master Medicare. Second, she had skipped the annual Gray Panther banquet, though a place had been set for her at the head table; she wasn't eager to spend an evening with all those senior citizens complaining about their ill-fitting dentures and negligent grandchildren. Third (this was her biggest bombshell), she had let lapse her charter membership in St. Isidore's Sodality, a membership going back to 1933; and not only that, she had quit in the middle of her seventh non-consecutive term as president. Well, what was the Sodality after all but a slavish cooking service for weddings and funerals? She was sick of preparing nutcups and goulash.

Poor Lillian would never understand her. She put her mouth close to Lillian's ear, deciding that her old friend deserved better than a falsehood. If not the entire truth, she owed her at least a piece of it. "To be honest, Lillian, I've always wanted more out of life than is given to groups."

But Lillian, diverted by a spaceship, wasn't listening. She adjusted her earphones and let herself be drawn back into the movie, where she remained until it ended, her lips shaping a little smile or grimace at each dissolve.

At break of day the movie ended and Lillian fell asleep. Agatha, numb with fatigue, searched the dawn for a sign that the earth would be down there when it came time to land, but because the sun hadn't yet risen and the sea was concealed by cloud, the morning was absolutely featureless, gray above and gray below. How could she be sure she wasn't flying off course to Iceland? Or upside down to Mars?

She took out her mirror and did what she could with her face, wondering what James O'Hannon would think of it when she met him tomorrow in Dublin. Only last week she had sent him a new snapshot of herself, taken at her retirement dinner. There was something sappy about her expression, her face twisted in deprecation and pleasure as she accepted the envelope containing the gift from her former students (money—twice as much as she needed for this flight), but she sent the photo anyway because it was flattering as to age, yet not so flattering that James wouldn't be reminded that four years had passed since the last photo she sent; she didn't want him to be disappointed or shocked when they came face to face. Her letters, she knew, conveyed a certain liveliness that made her seem younger than she really was and might lead a man who knew her only through the mail to expect more of her than he should. Or was it less?

Agatha dozed off, then awoke to Janet's voice: "Look, Miss

McGee, there it is!" Janet was straining forward against her seat belt, pointing.

Agatha looked out. The plane had passed down through the bottom layer of cloud. She saw the coast of Ireland outlined in white foam—the gray Atlantic beating against the gray rock of County Clare.

"Did you ever see so much green?" Janet's voice broke with excitement.

"Never," said Agatha. The plane rushed low over fields of lush wet grass, which even on this sunless morning were an iridescent green.

Lillian, awake now and ready to spring out of her seat as soon as permission was granted, sat clutching two tote bags on her lap as well as her purse, the three plastic handles nudging her under the chin. She held several newspapers clamped under her arm; they were folded tightly and bound with the rubber bands she had brought along for this purpose. She had promised Imogene she would bring home a newspaper from every stop.

"See you in Dublin, then," Lillian said out of the corner of her mouth, keeping her eye on the exit ahead.

"Yes, I'll be at the Gresham when you check in."

"If you get lonesome, just tough it out, as Imogene says. Starting Sunday I'll be with you every minute."

As Agatha feared.

Janet said, "Look, we're landing in a pasture. I thought Shannon was a city."

The plane touched down not in a pasture, but adjacent to one, and the first Irish faces Agatha laid eyes on were those of a dozen Holsteins.

10

AGATHA'S FIRST FOOTSTEPS in a foreign land echoed loudly through the Shannon terminal, for the heels of her sensible black shoes were hard, and the terminal at six in the morning was nearly deserted. It was shadowy and unheated as well. As she passed through customs she could hear the DC-10 roaring back into the sky, aimed toward the Continent. Only about thirty people had deplaned with her, a much smaller touring party than she had estimated when she joined them in the crowded Twin Cities airport. No wonder C. H. Garvey and the bishop had given her the hard sell.

After customs, Agatha and Janet exchanged their traveler's checks for Ireland's cabbage-leaf currency—large red and green bills covered with arcane lettering and engravings of poets and fish. Then they went to the floor-length windows near the terminal exit and stood guard over six suitcases, four of their own and two belonging to the bishop, who was seeing about the car.

They watched the rest of the touring party straggle outdoors and along the portico toward the dun-colored bus that awaited them in the rain. At the head of the line was Lillian Kite, who was determined to claim the front seat so as to have an unobstructed view of Ireland and to tell the driver the many facts he would surely want to know about Minnesota. Considering their lost sleep, Agatha thought it remarkable that so few of the travelers showed signs of the weariness she felt. Only their clothes seemed worn out—neckties crooked, collars limp, coats sagging open. When the last traveler climbed aboard the bus, C. H. Garvey, whose olive suit wasn't nearly the fit it had been yesterday in Minneapolis, put his head in at the glass door and said, with a smile he assumed was alluring, "Last call, ladies." He had thinning gray hair and a brushy moustache the color of nicotine. He repeated, "Last call."

Agatha smiled back. "Thank God for that."

Ignoring her guile, or not understanding it, Garvey turned toward the distant car-rental counter where the bishop was standing. "See you in Dublin, Dick." His call produced three echoes.

"Right, C.H., Sunday afternoon." The bishop waved energetically. "Happy highways."

Agatha and Janet watched Garvey carry his suitcase out to the end of the portico, where the bus driver stood waiting beside his open luggage door. The driver extended a hand to take the suitcase. Garvey set down the suitcase and shook the hand. The driver doffed his cap and straightened his tie. Garvey gave the driver a cigar. The driver gave Garvey a broad, toothless smile. Garvey shook the driver's hand again. The driver put on his cap and straightened his tie again. Garvey drew a notebook from his pocket and climbed aboard to count heads.

Agatha looked beyond the bus at a parking lot across the road. She was weary. She was chilly. Her new bronze-colored coat, though rainproof, was thin. Beyond the parking lot she saw a line of power poles and a cluster of traffic signs. Beyond those she saw the hill of wet grass where the dozen Holsteins were grazing. "So this is Ireland," she murmured. It was all very much like a rainy day at home.

"Maybe I should get out my raincoat," said Janet, looking to Agatha for instruction. Janet was dying to wear her new mail-order slicker—it was bright green with a dark blue corduroy lining—but did one open one's luggage in public?

"By the time we get to the coast the sun may be out, Janet." Before heading for Dublin tomorrow, they would be spending today and tonight in a coastal village recommended by the bishop. He had told them that the best cure for jet lag was sitting or lying still for the first twenty-four hours, and no tour of Ireland should begin without a good, long look at the sea. "They say Irish weather changes by the minute," she added.

Janet responded with a nod and a smile, hooking her straight dark hair behind her ears. She was wearing a new pair of blue jeans with bright white stitching and a gray sweat shirt with a drawstring hood hanging down her back. Sensible clothes for travel, certainly, but Janet's manner of dress was always a degree less formal than Agatha recommended.

Or would have recommended if she hadn't resolved to quit being so bossy. Retirement had propelled Agatha through some deep soul-searching, and one result was her vow before God that she would not spend her old age minding other people's business. As though by divine right she had served a lifetime as Staggerford's moral arbiter and chief of protocol. She had treated her fellow townsmen much the way she treated her sixth graders, which at least half of them had been at one time or another. With the passing years her influence had outgrown the village limits; for example, among the priests of the Berrington diocese she was known as Her Excellency for her efforts at holding back Church reform—a nickname they assumed (mistakenly) she was ignorant of.

Well, she was done with all that now. After all these years of showing the way, she had lost faith in herself as standard-bearer. Just as her teaching career struck her as depressingly plain in retrospect, so her efforts to improve people's lives, or at least to keep those lives from deteriorating, seemed ineffectual. Looking back at her record of wins and losses, she wasn't impressed. The people who had most depended on her for direction were the very ones who made the most ill-advised decisions when left on their own. Janet's hapless marriage to Randy Meers was but one example. Conversely, the people who had made a habit of ignoring Agatha or going against her wishes seemed to be getting along very happily in life. Bishop Baker, for instance. Witness the love lavished on him when he turned fifty last winter. Tributes poured in from far and wide. Gifts from every rank and stripe of the faithful. The Pope sent him a golden fish. Lillian Kite gave him a goldfish.

"Look, she's waving," said Janet.

The dun-colored bus began to move, and framed behind the large, frontmost window was Lillian, waving like crazy and throwing kisses, while with her other arm she was still clutching to her breast her purse, her two tote bags and her bale of newsprint.

Agatha and Janet waved. They watched the bus move along the drive and out onto the main road, picking up speed in the rain. What a curious rain. Not rain but mist. Not falling but hanging suspended. Was this the rain James called soft? It was scarcely visible to the eye, yet it shrouded the departing bus like fog. And the Irish light was so strange, so fragile, changing every few seconds, flickering.

"I'll only be a minute," said Bishop Baker, coming up behind them and hurrying out the door, jingling a keychain. He trotted across the road to the parking lot, his coattails flying.

Janet breathed on the window and wrote *Stephen* in the steam. "Why isn't he going with the group? Did he tell you?"

"Yes, he calls this his problem-solving vacation."

"What's his problem?"

"He's running out of priests."

In the parking lot Dick Baker walked briskly through the mist, searching for the car with which he would search for priests. For a hundred years the diocese of Berrington had been blessed with a trickle of priests from Ireland, three or four every decade, but now with the worldwide shortage of seminarians this foreign supply was drying up. Not one young man in the two major Irish seminaries was currently studying for the mission fields. So although Bishop Baker was the nominal leader of Garvey's tour, his primary business was to visit the two seminaries and remind the rectors and seminarians of their old Minnesota connection. It was a touchy business, of course, seminarians being the closely guarded property of their Irish bishops, so he must avoid looking like a pirate. And really it wasn't his purpose to abduct anyone—though if he tempted one or two men to follow him home, he would not protest. No, his purpose was simply to make sure the Berrington diocese was planted firmly at the back of their minds, so that when these young men became pastors in Ireland they might now and then steer a younger man his way. You never knew if something like this would pay off. It might be a generation or a century before Ireland again built up a surplus of priests. But twenty centuries had taught the Church patience, and Dick Baker was not dismayed to think that what he sowed today might not be harvested until long after he was dead.

All this he had explained to Agatha the other day when he phoned to confirm their travel plans. He said nothing of his ulterior motives, of course, his designs on Agatha herself, which were growing more and more elaborate; now, in Ireland, they were all one design and very baroque. First of all, he wanted Agatha's friendship for its own sake. As a mother's boy with no mother, he felt a strong attraction to her. He sensed that they might have a lot to share. As an only child he had spent most of his boyhood in the company of his mother, a vital, talkative, witty woman, and ever since leaving home thirty years ago he had been searching for her double. His mother, a young widow, had been inspired rather than dismayed by the prospect of earning a living, and she had done a fine job of it. Her job was secretarial and her hobby was politics. Eventually, in return for outstanding campaign work, she was appointed postmistress, from which position she kept her finger on the pulse of the town Dick Baker grew up in. In appearance his mother looked nothing like Agatha McGee (she was large and loud and wore a full frizzy head of dyed red hair), nor was religion one of her interests (she worshiped musicians instead, possessing the largest collection of jazz records in town); but she had Agatha's drive and resourcefulness, and she taught her son just how much an articulate, intelligent woman had to offer a man.

Then there were his churchly reasons for winning her favor. It was imperative that he harness Agatha's power to the changes he was planning in Staggerford. His latest idea—it struck him as late as yesterday, in fact—was that Agatha must take over as principal of St. Isidore's, replacing Sister Judith, who was to become Father Finn's assistant in parish work. Who better than Agatha to manage the school through its last two years of life? Whereas the schools in Owl Brook and Linden Falls had gone through prolonged and debilitating death pangs before expiring, Agatha would not allow any school in her charge to fall below standard. She'd keep it a dignified, efficient operation to the end. The bishop understood that after retiring the first time, Agatha had come back for four more years of work. He was giving himself these ten days in Ireland to convince her to do it again, for two more.

* * *

Dick Baker found the car, a sleek, yellow Mazda, and he drove it up to the portico. With the luggage stowed in the trunk, Agatha made a move to join Janet in the backseat (what was protocol for riding with a bishop, anyway?), but he said, "Nonsense, Miss McGee, don't treat me like a chauffeur. I could use some company up front."

"You'll find me poor company, I'm afraid. I'm half asleep."

"Well, if not company, at least a map reader. Somebody to point the way."

"All right—if you wish." She opened the front door and found herself on the driver's side. She went around and settled into the bucket seat on the passenger side.

The bishop got in behind the wheel and handed her a map. He chuckled as he strapped himself in—an impish chuckle.

"What is it?" said Agatha.

"It's this right-hand drive. It's this rain. It's Ireland. Why do I love this land of rain and rock and poverty?" He was beaming with delight and pointing to the windshield, opaque with mist. His sparse, dark hair was wet and curly.

"You've been here often?"

"This is my fourth visit." He started the engine. "I came here the first time when I was a seminarian. Three of us spent nearly a month on bicycles. We started in Cork and bicycled all the way to Donegal. Thought I'd never dry off. Then next I was here with Tom Dunn one summer when he came home on vacation. You know him, surely."

"Father Dunn in Pine Creek?"

"The same. We've got six priests from Ireland active in our parishes, and Tom is one of them. In the Irish scheme of things Minnesota is mission territory. I spent two weeks with him in Connemara, most of the time fishing. Tom loves to fish."

The bishop shifted gears and pulled away from the portico. "Then I was here a third time when I was chancellor, seeing about new priests, and that's what brings me back again."

He came to an intersection and stopped. "Which highway to the coast?"

Agatha took up the map. "Eleven. Turn left."

"Ah, yes, good old Eleven." He drove on. "Are you comfortable back there, Janet?"

"I'm fine." Janet spoke absently, sounding far away. She was staring sleepily out her side window at a green hill capped with gold blossoms made beautiful by the suggestion of sunlight filtering down through the thinning mist. She said, breathlessly, "All that gold."

"Gorse," the bishop explained. He turned to Agatha. "Wasn't it Robert Frost who said, 'Nature's first green is gold'?"

She nodded. " 'Her hardest hue to hold.' "

"Ahhh," said the bishop, speeding up. He chuckled and said "Ahhh" again, pleased with Agatha for knowing the poem, pleased with Janet and her eye for beauty, pleased with himself for being in Ireland.

Agatha turned to Janet. "Are you missing Stephen this morning?"

"Am I ever. And Randy."

In the mind's eye, each of them saw Randy. The bishop recalled Randy's less than friendly manner, his impervious eyes, at the Knights of Columbus banquet. Agatha thought of his clammy handshake at the wedding. Janet felt him cuddling her in bed; she wished with all her might that he had come along.

11

MEANWHILE, RANDY, unaware that he was being carried along a winding Irish road in the minds of three people in a yellow car, was sitting on the edge of his bed in his underwear. It was 3:00 A.M. in Staggerford. Randy couldn't sleep. Besides being inebriated and remorseful, he was elated. When had he last been elated? He was too full of beer to remember, too remorseful to care. What elated him was the water softener he had sold today, netting himself a commission of a hundred and forty dollars; how pleased Janet would be. What caused him remorse was what he had done next; how displeased she'd be.

This afternoon a woman named Ms. Ecklund had phoned the office in response to the Spring-Flo newspaper ad. She told Polly that she had lived in this town for only a week—she was the new pharmacist at Staggerford Drug—and already the hard water was turning her complexion to sandpaper. Could Polly arrange to send a softener expert over at six o'clock when she got home from work?

According to office policy as drawn up by Archie, the sales manager himself was entitled to first chance at all telephone inquiries, but Polly, with a conspiratorial wink, slipped this one to Randy. When Randy called his mother to say he wouldn't be home for dinner, his mother made a fuss. She had planned all the dinners she would serve Randy while Janet was gone, and this one was already in the oven. Salmon loaf. She and his father and Stephen would wait for him. No, Randy, insisted, you never knew how long a house call would take. "All right," his mother said, sighing with fondness and disgust, "if that's it, that's it"—the very words with which she had consented to Randy's marriage.

Later, over their cocktails before dinner, Mrs. Meers told her husband that Randy had sounded a little brighter over the phone, no longer so downcast, probably due to Janet's being away. "That's not it," said Mr. Meers, who felt a twinge of regret upon being reminded that Janet was gone from downstairs—not a bad girl, Janet.

"Well, why is he sounding brighter, then?" asked Mrs. Meers. Mr. Meers could only shrug. Far be it from him to define Randy's state of mind. From what he'd heard from Dr. Maitland at a party recently, the brain was full of chemicals, and it would take a team of biochemists to understand the repeated establishment and overthrow of the states of Randy's mind. After dinner Mr. Meers read to Stephen, and when it was Stephen's bedtime it was the man who objected, not the boy. He got a kick out of reading to the kid. Nice kid. Had his head on straight. Lucky thing for the kid his father wasn't Randy.

Ms. Ecklund, pharmacist, was a knockout. Wide smile, perfect teeth, brown hair falling in thick, soft curls to her shoulders. Complexion ruddy perhaps, but not sandpapery. She chuckled happily throughout Randy's suds demonstration and signed without question an order for the heavy-duty, deluxe softener. She asked him to call her Connie and offered to serve him dinner. Randy took a beer but refused dinner, saying he had eaten. Connie told him that now that her complexion problem was solved she would turn her attention to her social problem, which was a case of loneliness. She knew practically no one in town. The senior pharmacist at the drugstore was such a stuffy grouch, and the salesgirls were such brainless twits she didn't see how she was ever going to make friends. Did Randy have lots of friends?

Randy evaded answering, finished his beer and left. He drove out to the Brass Fox, where he sat at a wobbly little table and ordered a beer and a hamburger. The sale had excited him, and so had the buyer. He wondered why he hadn't stayed for dinner. Because he was married, that's why; one thing often led to another. But why (he asked himself halfway through his second beer), why, if he was all that firmly married, had his wife flown halfway around the world without him? Because she had been talked into it by that nosy old bird Miss McGee, who had convinced Janet she needed time away and had even convinced his mother of it. So here he sat, alone, following a course dictated by strong-minded women. As usual.

But Janet was no less strong-minded than Miss McGee (this came to him with his third beer), and how could anybody have pressed her into leaving him for ten days if she hadn't wanted to go? No, she truly needed to be away because Randy was such a glum husband. Yes, and he was worse than that—he was a heel. If he wasn't a heel he would have gone with her—she had begged him to go. Poor Janet. She deserved a better husband. He was moody and irritating and probably dull as dishwater. He drank his third beer and ordered a fourth.

He'd *be* better, damn it, he'd change. He'd be cheerful. As cheerful as Janet. If only she were home tonight, he would go to her and show her how cheerful he could be. He missed her acutely. This was the first night in ages he would step into the house and not find himself up to his ears in her embrace. How could he wait ten days?

It was also the first night in ages he wouldn't be pestered by Stephen. God, what a relief to have that kid out from underfoot. It was such a drag having a kid around who always wanted to be read to, and when you finally talked him into watching TV, he never liked your channel.

But halfway through his fourth beer it occurred to Randy that he missed Stephen, sort of. Having a little kid around sometimes made you feel good. Well behaved for a four-year-old. Not a whiner. Liked to have Randy wrestle with him. Liked to have Randy teach him songs. They were getting pretty good together on "Rocky Mountain High." The kid hit high notes the way John Denver did.

Randy ordered his fifth beer. He liked beer. Beer lowered his spirits. He had come dangerously close to being happy this evening. Selling a softener to the classy Ms. Ecklund in her clean little kitchen had elated him. Elation was not to be trusted. It never lasted. Happiness was risky. Beer was comfortably depressing. He turned his mind back over his unpaid bills and his wretched behavior as a husband. His parents and Janet were always on his back for the bills he ran up, but he couldn't help it. His buying was beyond his control. Certain things in life could not be resisted. When he had first heard about cable TV coming to town, he felt he would surely suffocate and die if he didn't arrange to have it piped into his living room immediately. The same with the earphone radio he had seen in a store window; it had made him short of breath; he had rushed into the store and come out with the earphones clamped over his head, having charged it without even asking the price. But didn't he buy things for Janet as well? That ceramic crock pot she never used? The bicycle she hardly ever rode? Yes, he bought as many surprises for her as for himself, but they never worked out the way he hoped they would. Janet nearly always ended up paying for them.

"Hiya, Randy, how's it going?" Eugene Westerman was marching toward him from the bar, bringing his bottle of Bud and his glass. He sat down at Randy's table and shook his hand. "How you doing, Randy?"

"So-so."

"I understand that. I know all about so-so. I been there." Eugene Westerman, too, was in sales. He was a big man, shaggy and glib. As a salesman he had all the qualities Randy lacked— self-assurance, belief in product, eye contact and a handsome moustache. He had been five years ahead of Randy in school and after graduation had left town, had gone on the road. He returned every few months to tell you how well he was doing, and you had to believe him—he was the picture of success. When leather coats were in he wore one, and when they weren't he made fun of yours. His line varied—pig feed one time, jewelry the next.

"You still working with your dad, Randy?"

"Naw, I'm selling Spring-Flo water softeners."

Eugene Westerman made big eyes and nodded approvingly. "There's money in Spring-Flo. You getting your share?"

"Yeah, today I am. I sold a top-of-the-line unit today."

"Oh, God, that's wonderful." Eugene clutched his heart. "I love hearing that. I always love hearing about a big sale, it wires me. God*damn*, I'm glad for you. How much commission you rake off?"

"Hundred and forty."

"Is that all? Hundred and forty on a top-of-the-line Spring-Flo? My friend, you are being taken to the cleaners. I know all about Spring-Flo. Got a friend in Berrington selling Spring-Flo. I happen to know that on a top-of-the-line Spring-Flo you've got over two hundred bucks coming, but you'll never get it unless you stand up to your sales manager and demand it. That's the way they operate. Who's your sales manager?"

"Archie Andrews."

"That explains it. I know Archie. Comes into a town, sets up an office and hires himself a local boy who's never seen the big time. Archie's hoodwinked yokels in every town around here. He's got you in his pocket, Randy. Sixty dollars of what you earned today Archie's putting in his own pocket. Call him on it."

Randy turned away from Eugene's powerful gaze. He wanted to weep. The beer was making him sad, and so was Eugene Westerman's fighting spirit. Randy wasn't a fighter. And if he were, would it be money he'd fight for? Of course not. Then what would it be? he asked himself. What was worth fighting for in the larger context of life? Love. He'd fight for love. God, if only Janet were home, he'd go straight home and tell her he loved her. He'd pick her up something nice on the way, a gift.

"I hear you're married now, Randy. Got yourself one of the Raft girls. The good-looking one."

"Yeah. Janet." He hazarded a glance at Eugene's intimidating eyes. "What you selling these days, Eugene?"

"Nothing."

"What do you mean, nothing? You're never selling nothing."

"Every so often I have to drop out of selling and let my income sort of flatten out, otherwise I pay too much taxes. Right now that's what I'm doing, taking it easy. I made too much money the past few months."

Randy finished his fifth beer. He drew himself up in his chair, looked steadily into Eugene's eyes and said, "How does a guy make too much money?"

"Main thing, get yourself a line that sells itself, that's how. Spooner vacuum cleaners. I sold so many Spooner vacuums in the past six months they couldn't hardly deliver them fast enough."

"Aw."

"Listen, Randy, I averaged four Spooners a week, and I raked off two hundred and thirty-five dollars every damn time."

"Really?"

"And that didn't include my bonuses. Seemed like every time I turned around I got another bonus. I sold vacuums to people who didn't even *want* vacuums." Eugene lowered his head and shook it, incredulous himself at what he had accomplished. "I sold vacuums to people who didn't even have *rugs*."

"How?"

"How? What do you mean, how?"

"How do you sell so much?"

Eugene studied Randy closely, as if to determine if Randy was worth an investment of his wisdom. "Listen, it's simple, and I wouldn't be telling you this if we weren't friends."

They had never been friends, but Randy nodded as if they were and moved in close to hear the secret.

"You sell to the buyer's weakness. Understand me?"

Randy thought of his sale to Ms. Ecklund, her complexion worries. "Yeah, I guess I do."

"Good, that's all you got to know. You can break down the most hard-ass customers in the world by finding their weakness and selling to it. Want another beer?"

"Sure."

Eugene called out, "Herb, bring us another beer." Then softly, "So how's married life, okay?"

Randy nodded unhappily.

"Tell me this, Randy: Does a guy get more before or after he's married?"

Randy shrugged. "You get about what you want either way."

"You don't sound like you're getting much."

The bartender brought two bottles and said, "That'll be a dollar and a half."

Eugene gave him seventy-five cents. The bartender held out his hand to Randy, who said, "I thought you offered to buy, Eugene."

"Like hell I did. I said you want another beer and you said sure. Is that offering to buy?"

Randy dug his share out of his pocket.

"Listen, Randy, tell me about being married."

He did. He told about his pesky stepson, his bills, his over-bearing father upstairs and the monotony of the Spring-Flo suds demonstration. He said he and Janet got along okay. Some problems, but who didn't have problems? One of their problems was that Janet wasn't crazy about living in the same house with his parents, and he could see that, but they were getting a nice break on their rent.

"Janet's really a good person," he said sadly. "Maybe too good for me."

He fell silent. They drank their beer and listened to the pained wail from the jukebox, hearing it through to its heart-breaking fade-out. Randy hung his head. Where was Janet at this moment? Did she miss him? Was he worth missing?

"Who does the vacuuming in your house, Randy?"

"Janet."

"She got a nice vacuum?"

"My mother's got one upstairs. We use that."

"Randy, let me sell you a vacuum."

He looked up. "What would we want with two?"

"A guy's wife ought to have her own vacuum, Randy, and she ought to have the best."

"My mother's is pretty good."

"But it's your mother's. It's no good sharing a vacuum, Randy. To a woman it's like cosmetics. A woman doesn't share her cosmetics, and when we're talking vacuums we're talking household cosmetics. Understand me?"

Randy forced down the rest of his beer, and although he felt bloated and dizzy, he called for another.

"You know, I can still get myself a Spooner at cost if I want it."

"What's cost?"

"Three hundred dollars less than the selling price. Can you believe it?"

"What's the selling price?"

"Nine twenty-five."

"Christ," said Randy. "Almost a grand for a measly vacuum cleaner."

"Wrong, my friend—for a top-of-the-line Spooner. A Mark Four. Anything comparable on the market would cost you fifteen hundred. It's got all the attachments and a lifetime warranty. Shampooer for carpet, buffer for wax."

"That would be something to have. Janet says we need a shampooer."

"See, when I left Spooner I made the boss promise me a vacuum at cost, figuring a guy never knows, he might find himself with a wife and a house some day. You want it?"

"At cost?"

"Yeah."

"Six twenty-five?"

"Right."

"But it's yours."

"Changed my mind. Decided I'm not the type to be owning a vacuum. Not domestic, you know what I mean. Now, you, Randy, you got the house, you got the wife, you got the kid playing on the carpet, you got everything but the vacuum. You can have mine."

It was usually Randy who had to go upstairs for the vacuum; Janet hated to go and ask for it. He sipped his beer. He said, "I'm not sure."

I'm not sure was a signal Eugene recognized and Randy didn't. Eugene drew a glossy folder from his pocket and spread it on the table—the Spooner Mark IV with eleven attachments and six bottles of blue shampoo thrown in on the deal. It was magnificent.

"Wives go absolutely out of their tree when they see this, Randy."

So strong was Randy's desire to please Janet, to get as much love from her as Stephen always got, that he imagined with no effort her rapture upon coming home from Ireland and finding this scarlet canister in her living room. Surely for something this beautiful she would overlook the extravagance. On the scarlet canister, above the wide chrome bumper, the numeral IV was stamped in gold.

"I could drop this off at your house tomorrow night. All I'd need would be a fourth of the money down, so I can pick it up at the Berrington office in the afternoon. Say a hundred and twenty bucks."

"Hell, Eugene, I only got enough money for one more beer."

"No problem, get your commission from Archie tomorrow and I'll stop by your office around noon and pick it up on my way out of town."

"I don't know, Eugene, my commissions never come through that fast."

"Listen, that's your own damn fault. Archie's screwing you from the word go. You got to stand up to him, tell him from now on you'll take your commissions on the day of the sale or he can stuff his softeners in his ear. You should be drawing interest on that money instead of Archie. It's your money."

Randy tried to picture himself standing up to Archie.

"Man, this is a honey of a machine and your wife's going to love it. It'll outclean any other vacuum on the market, and it's the only one in the world with a shampooer for carpet and a buffer for wax."

"Okay, Eugene!" Randy shouted, slapping the table with both hands. "I'll take it!"

"Oh, God, that makes me happy." Eugene clutched his heart. "The only thing Janet'll love more than this Spooner is you, for giving it to her."

Randy's spirit lifted like a bubble of gas.

"Now, how do you want the installments? Ninety days? A year? On ninety days the interest is a lot less. If you decide now, I can drop off your payment book with the vacuum tomorrow night."

"What do you mean, payment book? I'm paying you for your machine."

"Right, it's my machine, but you pay through the Spooner office in Berrington. It's just easier that way."

"But the office will want me to pay the full price." For an awful moment he lost his faith in Eugene. Maybe six twenty-five *was* the full price.

Eugene saw Randy's spirit drop. He gripped his wrist and steadied him. "See, I'm good friends with the girl who makes out the payment books, Randy. I just tell her six twenty-five instead of nine twenty-five and it's no problem. I happen to have a contract right here. You can watch me write six twenty-five where it says total price, and that includes the eleven attachments and the six bottles of shampoo." He pulled papers from his pocket. He bent back the creases, spread them on the wobbly little table. "Okay, Randy?"

Randy hazarded another look at his powerful eyes. "Okay, Eugene."

"Okay, my friend, sign here."

Randy signed.

12

THE THREE MINNESOTANS beheld the sea, lost it and beheld it again as the road lifted them into great rolling clouds of mist and dropped them down beside the crashing waves. This was like nothing Agatha had ever seen, and it took her breath away. Rock and water. Water and rock. The marriage of sea and land seemed to have given birth to rock the color of the sea—dark gray with a tinge of blue.

"Listen to that," said Janet, her ear out the window, her hair swept with rain, the sound of the roaring surf filling the car.

"Look there," said the bishop, pointing to a hill where five sheep and a horse were climbing among rocks and disappearing into low clouds, animal and cloud alike the color of the gray-blue sea.

"So *this* is Ireland," said Agatha, her heart thudding.

They came to a peninsula bending out into the water like an arm with two elbows. Overlooking the cove was a village called Knob. A number of fishing boats were moored to a concrete pier. Facing the pier from across the street was a guesthouse with gray stucco walls and a gray slate roof. *St. Margaret's B & B* was lettered in violet over the yellow front door. A waist-high stone wall enclosed the small front yard.

"Are they expecting us?" asked Agatha. The bishop had driven up and stopped with such assurance she assumed this was his customary first-night lodging.

"I've never been here before," said the bishop, "never traveled this road before. In Ireland you pick your rooms at random. It's more fun that way." He opened his door. "Come with me—the lady of the house will want each of us to pass judgment on the rooms. And do me one favor please"—he looked

115

from Agatha to Janet—"don't let them know I'm a bishop."

"How come?" Janet asked.

"Their faith is very strong in the West of Ireland, you see, and sometimes it's misdirected and can be embarrassing."

"What do you mean?"

"They've been known to confuse bishops with saints."

"Now, *that's* misdirection," said Agatha, unbuckling her seatbelt.

The door to St. Margaret's opened as they hurried up the walk in the rain. A small, elderly woman wearing a flowered pink apron over a raspberry dress stood in the narrow hallway. "Come in, come in out of the desperate weather," she said. One by one she pulled them indoors by their wrists. She shut the door and sized them up as they introduced themselves.

"And I'm Mary Plunkett," she said. She had small, piercing eyes. She led them into a dining room crowded with worn furniture and a hundred knickknacks. Whatever glowed in the fireplace had a fibrous texture and gave off an odor Agatha had never smelled before.

"Oh, is that peat?" she asked.

"Aye, turf we call it," said Mary Plunkett. "You're early arrivals, I must say."

"I guess we are," said the bishop, glancing at his watch. "It's only noon."

"No, you don't get my meaning at all. It's only May."

"You're not open yet for the summer?"

"Oh, I have rooms right enough, grand rooms, you'll not be wanting to leave for a week. Come along, I'll show you." She led them up a narrow stairway with a turn in the middle, the bottom flight carpeted blue; the upper, orange. "Will you each be needing a room of your own then?"

"If you please," said Agatha.

"You've just landed, haven't you?"

"Yes, we have."

"I thought so. Nobody comes looking for beds at this hour unless they've spent the night in the sky."

They were small, clean rooms made smaller by their busy wallpaper. In Agatha's room the motif was butterflies—tiny orange wings rising diagonally from floor to ceiling. The wallpaper overlapped the frame of the only window, which looked out on the fishing boats across the street.

Having obtained Janet's approval and the bishop's, Mrs. Plunkett returned for Agatha's. "The room will do then?"

"It's fine."

"Grand, that's grand. Tonight I'll be giving you each a hot water bottle for your feet—you Americans chill so easily. And now you'll have a cup of tea straightaway, will you not?"

"A cup of tea would be lovely."

Mary Plunkett went to the head of the stairs and called out, "Percy! George! Start the tea and get out the brown bread and scones and the plate of ham, these poor souls have a famished look to them!"

"Right!" called a small male voice from below. "Right, right!" called a stronger one. "Will we set out the jam and applesauce as well?"

"The lot," said Mary Plunkett.

They were six at tea, Percy and George included, two men in their sixties wearing matching white aprons over their suit-coats and ties. Percy was Mrs. Plunkett's husband. He was a shriveled, furtive man with a twitch in his cheek. He had a timid, recurring cough and not much to say. George was his brother, a husky, red-faced bachelor with humorous eyes. They looked nothing alike, these brothers, except for the family nose, liverish and bulbous.

After studying Agatha for a time, Percy said, "Tell me, Mr. Baker, are you this woman's son?"

"No, we're no relation."

"Ah, you Americans," said George, looking highly amused as he handed around the bowl of applesauce, "you're all so full of beans."

The brown bread was fresh and delicious. Agatha, biting into it, discovered she was starved.

Mary Plunkett said, "Now tell us where Minnesota is in relation to Texas, Miss McGee."

"Far north. Nowhere near Texas. It's near Canada."

"And near Ohio," said George Plunkett. "I should know, I've been to Ohio."

"Not very near," said Agatha.

"But closer to Ohio than to Texas."

"Yes, that's true."

Percy piped up: "Then you know our cousin's boy in Cincinnati?"

"No, I'm afraid not," said Agatha.

"But you must. He's the one living next door to the hospital."

"No, I'm not acquainted in Cincinnati at all."

George explained to his brother, "The States are vast, Percy." The vastness made him laugh. "Oh, they're a place apart, the States, and who knows better than I, being a cowman in Ohio for seven years." He turned to Agatha. "I went to Ohio and worked as a cowman for seven years, and why did I ever come home?"

"Why did you?"

"It's *me* asking *you*, it is. Why did I ever come home to this rocky spit of land? Lord God, how I wish I was back in Ohio."

"Mind how you use the Lord's name," said Mary Plunkett.

"The food markets. You can't conceive of the food markets in Ohio until you've seen them yourself. And the broad roads, straight as a string. But you know what I liked best about the States over every other thing? I'll tell you. Everybody's so full of beans over there." He laughed and spilled his tea.

Mary Plunkett leaned close to Agatha. "He's always doing this when it's somebody from the States, always telling them what they know better themselves. And what's your business in Ireland if I may ask? Is it a holiday?"

"I'm looking up my family tree."

"McGee is it?" said George. "I knew McGees in Cork. They worked on the boats." He turned to Janet and pinched her upper arm. "And what about you, my lass, what brings you to Ireland?"

"I'm visiting Dublin. My husband has family there."

"Aha, a husband, I knew it. A young thing with eyes pretty as yours gets snatched up in a wink."

Mary Plunkett asked, "Where's your husband, dear, home with the little ones?"

"Yes, home with Stephen. He's four. I'll show you." She ran upstairs for her snapshots.

"Ohhhh four, a lively age," said Mary Plunkett. "Remember when our Teddy was four, Percy?"

Percy had been woolgathering. "What's that?"

"I say, remember when our Teddy was four?"

"No."

"Teddy's our boy in Galway," she said to Agatha. "He's clerk at the Yardmore Hotel where the president of Ireland stayed last summer and our Teddy shook his hand."

"How nice," said Agatha. "And who is the president of Ireland?"

She thought. "Percy, who's the president of Ireland?"

"I've no idea."

"George, who's the president of Ireland, Teddy shook his hand."

"Oh, he's that toff pictured in the *Times* whenever there's a benefit ball in Dublin."

"But his name, I'm asking."

"Who knows his name? He's always the toff in the middle holding a glass. The one losing his hair."

"It's somebody different every few years," she explained to Agatha. "It's not like having a king."

Janet returned and showed them Stephen on his trike at three, Stephen with his three Raft aunts at three and a half, Stephen with his Grandfather Raft on the tractor. And here were Randy and Stephen at Christmas. And Randy and Janet on their wedding day.

Mary Plunkett said, "Such a lovely little boy and such a handsome husband, you must be very proud."

Janet nodded, smiling and then not smiling. Then smiling again, absently, wishing they both were here with her.

Percy pointed to Janet. "Is this lass here your granddaughter, Mrs. McGee?"

"No, no relation. We're friends."

George said, "Besides the food markets there's the lovers living together in Ohio. You'd not believe it, young people living together man and woman without the wedding and nobody batting an eye."

At this, Percy jumped slightly in his chair. "Think of it!" he said.

"Don't think of it," said his wife. "It's a mortal sin."

Percy subsided. "Tell them about your wallet in New York, George."

"Oh, New York!" George was overcome at the thought. He spread his hand on his chest and sighed. "You go to the pictures day and night in New York, and at least once a week you get what they call mugged. Well, it happened this way. I was walking down Broadway holding myself in, cautiouslike, you know, afraid every step I'd be beaten and robbed of what little money I was carrying back to Ireland. I'm stepping along like a wary old fox, I am, and what do you suppose but this chap comes up to me from behind and gives me a rough bump and runs on ahead and I feel my pocket and sure enough my wallet's gone. But I keep him in sight. He's ahead of me at the corner, standing, waiting for the traffic light. He's wearing a checkered suitcoat. For a scoundrel he's not so large as you'd expect. He's shorter than me and I'm only five-nine."

George leaned across and gripped the front of Dick Baker's shirt. "I came up behind him, I did, and I turned him around rough as you please"—he gave the bishop a shake—"and I took the lapel of his checkered coat like this"—he twisted the bishop's shirt—"and I said, 'The wallet now, hand it over and be snappy about it,' and God in heaven strike me dead if he didn't reach into his pocket and take out the wallet and slap it into my hand, swearing like a sailor as he did so, disgusted, you could tell."

He released the bishop and sat back, shaking his head. "I slipped it back in my pocket proud as could be, saying to myself, 'If only more people took it upon themselves to stand up to muggers, then muggers would soon change their ways!'"

George looked at his listeners one by one. "And then I went back to my hotel room and what do you suppose? There lying on my bed was my very own wallet."

Janet laughed. Agatha gasped. The bishop said, "No!"

"My very own wallet. I'd come away without it, and the cleaning woman found it and left it there on the bed as neat as you please."

"*You* were the mugger," said Agatha.

"*I* was the mugger and that poor short man in the coat of checks was my victim. I was the hooligan I thought *he* was, and he was the poor wretch I thought *I* was, and what do you make of that?" He sipped his tea. So did Mary and Percy. All three Plunketts waited expectantly to hear what the Americans made of it.

Agatha offered this: "It shows you, doesn't it, we're hasty to judge."

They agreed, yes, yes, right enough, indeed, you hit on it there, yes, indeed.

"But I know the feeling," said Janet. "When you think something's going to happen, you can't believe it won't."

Total agreement again, and more effusive this time, because Janet was so young and pretty. Right enough, right as rain, truer words were never spoken, yes, indeed, and isn't that the way of it.

"I'll tell you what it shows," said Dick Baker, smiling broadly over his teacup. "It shows that George is full of beans."

After an hour or so, Agatha, warmed and lulled by the turf fire and the six-sided conversation covering two hemispheres, went upstairs and put on her flannel nightgown.

As the Plunketts cleared away the tea things, Dick Baker said to Janet, "Before I turn in I'm going out and have a look at the harbor. Want to come along?"

Janet went upstairs for her green raincoat and joined him on the front stoop.

The rain had stopped but the wind still blew. The fishing boats at their moorings were lifting and dropping on the swells pushing in around the breakwater.

As they were letting themselves out the gate, the front door opened behind them and Percy Plunkett called, "Mr. Baker, before you go, may I have a word with you."

The bishop returned to the stoop. Percy stepped out, shutting the door behind him. He blinked in the bright, gray daylight.

"Mr. Baker, did you bring any magazines from the States?"

"No, I didn't."

He nodded, frowning. "Then you wouldn't have a copy of *Playboy* in your luggage."

"You're right, I wouldn't."

"I've never laid eyes on it myself, but my brother George goes on about it. It comes spang through the post, he says."

"So I understand."

"But not to your house."

"No, I don't subscribe."

"It's for George I'm asking. He's had his eye out for another look these fifteen years past, and for his sake whenever I see a chap from the States I ask. George says I wouldn't believe my eyes. Flesh totally open to view."

"You've been asking for fifteen years?"

Percy nodded. He coughed. He wiped his mouth with a dingy handkerchief.

The bishop had known Percy's type in the confessional, the man whose sexuality had outlived his means of satisfying it. This was the dirty old man the world found so unsavory—old wine with the chemistry still working, turning it to vinegar. The bishop was not repelled. He was moved to pity. "I'm sorry, Mr. Plunkett."

"Carry on then, Mr. Baker. No harm in asking, I always say."

"No harm, certainly."

With a swirl of his white apron, Percy Plunkett slipped back indoors.

The bishop crossed the street and caught up with Janet. He walked with her out along the pier, passing two dozen boats painted two dozen colors, the paint peeling, the decks a jumble of tackle. They were greeted by a man standing in an engine hole. He wore a black turtleneck and a blue stocking cap. Taking his pipe from his mouth he said, "We're in for a clearing afternoon, I would say." Farther along, a man in a dirty yellow slicker tipped his cap and said, "Don't wander far from the Plunketts', the rain will be soon back."

As they approached the end of the pier two gulls, which had been standing on either side of the lamppost like sentries, flew out over the water.

"This is when I always know for sure I'm in Ireland," said

Dick Baker. "I find a pier like this and I look west and I think of all the water between me and my everyday life and I feel so free I want to sing."

"Do it," said Janet.

"Thank you, I was about to." He gave her a little bow. The gulls glided back and stood near them. "This is my Irish ceremonial song, composed for this occasion. Here goes." He threw his head back, closed his eyes and sang nasally to the tune of "My Bonny."

> My troubles lie over the ocean.
> My troubles lie over the sea.

He was flat, but his volume was impressive.

> My troubles lie over the ocean.
> Don't speak of my troubles to me.

He opened his eyes. He stood silent for a time, smiling blissfully, while Janet wondered if it was improper to ask what a bishop's troubles might be.

She asked, "That's it?"

"That's it. Both of us together now."

They sang it through twice. The second time the bishop threw his arms out in operatic gestures, scaring off the gulls. Agatha saw them from her room across the street and thought the bishop must be shouting. She opened her window to catch the words.

The gulls returned a second time. Dick Baker drew from his coat pocket a shiny steel tube with six fingerholes and a blue plastic mouthpiece. He blew a strident high C, and the gulls took flight again.

"My penny whistle, Janet. I bought it when I was here last time, and I've been teaching myself to play. Would you please sing 'My Troubles' once more and I will accompany you?"

He tooted a measure. "Can you sing in that key?"

"I think so."

"Good. One, two, three."

Her voice and his plaintive piping carried clearly across the street to Agatha's window. She stood in her nightgown listening, sleepy and charmed.

Agatha slept deeply for five hours, woke, turned over and slept for two more. She dreamed little shreds of dreams. Visitors were coming to her house for dinner but she was unable to unlock the door to let them in. Someone in New York (where she had never been save for two hours at JFK) congratulated her on the firmness of her handshake. A man stood in the middle of a field holding a glass of water up to the sun.

The sun was shining when she woke. It stood an hour above the sea and faced squarely in through her window. The boats in the harbor were bobbing gently. Below her window she saw Mrs. Plunkett cutting blossoms from the moss roses lining the sidewalk.

She dressed and went downstairs. In the dining room George was feeding the peat fire, and Percy was setting the table.

"You slept?" asked George. "You were warm enough?"

"Yes, I was dead to the world."

Percy said, "What's become of the spring weather I'd like to know. It hasn't been fine since Easter."

Janet came down wearing a green sweater and brown corduroy slacks. A thin, gold chain would set off the sweater nicely, thought Agatha. She would find something for her in her jewel box at home.

Mary Plunkett came in with a centerpiece of red and yellow blossoms, then went to work with her men in the kitchen.

Dick Baker came down wearing a red tie and a gray sportcoat. He chatted with Agatha and Janet as dusk darkened the room. Lamps were switched on. Dinner was served.

Dinner was salmon with a dozen side dishes, wine during and Cognac after. Harmony during and discord after. George, coming in from the kitchen with the Cognac, said, "Another shooting in Belfast, it just came over the wireless."

"God be praised!" said Percy, his small, pallid face taking on color. "Long live the IRA."

Mary Plunkett ordered, "Don't be bringing that up."

George said to the Minnesotans, "You know of our troubles, do you?"

"Yes," said Agatha, "it's in our papers."

Percy got to his feet, held his glass out for Cognac and said, as George poured, "It's the one glorious thing we know how to do in Ireland. We know how to back the British against the wall, the bloody tyrants. They'd rule us if they could."

"What do you mean if they could?" said George, cutting him off with a short portion. "The British have had the upper hand for four hundred years because they're smarter than we are, and what they're saying over the wireless is that a whole family of Catholics has been wiped out by the Brits, a father and his three little ones."

Percy held his glass high and thrust his jaw forward. He spoke through clenched teeth. "Long live the IRA!"

George said, "Percy, would you give over with that rubbish? All we've ever known how to do in this godforsaken country is go out and lie down and die in a hopeless cause and call our dying a great victory."

"No more talk of it," said Mary Plunkett. "I won't have it."

George poured for the guests. "The Irish heart is so topsy-turvy it doesn't know defeat from victory. We're always going into battle outnumbered, outarmed and outsmarted and getting butchered for our efforts."

"Get out with you!" Percy's cheeks were now the color of his livid nose. "That's unholy talk and we'll not be having it in this house. You never were the same after you came back from America, George. America made you weak in your national spirit."

Springing out of her chair, Mary Plunkett went for her husband with murder in her eye. Percy tried to duck but she caught him by one of his large ears and pulled him into the kitchen. "Get busy with your dishes and let me not hear another peep out of you."

"Watch now," said George to the guests, "she'll be back in a second to throw me out the front door." He was grinning gleefully.

When she returned he stood up and bent over and presented her with his ear. She gripped it and steered him into the hallway. He called as he went, "Come with me, Mr. Baker, we'll have ourselves a farewell pint at the pub." She steered him out the front door, then held it open for Dick Baker, who hurried after him, saying, "Delicious dinner, Mrs. Plunkett, simply delicious."

She said "Thank you" and slammed the door.

Peace settled over the dining room. Janet finished her spot of Cognac and said, "I'm going upstairs and write to Stephen and tell him about the ocean." Agatha helped Mary Plunkett clear the table, and then, alone at the hearth, Agatha put on her reading glasses and scanned a newspaper. An hour passed. She had expected the Plunketts to join her, but when they finished their work (the dishes and silver ringing angrily in the kitchen), they had apparently retired to a room at the back of the house.

She went upstairs and knocked on Janet's door.

"Come in." Janet was sitting on her bed, writing on her suitcase. "Hi. Want to sit down?" She made room on her bed.

"Janet, would you care to go for a walk?"

"Sure."

They put on their coats and went out through the front gate to the dark street. The night was still. Overhead hung a small fraction of moon.

"Well, Janet, you're glad you came?"

"Sure. Why wouldn't I be?"

"Because of Stephen—you've never been gone from him overnight before."

Janet thought of her nights alone with Randy before they were married. "You're right," she lied, "but it's sort of nice being free for a few days. Stephen's in good hands with Mrs. Meers."

"You're still calling her Mrs. Meers? Don't you call her Louise?"

"She wants me to call her Louise, and Mr. Meers wants me to call him Carl, and I do to their faces, but it's an effort. I always think of them as Mr. and Mrs. Meers, just like you're always Miss McGee."

"But you're their daughter-in-law."

"But still not close to them, if you know what I mean. Mr. Meers babies Stephen and Mrs. Meers babies Randy and I feel sort of left out. Not that I'd want to be babied like that, but I wouldn't mind getting right down to it when we talk."

"Right down to what?"

"Oh, you know, right down to the basics. I never feel like I'm saying what's on my mind when I'm with Mrs. Meers. And neither does she. We never talk from the heart, is what I mean. It's always sort of stiff, like what's happening with the price of groceries and whether it's going to snow."

"I should think you'd talk about Stephen."

"Oh, we do, I guess, but . . . Randy's dad, he seems so bitter sometimes. Of the two, he's easier for me to understand, though. I guess I know dads better than mothers, anyway. Mr. Meers is like most people's dads. He wants his son to do his best all the time and he acts bitter when he doesn't. I don't think he'd drink so much or do so much swearing if Randy was more of a success."

They crossed the street to the pier. The boats were standing motionless at their berths. The harbor smelled fishy. They walked out to the end of the pier and stood in the circle of yellow light under the lamppost. Beyond the breakwater the ocean sounded like the rumbling of an endless train. Somewhere in the hills behind the town a dog barked.

"Janet, I have to tell you something. There's a man in Dublin I'm going to be seeing."

"There is?"

"He's a teacher. He lives in a small town not far from the city. We've been corresponding for four years, and tomorrow evening . . . It's a correspondence that . . . You see, Janet . . ." She fell silent. She felt confused. Never in her adult life had she been at a loss for words.

"What's his name?"

"James O'Hannon. You may have seen his picture on my desk at home. He's . . ."

Janet looked at her curiously in the amber light. "Yes, I've seen it. I thought it was your cousin or something. What is he, your boyfriend?"

"Now, Janet."

"He is, isn't he! He's your boyfriend!" Janet squealed. "I can't believe it." Laughing, she took Agatha's arm and hugged it. "James O'Hannon is your boyfriend."

"Stop that and listen to me."

"Oh, Miss McGee, a boyfriend!"

"*Not* a boyfriend, Janet. He's sixty-six."

"A manfriend, then. How wonderful."

"Will you please be still and listen? It's nothing like that. We've been corresponding for four years, and I'm going to meet him in Dublin, and I thought somebody should know of my plans in case anything happened to me."

"What do you mean? What could happen?"

"Oh, you know—an old lady in a strange city. She might be set upon by thieves. She might turn her ankle and fall into the Liffey."

"You're not telling the bishop about him?"

"What possible interest would it be to the bishop?"

"And you're not even telling Lillian?"

"Lillian's the last person."

"But you tell Lillian everything."

"And she tells everyone else."

"But why not tell her? What's the secret? I mean, what's there to hide?" She squeezed Agatha's hand in both of her own and laughed again. "You've fallen in love."

"Janet, I have not."

"Well, what are you calling it then, a crush?" Her laughter rang out over the water. "You've got a crush on James O'Hannon."

Her laughter carried down the street to Dick Baker and George Plunkett, who were standing outside the pub, George with a mug of porter in his hand. The two of them saw Agatha and Janet at the end of the pier, under the lamppost, under the moon.

"Your lady friends are full of beans, Mr. Baker."

"Yes, aren't they."

"That's a right smart young one you've brought along."

"And a right smart older one as well."

13

AFTER THREE WRONG TURNS on city streets, Dick Baker located the Fermoyle house in Blackrock. It sat proudly on rising ground behind a high stone wall. The sign on the gatepost said BEECH GROVE in large pea-green letters. The driveway ran uphill beside a hedge of magnificent rhododendrons, pink and white, and led to a parking area behind the house. As Agatha and Janet stepped from the car, Nora Fermoyle came out the back door and greeted them warmly, kissing the air near their cheeks. "You're Agatha McGee, Louise has written so much about you. And you're Janet, how wonderful to meet you finally." She gave the bishop a slight curtsy. "Welcome to Beech Grove, Bishop Baker. Won't you all please come in?"

Dick Baker deferred to Agatha, who consented, saying, "For just a few minutes. My, what lovely flowers." The back garden was mostly roses.

"Yes, we have a new gardener this year, he's superb."

Though Nora Fermoyle smiled easily, it was a smile restricted entirely to her lips and did not spread as far as her eyes. Like Randy, thought Agatha. She was tall. She wore her graying hair short and straight. Over her sheer summer dress, light green, she wore a white Angora sweater and a short strand of pearls. She led them indoors.

Agatha was struck by the gallerylike aspect of the house—shoulder-high sculpture standing about, abstract watercolors and lithographs hanging on wires from the high moldings. "What beautiful rooms," she said. "So airy." Across the front of her house in Staggerford was a porch she was coming to regret because it cut off so much daylight.

Nora Fermoyle asked her, "Is this sort of art to your liking?"

Agatha paused before a pair of watercolors. Rectangles rendered in black and gray. "No," she said.

"My husband doesn't care for it either, but I tell him he'll come to understand it in time. I tell him it's good for Evelyn to have grown up with art like this. If she's going to be a modern woman she'd better be accustomed to modern art. Don't you agree?"

Agatha didn't answer. She had moved along the wall to a rectangle of great beauty and was standing before it, enchanted. It was a window. The range of hills on the horizon was luminous and stunning. The hills were a brilliant green mottled with cloud shadow. "What a gorgeous view," she said.

"The Wicklow Hills," Nora explained. "You may have come through them on your way into the city."

"No, but I hear they're not to be missed. I'd like to see Glendalough."

"Perhaps we could drive you out there. Are you free this weekend?"

"No, I'm sorry, this weekend I'm occupied."

"Oh, dear, and next week is the busiest week of my life, I'm going into business. A friend and I are opening a boutique in a shopping center in Dun Laoghaire. My first time out of the house since I married Alexander twenty-five years ago. I'm nervous about it. In the States wives have jobs and nobody cares, but Ireland isn't like that. I'm afraid my neighbors are going to give me the cold shoulder when they discover what I'm up to."

"You'd think she was taking over the Common Market" said Evelyn Fermoyle, rushing into the room laughing nervously and shaking the hands of Agatha and the bishop and giving Janet a little hug. "It's making her a wreck. It's making us all wrecks."

"Don't exaggerate," said her mother. "Come and sit down, everybody."

Facing the couch across a wide glass coffee table were two deep chairs into which Agatha and the bishop sank. Evelyn sat bouncing on the couch next to Janet. Nora Fermoyle pulled up a stool.

The bishop said, "A very lovely house you have here, Mrs. Fermoyle."

"Alexander will be home any minute," she said, "and he can show you around. He'll want to show you his den. What is there about you men that makes you love dens?"

Evelyn said, "We're going to have a wonderful time, Janet. My term is finished except for exams and I don't plan to study at all, the courses are a snap." Evelyn was loud as well as bouncy. She had a wide face, large features. Her gaping smile revealed small teeth. Though she had missed being pretty by quite a bit, she gave no sign of caring. "You simply have to meet my boyfriend Willie without delay. And his friend Jack. I'm not suggesting a double date or anything, only just getting together for a beer or something, because Willie and Jack are such fun together. They're a stitch."

"Fine," said Janet. Caught in the wind of Evelyn's talk, she felt blown off balance. "Great," she added.

"Jack is an actor, you'll love him. He's in a new role at the Peacock, and he got special mention last week in a *Times* review. My dad's with the *Times,* but that isn't why he got special mention, my dad hates theater. Do you like theater? We'll see the play he's in while you're here."

Agatha was disconcerted by the life-sized sculptures standing left and right at the edges of her vision—an American Indian, a stone ox, a wrought-iron bird. She felt watched.

"Will it be tea all around?" asked Nora. "Would anyone like wine?"

"Tea," said Agatha.

"Tea for me as well," said the bishop.

"Or beer?" said Evelyn. "I like beer."

"So do I," said Janet.

"Good, come with me." Evelyn popped up off the couch and led Janet through the dining room (more framed watercolors) and into the kitchen (framed cafe posters). "Willie's got me drinking Smithwicks." She drew two bottles from the refrigerator, uncapped them and swigged from one as she put water on the stove and got the tea things together. "Now tell me all of it, Janet, everything. Randy, Stephen, being a wife."

Janet put down her beer and went to the living room for her purse. She returned and spread her snapshots on the counter.

Evelyn bent over them, analyzing the faces. Stephen, she said, was the most beautiful child she had ever seen, Randy the most handsome man, Aunt Louise Meers the most military woman, and Uncle Carl the most bald-headed man. "*Bull*-headed too, as I recall."

Janet concurred on Stephen and Randy. She withheld comment on her in-laws.

Evelyn carried the tray of tea and scones into the living room. As Janet followed with the two beers, she heard Nora Fermoyle saying, "I hope you have an open evening while you're in Dublin. We'll all go out to dinner and a play afterward."

"Let's see, this is Friday," said Dick Baker, tapping his wide forehead and sorting out his seminary visits, All Hallows Seminary tonight and tomorrow night, a day visit to St. Patrick's in Maynooth next week. "Any evening after Sunday," he said. "What about you, Agatha?"

Better later than earlier, she thought. She wanted to keep her days and evenings open to see what developed with James. "Next Thursday," she said, covering her anxiety, her slipping confidence, for she was watching something strange and ominous happen to the light over the Wicklow Hills. She had been watching the hills change from green to deep blue and then to gray, and now they were fading away altogether as clouds of haze moved in from the sea and thickened. A cloud of foreboding moved across her mind as she came to realize how much she was expecting from a man she had never met.

"Thursday it is," said Nora. "Alexander will be so pleased. He loves seeing friends from America."

"Your husband is American?" asked the bishop.

"Oh, no, he's native Irish, I'm the American, but he loves my contacts from home. We lived for a time in the Midwest when Evelyn was little."

"It's the Peacock on Thursday then?" Evelyn asked her mother.

"Why don't we leave it to them which play?" said Nora.

"Oh, Mother, we've been round and round on this." Pouring tea into the bishop's cup, Evelyn explained to him, "You simply must be forced to see *Buried Child* at the Peacock because my friend Jack Scully is in the cast, and besides, it's the only interesting play in town."

She moved on to Agatha. "The Gate is doing ballet, and Daddy simply despises ballet, and the Olympia is doing a modern-dress *Hamlet* I've already seen and found absolutely dull, and the Abbey is closed for two weeks for refurbishing."

"Evelyn, dear," said her mother, "don't be cross." Her tone was not reprimanding. She had been receiving American visitors long enough to know that what pleased them most were strong tea and her daughter's amusing assertiveness, proclaimed in her charming brogue.

"Mother, let me finish. My friend Jack Scully plays this younger brother in this decadent family, and he comes home with this brassy new girlfriend, and he's just wonderful in the part." She went on to summarize the play.

"Sounds interesting," said the bishop when she finished. "What do you think, Miss McGee?"

"It sounds absurd."

"Exactly," Evelyn explained.

Somewhere a door closed.

"Oh, good, here's Alexander." Nora called out, "Alexander, come in and meet Janet and her friends."

Alexander Fermoyle was a young-looking fifty, his moustache and beard sharply groomed, his green eyes clear and icy, his voice high-pitched and staccato. "How do you do, how do you do, how do you do." He gave each hand a quick pump and then tucked himself into a corner of the couch, wishing he had waited longer at the office so that these visitors would have left by the time he got home. He hated meeting people from America because they came over here with no sense of his importance. The Irish were different; they were used to seeing the name Alexander Fermoyle on the masthead of the *Times.* But what did foreigners know? How tiresome to come home after a hard day's work and find three strangers who needed impressing. How tiresome to come home to tea instead of gin. Rotten, tiresome luck, he thought, but here goes:

"You know about the shooting of the three children and their father in Belfast, do you? We have the whole story now from one of our reporters in Belfast, and you'll see it in print in the morning. There's a road in Belfast named Curston Row and it's been trouble all along. Last evening there was an armored truck of the RUC driving along it, patrolling, when the driver saw a well-dressed young man walking along the street carrying a briefcase. Besides the driver there were four other men of the RUC in the truck, and they were armed with automatic rifles. There was also a police dog. Three of the men rode in back with the dog, and one of the men rode in the cab. The one in the cab was named Benjamin Wakefield. The sight of the briefcase made Benjamin Wakefield nervous, as he told our man later. The driver told him to relax, this man carrying the briefcase looked nothing like a bomber, his suit was clean and pressed and his shoes were polished. Terrorists when they came at you with bombs were a scruffy lot, he said."

As Mr. Fermoyle spoke, his wife and daughter began speaking of other things in a manner suggesting that he bored them. Or was it Belfast that bored them? Evelyn spoke to Janet about her classes at Trinity, and Nora, on the stool beside Agatha, went over recipes for salad dressings and baking powder biscuits. Though an adequate cook, Agatha had never considered recipes interesting enough to talk about, and she wished Nora would be quiet and pay attention to her husband. His voice wasn't easy to listen to—it had a high-pitched, grainy quality—but how could you not be gripped by a story so awful as this, the killing of three children and their father?

" 'But he's not the type for Curston Row either,' said Benjamin Wakefield to the driver. This was a street of factory workers who didn't wear suits like this man's suit. As it turned out, Benjamin Wakefield was right to be suspicious, for as soon as the truck drew abreast of the man, didn't the man sling his briefcase out into the street, where it slid under the truck and exploded? The noise was deafening. One of the men riding in back still can't hear a thing, totally deaf. The truck tipped over on its side. There was a broken skull and a lot of cuts and bruises and the one man deaf, but all five of them and the dog got away with their lives. They leaped clear before the gas tank went up."

Nora Fermoyle told Agatha about her experiments with custard. Evelyn told Janet about Willie Hughes's apartment as compared to Jack Scully's apartment. Willie's was neat, Jack's was a mess. Only the bishop was free to listen to the story from Belfast, though Agatha and Janet strained to do so.

"Now, all this happened in front of Number Twenty-four, the endmost house on Curston Row, a semidetached house of white pebbledash, fairly new, but sooty-looking—our chap took some photos. And who should be living in Number Twenty-four but Paddy Creely, a man I've seen giving speeches more than once in front of the GPO here in Dublin. Paddy Creely's an active sympathizer of the IRA, though not a member, I'm told. He's a small, redheaded fellow about my own age with a voice like thunder. He works in a factory, so he's been called the Lech Walesa of Ulster, but that's rubbish, of course. He's just a minion of the freedom boys, who like him for his voice. Or *liked* him, I should say, because now he's dead."

Evelyn told Janet she was expecting to work during the summer in her mother's boutique. Nora moved on to the manifold uses of the avocado.

"Now, the tragedy concerning Paddy Creely started last Monday when his twelve-year-old daughter Meg was out with some friends after dark. She and her friends were walking home from the library, where they had been studying, and they came upon a skirmish between a British soldier and a bunch of youngsters who were setting fire to a tree in a park. Don't ask me why they were setting fire to a tree, but there you are. They were splashing gasoline on the trunk and throwing matches at it. The Brit soldier patrolling the park fired off some plastic bullets to drive them away and he hit Meg Creely in the temple by accident. Killed her outright. Her funeral was yesterday at eleven o'clock. Paddy Creely and his wife, Annie, and their three remaining children came home from the burial in mid-afternoon. Some relatives came home with them and left around six. At six-thirty, the RUC truck exploded in front of their house. As soon as he heard the explosion, Paddy Creely ordered his wife and kids into the basement and he followed them down. Many's the time Paddy Creely used to tell his coworkers

at the Sampson Tractor Factory that the reason he bought the
house he did was because unlike most other houses in that part
of the city, it had a basement for sheltering the wife and kids.
Our chap picked that up by interviewing the men he worked
with. Shush, now, Evelyn, do you mind? Nora, do you mind?"

His wife and daughter fell silent.

"Annie Creely, who survived this, reports that she was
weeping the whole time in the basement. Weeping the whole
day, in fact. Weeping the whole week. The basement is a long
room with two windows at ground level, their sills about seven
feet above the floor. Our chap's been down there. He says the
one window faces the street and the opposite window faces the
back garden. Paddy was expecting rifle fire after the explosion, so he and his family huddled under the window facing
the street, assuming that any stray bullets entering the basement would come in overhead and strike against the back wall.
That was his fatal mistake, because the young bomber ran
around the house and plunged through the hedge into the
garden and there he collapsed, because he had been fired at
by one of the RUC and had been hit in the ankle.

"There are three concrete steps leading up to Paddy Creely's
back door, our chap took pictures of the whole house, front
and back. The young bomber crouched down beside those back
steps, in front of the basement window, and he took out a re-
volver and waited for the RUC to find him. They weren't long
finding him. The man named Benjamin Wakefield came into
the garden with the dog. The young man fired at the dog as
it leaped on him. The dog died instantly without a yelp. Benjamin Wakefield opened fire on the young man. He, too, died
instantly, falling flat to the ground. Benjamin Wakefield went
on firing, emptying his automatic rifle, and some of the bullets
entered the body and some went through the basement window, killing Paddy and his six-year-old boy and his four-year-
old girl and his two-year-old baby. Annie Creely wasn't hit. Our
chap says she's in and out of shock. She's able to talk coher-
ently, but her eyes have the look of a zombie."

It was a horrible story, and Agatha, who made the first move
to go (saying she wanted to be at the hotel by seven), was

stunned by it. The party moved out to the car mumbling, grieving for the Creelys, five dead and one alive. Alexander Fermoyle had succeeded in impressing all three Minnesotans with his importance. Stepping out the door, he looked at the sky and said it would rain. His wife pointed out her plot of vegetables near the garden wall. Evelyn helped Janet lift her bags out of the back of the car.

Agatha said, "Good-bye, Janet, you have the Gresham Hotel number if you need it."

"Yes, good luck with your family tree." She followed Agatha around to her side of the car and added privately, "Good luck with James."

"Thanks."

"Maybe you could bring him along to dinner on Thursday."

"We'll see."

"I hope you do. I'd love to see him."

Buckling her seat belt, Agatha noticed a tremor in her hands. Janet noticed it, too.

"Too much tea," Agatha explained.

At the bottom of the drive, Agatha looked back at the three Fermoyles and Janet clustered beside the showy rhododendrons, happily waving and calling good-bye.

She turned to Dick Baker. "Janet's in good hands would you say?"

"Capable hands." He drove out the open gate and turned onto the curving street. "We're both glad it's not us staying at Beech Grove, am I right, Miss McGee?"

She restrained herself from correcting his grammar. "Exactly what I was thinking."

They were silent for a mile or more. Part of Agatha's mind was on Curston Row, the bloody basement, Annie Creely zombielike, and the other part was on James, who as the time drew near was becoming more and more of a stranger to her.

Dick Baker's mind was on Agatha and the distance she had maintained all day in the car. The trip from Knob to Blackrock, designed to win her friendship, could hardly be called a success, for while she had been civil all the way, she had never really warmed up to him the way Janet had. Well, there was time. After his weekend at All Hallows he would be moving into the Gresham.

Rounding a corner, he nearly collided with a truck. He pulled over to the curb and stopped. "Where am I?"

"Oh, sorry." Agatha spread the map across her lap and found their place.

14

JAMES O'HANNON PHONED from the lobby. Was she rested from her flight across the sea, from her drive across the Midlands? Was she hungry—would she still have dinner with him? His voice affected her deeply. Of all his traits that she had tried to imagine, she hadn't thought to speculate about his voice. It was simply the most pleasing voice she had ever heard.

She put on her coat and hurried to the elevator. It was eight o'clock. She had checked into her room only a half hour ago, yet the wait had seemed eternal. She was famished. At home she ate supper at six.

But in the elevator she wondered if she should have waited in her room a while longer, calmed herself down after his call. She wondered if she was dressed correctly. Mightn't this dark blue suit be too formal? What if James weren't wearing a tie? He wore no tie in the photo outside the O'Hannon family pub. Oh, please, Lord, let him be wearing a tie. She had trouble taking any man seriously who wasn't wearing a tie.

The elevator opened and there he was. Tall. Coming forward. Smiling. His hand out to her.

"At last, Agatha, welcome to Ireland." He was handsome. He was older than his photo, considerably more than four years older, it seemed. He was pale, except for a ruddy spot high on each cheekbone. His dark suit was rumpled. So was his dark wool tie. His white shirt was brand new and hadn't been ironed—she could see the creases when he bent to her and his suitcoat fell open.

She was stirred by his direct blue eyes. She was calmed by his wonderful voice, by his hand at her elbow as they made their way to the door.

"I have a place in mind for dinner," he said, pointing down

139

O'Connell Street. "It's beyond the bridge. Will we walk or take a cab?"

"I don't have my walking shoes on, I'm afraid." How like a bachelor not to notice this. As they both looked down at her shoes, she was thankful for her trim ankles.

In the cab they sat discreetly apart. She couldn't take her eyes from his face, and when he asked, "What are you finding so interesting about my mug?" she felt suddenly girlish and said, "I thought your nose would be smaller." This set them laughing until their eyes were wet.

"There's the General Post Office," he said, wiping his eyes with a dingy handkerchief, "where the Rising of Sixteen took place." She leaned over and looked out his window. The tricolor flag over the portico—vertical bars of green, white and orange—struck her as surprisingly plain considering how many people had died to put it up there.

The cab moved on. The evening sun was clouded, and the light over O'Connell Street was pale. The buildings were grimy.

"I've lost my directions, James. Where is west?"

"Behind that monstrosity." He pointed to a Burger King. "We're laggards. It took us many generations to import your hamburger, but there it is at last. And there you see its matching piece." He was pointing at a McDonald's.

As they crossed the Liffey, James called her attention to the Ha'penny Bridge arching gracefully over the water. "And out that way"—he nodded toward her window—"would be the sea."

The taxi moved up through a narrow street. Children with smudgy faces stood in front of pubs and newsagents' shops, looking glum.

"Give the likes of them a wide berth when you're out on the streets, Agatha. They'll have your purse in a wink. Maybe it was always so, but there's a whole generation of no-goods growing up in this land." James, too, looked glum for a moment, then bright. "Tomorrow I'll give you a proper tour of the city. We've more to show than take-away hamburger places and pickpockets."

The driver stopped at the corner of a deserted street. James led the way through a narrow doorway and up a narrow stairs to a small restaurant on the second floor. Six tables overseen by a headwaiter in black. Candles, caned chairs, framed photos of racehorses. Two waitresses moved about softly, dressed in maroon and white. James and Agatha were shown to a table at the large window overlooking the street. Above the rooflines across the way, she saw a high pile of thunderclouds advancing upon the city.

After sending the headwaiter for wine, James spread his napkin on his lap, looked at Agatha and said, "Now."

"Yes," said Agatha, "now." For a long, awkward moment it seemed the only word they knew. Trying to think of a few more to go with it, Agatha realized how little correspondence had in common with conversation. She groped for something to say from James's last letter, but its main topic—marriage—was hardly the thing to be bringing up on this occasion. To her astonishment, however, James brought it up.

"What did you think of my letter on marriage, Agatha—the demise of marriage in the modern day? I don't know what set me off. You must have thought it strange."

"Such a disquisition. Are you really so pessimistic as you wrote?"

"Every bit and more. I used to keep count of the unhappy unions among the young who grew up in Ballybegs, but I've lost track. Lost interest, actually." He regarded her with serious eyes. "Agatha, why didn't you ever marry?"

She didn't know the answer, quite.

He prompted. "What I mean is, are you single out of principle, or was it circumstance?"

"Circumstance, I suppose. What about you?"

"Circumstance. An incident early in life. Whether one marries is determined very early in life, is it not?"

"No, I don't think necessarily."

"By the time we're ten or twelve, I'm saying."

"Oh, no, I considered the possibility of marrying until I was thirty."

"Yes, the possibility. We all do continually, until we're dead. But we're *disposed* not to marry from very early. Some childhood incident, I'm saying."

The wine came. Rosé. They raised their glasses.

"Welcome again, Agatha."

"Thank you, James. It's so good being here." The wine, even before her first sip, relaxed her.

Their talk veered away from marriage for a while. The flight over. Bishop Baker. Janet's host family in Blackrock.

The waitress came and they ordered. Then Agatha said, "I don't recall any childhood event setting me off on the single life. What was yours?"

"Well, of course we can never be sure about a thing like that, but I'm thinking it was the wedding I served when I was eleven or twelve. The marriage of a farm girl and her father's workman. Did I not write you about it?"

"No." Did he not remember, as she did, every last word of every last letter?

"I was going through my pious phase at the time. Loved the Church inordinately. Served Mass every chance I got. I was on my way to being a mystic. We had an old parish priest, Father Hogan. He was stern and ascetic and fit my image of God. Whenever he had a funeral come along, or an emergency wedding, he'd call on me to serve. He'd telephone my mother at the pub, or if it was a school day he'd telephone the brothers at the school. 'Send Seamus,' he'd say. It was a wet winter day. Lily Byrne was the girl's name. I forget the name of the man she married, if I ever knew it. He was nobody from our valley, or even the next. He'd been the Byrnes' cowman for a year or two. There was no one in church but Father Hogan and myself and the wedding party of four. Picture it, Agatha. Lily was big with child and the bridegroom looked like a captured criminal."

"Surely not."

"Exactly like a captured criminal. He was fifty or more, judging by his gray hair and wrinkles. Lily was seventeen. The two witnesses were Lily's older brother and the half-daffy woman who cleaned the church. Lily's parents stayed home. Not only was it a dark morning, but since there was no one in church, Father turned on no lights but those over the altar, and I remember feeling as if we were stranded on an island. Do you have the picture?"

"Yes, unfortunately."

"When the couple was called to the foot of the altar for their vows, I noticed how Lily's plaid skirt, which I had seen her wear to town every week on market day, was hitched high up over her growing belly, and the bridegroom's black suit was too small for him. The coat was tight across his back, his wrists hung far out of his sleeves. Somebody else's suit, to be sure. Rain was beating down. There was frost on the stone walls of the sanctuary. The inside walls."

"How dismal."

" 'Where were Lily's parents?' I asked my mother when I got home, and she told me they disapproved and were too ashamed to attend. She said there were some things in life so ugly that only the priest had the power to look upon them, and wasn't it too bad I needed to look upon this one at such a tender age. She had a mind to forbid me to be an altar boy anymore. Well, it wasn't my first wedding and it was far from my last, but it was the one wedding that left its mark on me, Agatha."

Their food came. Cod for Agatha, beef for James. A second waitress came and spooned out peas and potatoes from serving dishes. They ate in silence for a time, candlelight coloring their faces warmly as daylight failed outside the window.

"No bad impressions of marriage in your early life, Agatha?"

"No, my impressions were favorable. I got them from my parents."

"Happy every minute, were they?"

"If not happy every minute, at least content. Or, if not content, complaisant."

"But you have to admit to a bit of pessimism, don't you, never having married?"

"Yes, more than a bit, now that I'm older. I've come to know of so many marriages with nothing inspiring about them."

He agreed. "Many, many like that."

"And I see things like the annual renewal of marriage vows in church. You watch the dispirited way couples take that vow, and you wonder what holds them together. Do you know what I'm talking about—Holy Family Sunday, when the priest asks one and all to stand and renew their marriage vows?"

"We don't have it in Ballybegs."

"Our priest doesn't say, 'All of you who are married, please stand,' he says, 'One and all,' and isn't that typical of the little respect we single people get these days? We're thought not to exist. Well, needless to say, I keep my seat as the husbands and wives stand up on command, and it's one of the most discouraging sights in the world. They're told to hold hands, and most of them refuse. Last time, in a pew just ahead of me, a neighbor of mine, Mrs. Morrison, moved her hand tentatively toward her husband, not wanting to make the gesture too obvious in case he ignored it. And sure enough, he ignored it. He pretended not to see the hand. I wanted to drill him in the back with my umbrella. Poor Mrs. Morrison, she took her hand back and held it herself, as though it were wounded, held it with her other hand tight to her breast."

"Sounds like an odd ceremony."

"And when the husbands are asked to repeat their marriage vows, you can scarcely hear them whisper. It's the timid whisper of men ashamed. So you wait to see how the wives handle it. Wives, you assume, live more comfortably in marriage. But no, the wives, too, whisper as though in shame. The whole ceremony's a disaster. The priest concludes with a short prayer and gets on with the Mass, and everybody sits down relieved."

"So you *are* as pessimistic as I."

"Watch them fumble around with those vows, and you have to think their love for each other has died. You have to wonder if every last husband and wife sooner or later becomes unfaithful, either in reality or in their hearts, so the public pledge is false and they know it."

"Ah, hearts. So many people have difficulty knowing what's in another's heart, but surely not us, Agatha. Am I right? Aren't we the kindred spirits, though?"

"Aren't we."

"It's our being Irish, you know. There's always a bond between Irish hearts."

Eating, they looked down at the dark street. A neon light flickered over a pub. The door to the pub was low and a man in a dark coat and cap bent his head as he slipped in. Another slipped out. A car sped by.

"How is your cod?"

"Delicious."

"I come here quite often for meals, sometimes with friends, sometimes alone."

"You've never mentioned it."

"Ballybegs is at the farthest reach of the Dublin City bus line, you see, and the ride is inexpensive. Not a bad ride if you don't mind the stops and starts. I like sitting at the rear of the upper deck and watching the people get on and off and looking out over the tops of the hedges going by."

"I seldom eat out," she said.

"How about movies? Do you go?"

"Never."

"I sometimes come into the city for a movie. We see American movies here. Shocking language on the sound track these days. And even after being edited for Ireland some of the love scenes are outrageous. And the violence—guns, murders, wars. You Americans and your love of firearms. I would never cross to America. I'd fear being shot dead in the street my first day over."

"Nonsense, James. Ireland takes the lead in violence."

"The North, you mean."

"That's Ireland."

"But it's British."

"It's Ireland."

Silence for a time, then: "You spoke of your bishop, Agatha."

"Yes."

"What is your business with him, may I ask?" She heard something strained in his voice. Was he jealous?

"He's leading the tour I came over with. But not with much enthusiasm, I should add. He's here mainly to look for priests."

"He's the man you've written about? Not much to your liking?"

"He was no sooner consecrated than he began innovating like crazy."

"Your nemesis, I believe you've called him."

"You should have seen our cathedral before he went in with his wrecking tools. Granted, it was overdecorated, but now it looks like a warehouse. Without the wares. Absolutely unadorned. A Puritan meetinghouse. We're witnessing the successful completion of the Reformation, James, five hundred years after Luther."

"Not really."

"Of course we are. We should have all turned Protestant in 1517 and spared all those heretics we burned at the stake, spared all those Catholic heads Elizabeth and Henry the Eighth cut off."

James wasn't certain if he should laugh at this, or frown. He ate.

"But I have to say in his favor that he's been very agreeable on this trip. Crossing the Midlands today, I found him rather good company. He's one of those people you could almost like if it weren't for his beliefs."

Night fell, together with a squall of mist that pebbled the window and softened and blended the lights shining up from the street. One by one the other tables emptied, and they were left alone, lingering over dessert and coffee, Agatha speaking of her students, her retirement dinner, her misgivings about retirement, James listening alertly, cordially.

In the taxi, James said, "Agatha, let me ask you this." Then a long, portentous silence. Was he preparing an intimate question?

"Yes?"

"Is it true that Americans neglect Confession these days?"

How tiresome. "It's true."

"I see. And do you go to Mass on Saturday nights and call it Sunday?"

"Yes."

"I see. And do I understand that laymen actually distribute Communion?"

"And women."

"No."

"Yes."

"What does God make of it all, do you suppose?"

"I often wonder."

They crossed the Liffey. James pointed to a bus loading on Aston Quay. Number Sixty-seven. "That's the bus to Ballybegs and all points in between." He looked at his watch. "There's another leaving in forty minutes. That will be just right."

He came into the hotel with her. At the end of the long lobby a number of well-dressed people were sipping liquor at tea tables and listening to an elderly pianist play Cole Porter. Absently, dreamily, most of them turned to look at Agatha and James entering.

He accompanied her to the elevator. "Tomorrow I'll show you the city, Agatha. May I come for you at ten?"

"Ten will be perfect."

The elevator door opened. In plain sight of all, he embraced her.

Ascending, she felt that for a mere seven hundred dollars she had been carried not only from the New World to the Old, but also beyond it, to the realm of her happiest dreams.

15

HE CAME FOR HER AT TEN. His face looked different; there were lines of stress around his eyes. However, he shook her hand firmly with both of his own, and his voice gave her confidence.

Today she wore her walking shoes, but because of the rain they went by cab to their first stop, the National Gallery. There, outside the front entrance, they encountered a statue of George Bernard Shaw looking either amused or irritated; it was hard to know what to make of his grimace.

Entering, checking their coats and umbrellas, James said, "What's your manner of seeing paintings, Agatha? Will you roam free, or will I show you my favorites?"

"Your favorites, of course."

In a brisk, businesslike manner, without a great deal of pleasure, it seemed, he took her around to several Dublin scenes by a painter named Osborne. She liked them—the greens, the reds, the wind, the sun. Then on to a surprising number of Corots, and a pair of interesting faces by Goya. Next, a magnificent altar triptych featuring apostles with gold-leaf halos and somber eyes.

"Now my special favorite." He led her to a Brueghel. "Isn't this a wonder, Agatha?" He approached the painting as he would an old friend, crossing his arms, laughing, stepping nervously up to it and back. For the first time this morning he seemed relaxed. The painting was a peasant wedding with a lot of dancing and kissing going on. Heavy bellies, round cheeks, wine and food spilling. Treetop leaves turned by a breeze.

"Tell me what it is about Brueghel that people admire, James. I've never understood."

He gestured toward the canvas. "Surely you see it."

"What?"

"Life!"

For several minutes she regarded the brown earth beaten under the dancers' feet; their mouths wide, emitting cries and laughter; broken teeth; two lovers tumbling in a bush; birds rising.

"You see what I mean, Agatha?"

"Yes."

"You like it?"

Further scutiny. "Maybe."

Their last stop was in a mammoth room containing a mammoth Last Supper painted by someone Agatha had never heard of. There was a bench before it, and they sat. She studied Christ. He was intent on the bread he was breaking. All depictions of the Last Supper, even the cheap plaques in the Staggerford five and dime, reminded her how wonderful it was that in practically any city or town in the world she could walk in off the street and witness this ceremony of bread and wine at Mass, could feel united with these twelve Apostles and all believers ever since. She felt a sudden desire to attend Mass with James. Tomorrow was Sunday. But she didn't bring it up, and she didn't know why she didn't bring it up. Her eyes roamed over the faces. She counted them.

"James, why are there only eleven?"

"Eleven? I hadn't noticed."

They counted together.

"Look." She found the hint of a face in the upper right corner, a man standing behind the others. "Is that Judas, do you suppose?"

"Yes, indeed, all but erased by reason of the betrayal he's planning. I never noticed him before."

Because the painting was not brightly lit, the face was hard to hold in view.

"James," she said after a long pause, "I hope we can go to Mass together while I'm here."

"Ah." A sudden look came into his face, like Shaw's outside in the rain. Irritation or amusement? Or was it fear? "While I think of it, there's one more thing we must see."

He led her off to a portrait of a fisherman.

* * *

From the National Gallery they took a cab to Dublin Castle, where they spent an hour browsing through genealogy books. *McGee* was derived from *MacGeehan*, which was derived from *Mac Gaoithin*, a name found principally in County Donegal and derived from the word *gaoth* or *wind*; thus related to the *Wynnes* and *Gwynnes* of Wales. Agatha recited what she knew of her forebears to a helpful man behind a counter, who wrote it all down and promised, for a fee, to search out her Irish roots.

Their next stop was St. Patrick's Cathedral, which to Agatha's astonishment proved Protestant. They walked up and down the aisles reading memorial plaques and gazing at the red and blue stained glass.

"Here's their saint," said James, chuckling. He showed her the square in the floor under which Jonathan Swift was entombed with his beloved Stella. "Not his wife," he reminded her. "His lady friend."

"Astonishing," said Agatha.

They lunched at Bewley's. It was crowded. There was a steady din of chatter and teaspoons. Over their second cup of coffee James noticed Agatha's eyes losing focus. "What's on your mind, may I ask?"

"I'm thinking what a pleasure this is." She meant the smell of pastry and coffee, the dark paneling, the Irish faces over their plates, over their newspapers. She meant the gallery, the cathedral, the castle. She meant knowing there was wind in her name. She meant James.

"I thought you were getting weary. Your eyes looked so far off."

"Not weary at all. I was thinking about all I've seen."

Her eyes lost focus again. She was seeing Preston Warner now, the Staggerford farmer who proposed marriage to her in 1938. A close call. These days Preston Warner, though not much older than James, devoted his life to nothing more than sitting in his car on Main Street and watching people walk by. Every day, empty-eyed and emaciated, he drove into town from his farm, which was no longer under cultivation, and parked his old dusty car in front of Hanson's Hardware and sat motionless and stone-faced behind the wheel, interrupting his surveillance only at noon to eat soup at the Hub Cafe. To think she might have married him. He wore bib overalls, and his teeth were gone. Very little of what he watched registered in his mind—you could see that through the windshield when you walked past his car and tried to engage his eyes and failed. He never recognized Agatha, never recognized anybody, but he returned every day, addicted apparently to the movement and the color of Main Street even though it held no more meaning for him than the changing shapes in a kaleidoscope.

"What will it be this afternoon, Agatha? More antiquities? Or the sea, perhaps?"

"Do you have a preference?"

"None whatsoever. Old landmarks and the sea are one to me. Always there when you want them. Eternally in their place."

"The sea then. I can't seem to get enough of it."

Leaving Bewley's, they stepped out into sunshine. They took the suburban train to Dun Laoghaire and strolled along a magnificent pier that extended, it seemed, miles out to sea. They met young couples holding hands and men in business suits talking business. There were babies all over the place, in laps, on blankets and sleeping in harnesses on parents' backs. Here and there they came upon sunbathers exposing only a little of themselves because the wind was so chill off the water.

"I'd say they're rushing the season," said Agatha, indicating a middle-aged couple sunning their legs and faces and shivering; they wore wool jackets over their swimsuits.

"No, this *is* the season, Agatha."

"Really? It gets no warmer than this?"

"We'll see seventy degrees one day in July, and we'll all be on the verge of heatstroke."

"Oh, in that case I could never live in Ireland. I need more and more warmth every year. Even ninety is never too much anymore."

He shook his head vigorously. "To an Irishman eighty is hell."

At the lighthouse end of the pier they stood and watched a ferry steam in from Wales, travelers waving at the rails, gulls gliding and diving above the churning wake. James pointed east through the sunny haze to a fishing fleet on the horizon. He turned and showed Agatha the Dublin smokestacks at the mouth of the Liffey. "Now follow the land around to the north and you come to Howth Head." Howth was a hump of green rising up out of the sea. "Howth will give you a fine view of the sea as well, but its pier isn't nearly so fine as this one."

When she turned up her collar against the wind, he asked, "Are you cold?"

"A little."

"We'll walk back." He took her arm, and this made her as buoyant as last night when he embraced her in the lobby of the hotel. Far and near seagulls were diving, turning, soaring, gliding. As Agatha and James strolled along, he pointed out spires and headlands up and down the coastline, naming them.

"You can't see them now for the haze, but down there, behind Bray Head, are the Wicklow Hills."

"Could we go to the Wicklows, James? I'm told they're very beautiful."

"No convenient bus connections, I'm afraid."

"We could rent a car."

"I don't drive," he said.

"I do."

"Not on the left, you don't."

"I drive wherever I'm told." She waited for the irritation to drain out of her voice before she added, "Let's go to the Wicklows, James."

He changed the subject, pointing out some chimney or other.

She changed it back. "How odd that you've never driven, James."

"Not so odd. I've lived all my life handy to a bus stop or a bicycle. Now, over there you see the Martello Tower of *Ulysses.*"

"Would you like me to teach you to drive?"

"No, indeed, I'd have no use for the knowledge."

"Let's rent a car. Have it delivered here to the outskirts of the city."

"No, the risk is too great." Again his mouth was crimped like Shaw's. Was he losing patience or about to laugh? "Every week a new foreigner is killed in Ireland forgetting himself and driving on the right."

"We would not be killed. We would keep to the country roads and go slow. I've just crossed from west to east with one of the worst drivers I've ever known and I'm here to tell about it."

Rudely: "No!"

She gave up.

Halfway to land they sat on a bench against a sunny wall, shielded from the wind. Now in midafternoon the pier was growing busier. Agatha wondered why James was so edgy today. She watched the pale Irish faces going by, old and young. So many resembled her ancestors. Here was Uncle Charles with his small eyes and fat cheeks. Here was Cousin Min with her narrow face and dark eyebrows. And here in this open-faced child playing tag with her brother she saw her mother as a girl, a face straight out of the family album.

James startled her by saying, "Friend of mine died in this harbor." He opened his coat to the sun. He smoothed his hair. "Name of Desmond."

"Oh, I'm sorry."

"His brother had a sailboat. They went out one Sunday. Didn't stay out long because his brother was new at sailing and wasn't handy with the sails. Desmond, helping him, overdid it, apparently. They were skimming back into the harbor when he told his brother he felt weak and he lay down on the deck. By the time they reached the wharf he was lying there dead. This was many years ago. I first met Desmond in college."

"Did he leave a family?"

"He was a priest." James swept his arm landward, indicating the town. "Curate in a parish here in Dun Laoghaire. He would have been thirty the week after his funeral."

Basking in warmth, James and Agatha went on speaking of death, telling stories they already knew from their letters but that seemed to need telling in person.

James said, "No death affected me more than that of my sister Marian. You remember the snapshot outside the family pub. She died of leukemia about two years after that snapshot. Then two months after that my mother died."

"She didn't know about Marian, did she? She was losing her memory."

"Lost her mind entirely. Didn't know us from cats. It's been grim going home since the two of them died. My brother Matt's letting the pub go down. Chilly and dirty it is. He's drinking too much, not tending to business as he should. A cozy old place in Marian's day. Cozy and wholesome in my mother's day before her, far back as I can remember. About once a month now I take the bus home and spend the afternoon with Matt, take him out for a meal at the hotel, sit with him in the pub, but there's no joy to be had from it, the female presence gone."

Agatha gave him five minutes of silence, then countered with the story of Miles Pruitt, the young lodger who had been like a son to her. "He had grown up in Staggerford, I'd had him in school. After college he came home to teach. By that time his mother had died and his father was senile and living in a nursing home, so Miles took a room at my house. Took his meals with me. Helped me with the house and yard. He lived with me ten years before he was shot and killed by the deranged mother of one of his students."

Though he already knew the story in every detail, James bent his ear to her.

"The girl's name was Beverly. She and her mother lived on a small farm near the Indian reservation. The National Guard was alerted for an Indian uprising that never occurred, and they camped overnight in their barnyard. The sight of jeeps and guns and soldiers drove the poor woman over the edge. When the bivouac was over she barricaded herself in the house with a rifle, determined to defend her farm against the next stranger who set foot on her property. The next stranger was Miles, poor Miles, who came looking for Beverly, fearing for her safety. Beverly wasn't in danger. She had fled before the soldiers arrived and was staying with friends. The madwoman took aim from an upstairs window and shot him through the head. Oh, the horror of it. I thought I would die of it at the time." Even now, telling it, she had a hitch in her voice.

James took her hand and they sat for a long time in silence, the sunlight falling across their laps.

"What saved me was Beverly. Her mother was put into an institution, and I took Beverly into my house. By the time she finished high school and went away to junior college, both she and I felt strong again. She was the first of my hardscrabble girls."

"What became of her, Agatha? You've never said."

"She met an Army recruiter in Berrington, where she went to college. She married him and cut all her ties with Staggerford, except I get a brief note at Christmastime. Last Christmas it came from Australia."

Silence again. Repose. Comfort. James cupping her hand in his own. Agatha wouldn't mind if she never moved from this bench. She felt whole and complete and exhausted, as though bringing this story of Miles Pruitt to Ireland and handing it over to James were the major work of her life. Gone now, for the moment at least, was the old ache caused by that rifle shot.

After a while they left the pier and climbed to the station. On the train, rocking around a curve, James took her hand for the second time and held it until they got off at Pearse Station.

They walked through the grounds of Trinity College. They went into the library there and bent over the Book of Kells, open this day to an illuminated page of St. John's Gospel. How could thirteen-hundred-year-old ink be so vivid? The red and black serpent winding down the left margin glistened like gems.

They left Trinity and walked to the Liffey, James going into a bakery along the way and buying a loaf of day-old bread.

"I dare say you've never seen a whirlpool of gulls," he said. He led her up the steps to the Ha'penny Bridge. Stopping midway across the water, he asked her to hold the paper sack as he reached in and crumbled the bread. Then he began throwing crumbs over the rail, attracting gulls from upstream and down. As he continued flinging the bread, the birds flew round and round, dozens of them, some higher some lower, and with each pass near the bridge they slowed or speeded up to snatch the morsels in midair. Circling, circling, they formed a white-winged whirlpool above the dark water. People stopped along the quays to watch the birds and the man's astonishing control over them. The gyre speeded up or slowed down as he dispensed the food faster or slower; it moved back and forth across the water as he moved along the rail. When the last of the bread was gone, he turned to Agatha and laughed heart-ily, taking her arm to help her down off the bridge, but she held back. She stood there watching the birds dispersing, climbing east toward the sea. She felt airborne herself.

With so far to fall, therefore, her spirits took a dizzying plunge when, after escorting her up O'Connell Street to her hotel, James said at the entrance, "I'm desperately sorry to tell you this, Agatha, but something has come up . . . a crisis . . . and I can't say just when I'll get back into town. You're here till the end of the week, are you not? We'll be in touch before you leave."

"But James—"

"For now let me just say how very much you mean to me." He was looking at the sky in a grief-stricken way.

"What is it, James? Can I help you somehow?"

He took her hand in both of his own. He pierced her for a moment with his deep blue eyes. "I trust we'll continue to write to each other." He turned and walked away.

She felt as if she'd been struck. She put her hand to the lamppost at the curb to keep her balance. She watched him flow away with the crowd, his white hair visible for a block or so, then gone.

16

AGATHA WOKE EARLY. She got up and put on her robe. Last night's ache returned and gradually filled her breast as she stood at the center of the room absently straightening her hair. She pulled a chair up to the window and sat looking down at the street, which lay submerged in shadow. Two men with a wheelbarrow were sweeping the gutters. Minutes passed between cars going by. No one was out walking.

Agatha had lived her life believing that nothing was hopeless in the morning, particularly if the sun was out. Throughout forty-six school terms most of her sanguine ideas and inklings had been conceived between 6:00 and 8:00 A.M. No student was dull enough to be despaired of before school started. In her breakfast nook no morning headline—street crime, inflation, the arms race—was ever dark enough to distract her entirely from the sunlit diamonds in the dewy grass.

It was clear what to do. She must offer to help him through his crisis. She must go to Ballybegs this morning. She would find James in church. She knew which Sunday Mass he preferred—not the early, austere Mass at nine but the baroque Mass at eleven-thirty with the choir and the six acolytes. It was unthinkable that they should be on the same island together without her experiencing, at least once, what it felt like to sit, stand and kneel in church beside the man she loved. Loved? Yes, the pain in her breast had to be love. Either that or a coronary.

She dressed and went down to the lobby. The man behind the desk was helpful, a thin, elderly man with a frail smile. He looked up the schedule for Route Sixty-seven. The first bus out on Sunday morning left Aston Quay at nine-thirty and arrived in Ballybegs at ten-fifty. Perfect.

She went into the coffee shop, where she passed an hour over coffee and toast, assuring herself that James cared for her. Hadn't he beamed fondly at her Friday night at dinner? Hadn't he embraced her here in the lobby? Twice yesterday he had held her hand. Now, having met him, she had a million thoughts to tell him, and letters would no longer do. Either she must see more of him or know the reason for not seeing him.

She bought a newspaper and went up to her room, where she read the front page with a kind of desperation, as though searching for a cure for her disappointment, but none of the news was diverting enough to register in her mind, and the bottom of the last column was blurred by tears. She threw down the paper and allowed herself one minute to weep like a jilted girl. Then she dried her tears, put on her coat and walked down the sunny side of O'Connell Street to Aston Quay.

Bus Sixty-seven stood open and empty. It was a new green bus with a garish ad painted below the windows of the upper deck, a euphoric-looking child biting into a cookie as his mother smiled her approval. "The biscuit Mum would bake if she had time," was the legend. Agatha entered and took a seat near the back. In a few minutes the driver climbed aboard with a Sunday paper. "A grand day," he said, tipping his cap.

"Yes, lovely," Agatha called to the front.

He spread the paper across the steering wheel and sat down and read it, looking up and saying "Grand day" as others climbed aboard. A man with a suitcase. Two women in flowered hats. A young man and woman carrying a picnic basket. A family of five, the youngest a wailing baby.

The bus moved north out of the city, making very few stops, the bus stops deserted, the streets deserted, the city no more animated at ten than it had been at sunrise, except around churches, where cars were clustered and the faithful were crowding in and out of the doorways. They passed Dublin Airport on the left, a jet lifting off. Then countryside with a glimpse of the sea on the right. Then Skerries, a many-masted fishing harbor. Then Carrington. Then Ballybegs, a stony village with doors shut and curtains drawn. Jackdaws fluttered around the chimneys. The bus pulled up in front of a newsagent's shop, and Agatha got off with the others.

The street was narrow. The row houses and storefronts were stucco and stone, here and there a blue or pink façade among the gray, the noise of the idling bus echoing off the walls. The riders dispersed.

Agatha put her head in at the open doorway of the news-agent. Standing behind the counter and wearing a colorless suit was an old man who told her she would find the church by going downhill to the street leading off toward the sea and taking that. To the right, it was. He asked her to pray for him.

She went down the hill and off to the right. It was a pretty street, lined with beeches and another sort of tree she didn't recognize. She came to a large grassy area with a flower bed and benches. She sat down. A cuckoo called from the top of a tree. No tears now. She would see James within half an hour. No abrupt parting this time. This would lead to more meet-ings, or it would not. If not, she would know why.

Sitting there, she became conscious of a strange sound car-rying to her from the end of the street. It was like nothing she had ever heard before, a steady moaning, low and mysterious; a choir of bass voices in agony; an organ in a deep cave. She left the bench and followed the street to its sandy turnaround. From here a path led up to the top of a ridge. The moaning was louder now. The path was soft sand, cushiony under her feet; it wound up between tall clumps of waving grass. Panting a little, she climbed to the crest of the ridge and beheld, to her surprise, the sea. Waves roared as they curled and spilled onto the beach and frothed at the foot of the dune she was on. She trembled with cold, the wind catching at her hair and coat. Gulls hung overhead, waiting for the edible dregs of the turning tide. Off to her left she saw the young man and woman from the bus, holding hands, running barefoot in the froth, yelping whenever a cold wave larger than the others took them knee-high. Agatha stood there entranced. The roaring soothed her, enveloped her like a drug, like sleep. Only when her trem-bling grew to quaking did she turn and go back down into the town, where the sound of the sea died away and bells began to ring.

The gray stone church, St. Brigid's, was set far back from

the street behind a tall iron fence. At the gate were two women collecting money for cancer research. Halfway up the walk stood a card table onto which you were to drop money for African missions. The church was sharply gothic, embellished outside with layers of curlicues and pigeon droppings and angels in half relief, embellished inside with fluted stone columns entwined with dark stone grapes. The stained-glass windows were very small, the light dim, the woodwork dark—a cheerless church overall.

The pews were filling fast. She knew where James would be sitting; he liked the front pew near the Virgin's altar. He wasn't there; she walked partway down the aisle to make sure. She returned to the back and stood waiting. The bell stopped ringing. Half a dozen men came in quickly at the last minute, unceremoniously, dipping in a perfunctory genuflection and slipping into pews. Still no James. She saw a place for herself near the back and went there and knelt. She looked about her at the preponderance of red- and black-haired women, at the exquisite lace and flounces on the dresses of the little girls, at the suits and ties on the little boys. The teenagers looked about as unkempt as teenagers at home—jeans and sweat shirts. All the men seemed to be wearing the same drab sport coat of earth-colored tweed. Agatha's eyes settled on a heavy woman in a print dress and a pretty blue shawl who looked serene and knowledgeable. If James didn't show up, this was the woman she would approach after Mass and ask where he lived.

There was a long wait. Eleven thirty-five. Coughing. Two or three babies whimpering. Then a small bell tinkled over the sacristy door, and six altar boys stepped out into the sanctuary, two abreast, carrying candles. They were followed by the priest wearing white for Corpus Christi. He was a tall, white-haired man. He was pale, with ruddy spots high on his cheekbones. He was James.

Number Sixty-seven, standing open and nearly empty in front of the newsagent's, was like a private conveyance; the moment Agatha took a seat the driver closed the door and set off for Dublin. Not that she was aware of this. She hadn't been conscious of the bitter laugh she had uttered as she fled the church, and now, though her eyes were turned to the window, she was blind to the fields, the hills and the glimpses of the sea. She was thinking back to the time when she was nine years old and introduced to chaos for the first time. That same devastating shock she felt on the Quimbys' front porch when she was nine she felt now leaving Ballybegs. It was a summer evening. She was playing in her yard on River Street with the Wickwire sisters, Kathleen and Jane. They were playing hide-and-seek. Her mother came out of the garden with a great armload of blue and white irises and asked Agatha to take them down the street to the Quimby house; they would brighten up the rare luncheon party that Mrs. Quimby, ancient beyond belief, beyond gardening, would be giving the next day. The three girls ran off on the errand eagerly, because the Quimby house was beautiful and mysterious and contained, everyone said, an idiot child.

On their way they passed the Wickwire house, and Mrs. Wickwire saw them and came to the door and called her daughters in. It was to be expected. Kathleen and Jane were the most tightly reigned girls in town. They protested, but of course it was no use. Agatha went on alone.

It was growing dark. The Quimby house loomed over the street, with the moon rising out of the chimney. Agatha went up the steps and crossed the wide, vine-covered veranda. The heavy front door had a tall oval window, and through its gauzy curtain she could make out, in a room beyond the foyer, a lamp burning on a table beside a sofa. She rang the doorbell (it rang like a phone when you turned the handle), and after a long wait the door was opened by Mr. Quimby.

In Staggerford's hierarchy of esteem, Mr. Quimby ranked higher than Agatha's father, but Mr. Quimby had grown so old that Agatha's generation had no idea why the town respected him so much. Had he been a judge? A doctor? One look at him and you knew that he was declining decorously toward death from a great and distant height, never mind what that height had been. He peered out into the dark, squinting to see who was calling. His hand shook as he groped for a wall switch and turned on a dim yellow light over Agatha's head. He jumped a little, to see a child. He said, "How do you do."

"These are for Mrs. Quimby." She thrust the flowers up into his arms. "My mother sent them."

"Oh, yes," he said, as though expecting them. He stooped for a better look. "Who are you?"

"Agatha McGee."

"Oh, yes. Wait here." Bowing slightly, he turned and hobbled off to another room, leaving Agatha defenseless against the shocking sight in the room beyond the foyer. There, lying on the ornate sofa under the lamp, was the idiot girl. Agatha's first shock was in realizing that the pile of fabric she had assumed was a blanket or a sheet was actually clothing on a human figure, and the second shock was in discovering the inhuman aspect of the human figure. The girl lay on her back without a pillow, her head rigidly horizontal, her face turned toward the door, her lashless eyes staring at Agatha. Her face seemed not to correspond to God's plan for human faces. Both Mr. and Mrs. Quimby had long faces, but this face was long beyond belief, and since she had a shallow chin and no forehead, most of the length was between the eyes and the mouth. On her feet were patent leather shoes that must have been very old; they reflected the light like new shoes, yet were of a fashion never current in this century. Her white dress fit her the way baptismal dresses fit infants, with no conformity to the lines of the body. So this was the creature who had existed only in whispers and rumors for forty years. She had spent her entire life in two rooms of this house, it was said; she was dressed and fed by her mother and a maid and carried in her father's arms.

Mr. Quimby came stooping back to the door. "Mrs. Quimby is so sorry she cannot come to the door. She has retired early this evening. She thanks you and your mother ever so much for the flowers." His smile was very kindly. The solicitude in his eyes was that of a man who had been carrying his child from crib to couch and back again for forty years.

Agatha raced off the porch and ran home in the dark, wondering how two people's reactions to laying eyes on one another could be so one-sided. Certainly her presence in the doorway had made no impression whatever on the Quimby girl, but the girl's presence caused in Agatha a bowel-churning shock

and a confusing chain of thoughts that would last her a lifetime. Why had God given the Quimbys this cross? If Agatha
bore a child someday, what were the chances of its being an
idiot? Could the Quimbys love this girl the way parents loved
normal children? Deprived of understanding and free will, did
this girl have a soul? Where did she fit in God's plan? Agatha
lay awake for a long time that night, feeling sick to her stomach the way she felt now, leaving Ballybegs.

The bus stopped in Carrington, Skerries and Dublin Airport and at dozens of street corners in the city, but Agatha
didn't notice. She kept going back over the evening when she
was nine and first confronted chaos. The memory carried her
all the way to Aston Quay beside the Liffey.

She went directly from the bus to Pearse Station and boarded
the suburban train to Dun Laoghaire. She must see the sea.
To keep her balance, she must fix her eyes on the perfect horizontal of the sea. Would the train arrive at the pier soon
enough to save her, or would she utter the cry she felt building up inside her and shock the scrubbed, smiling family sitting in the long seat facing her? It arrived in time. She uttered
no cry on the train. She walked down to the long, long pier.
Ah, the sea, the waves, the wind, the birds. The flat blue horizon. Her breathing came easier. Walking swiftly out to sea
and taking great gulps of air, she felt the shout or cry still taking shape in her throat. She wasn't yet sure of the words or
for whom they were meant, but already in its unformed state
the cry was giving her confidence. Throughout her life whenever she was bowled over, Agatha invariably got to her feet
again by finding the precise words and the proper listener to
hear them. Today's listener was God, no doubt, this being
Sunday and God being her only friend within earshot. She
strode swiftly on, and when she came to the lighthouse end of
the pier she stopped and lifted her eyes eastward, as though
God were positioned in the sky over Wales, and she cried, "Who
said there are no snakes in Ireland?"

17

It was late on Sunday afternoon when Bishop Baker left All Hallows Seminary and drove to the Gresham Hotel. In his room on the fourth floor he took off his tight black shoes and his tight Roman collar and lay on the bed and looked at the ceiling. He was weary from his weekend among strangers. He was queasy from the cocktails and roast pork dinner pressed upon him by the rector and the dean. He was sorry not to have spoken to more seminarians. For nearly forty-eight hours he had been handed around from one chatty faculty member to another, all of them careful not to give him more than a minute with any of their prospective priests. He couldn't blame them, of course, vocations in decline now, even in Ireland, all seminarians spoken for.

He looked at his watch. The Minnesota tour bus was due in at six o'clock, which gave him time for tea with Agatha. He sat up and phoned the desk and was told that Agatha had checked out of the hotel.

"What? You're sure?"

"Yes, sir, she paid for two nights and checked out."

"Did she say where she was going?"

"I was just coming on when she left, sir. A porter carried her suitcases out to a taxi. She seemed upset."

"You've no idea where she went?"

"No, but the man on duty at the time is still here if you'd like me to ask him. He's in the grill room."

"Please do. I'll come right down."

Dick Baker changed his shirt and went down. The clerk from the earlier shift was standing near the front desk waiting for him. He was a frail, elderly man whose starched collar was a size too large.

"Her checking out was unexpected," he said. "Her plans took a sudden change, she told me. She asked if I might recommend a lodging away from City Centre."

"And did you?"

. "I did indeed. It's not a service we normally provide, but hers was a special case, don't you know, and I'm acquainted with a dear lady who runs a B&B on Leeson Street, so I put her in touch."

"A special case? In what way?"

"She appeared to be in urgent need, sir."

"Of what?"

"Of escape, you could say."

"Did she explain?"

"She didn't at all." He shook his head and looked sad.

"But it was obvious she was under some kind of stress?"

"Under stress right enough."

"Was it anger?"

"I shouldn't say anger." He closed his eyes and thought back. He opened them. "I should say agitated in a downcast way."

"May I have her address? I'm responsible for the touring party she's with."

"Twenty-four Leeson Street is the house. She's in good hands with Rosella Coyle. Rosella's a widow. A large woman she is. Salt of the earth."

"Can you give me her phone number?"

"We'd have to look it up." He went around behind the desk and opened the Dublin directory.

The young clerk on duty said, "Get out of the way, Cedric, there's business coming through the door." Cedric and the bishop moved out of the way. The bishop wrote down Rosella Coyle's number, then the Fermoyles'. He would consult Janet about this.

The business coming through the door was the Minnesota tour group, C. H. Garvey bursting into the lobby like a victor into a fallen city, calling to his followers, "Step up to the desk for your keys, folks, then go to your rooms and relax for fifteen minutes. Dinner's at six-thirty. Atta girl, Mrs. Kite, step right along. Atta girl, Mrs. Hardy, put your bags over there. Form a double line all of you, they'll get more clerks and bellhops on the job here if they know what's good for them."

Seeing the bishop with the phone to his ear, C. H. Garvey stepped over and put his arm around his shoulders. "Am I glad to see you, Dick. This group's a handful, asking questions a mile a minute and giving orders to the driver contrary to my own. Take over, will you? I'm going to find a quiet corner and have a drink."

Dick Baker nodded, pointing to the mouthpiece of the phone to show he was busy. There was a voice on the phone saying hello.

"Hello, Mr. Fermoyle, this is Bishop Baker. I'm wondering if Janet's available."

"She is, I'll call her. Nora, it's for Janet." There was a pause. "She'll be taking it downstairs in a second, Bishop. How is your holiday so far?"

"Very nice. The weather's good."

"Yes, you're fortunate, we've not seen this much sun since Easter." Alexander Fermoyle's voice seemed even raspier and higher-pitched over the phone. "You're following the Belfast story in the *Times*, are you, Bishop, the Paddy Creely story? We'll not hear the last of that shooting for quite some time, the Catholic groups are calling for demonstrations all over Ireland. You'll be seeing rabble-rousers gathering in front of our General Post Office anytime now, if they're not there already. It won't come to much, Dublin's hard to arouse. The real skirmish will be in the *Times*, the letters page."

"Hello," said Janet.

"Here she is, then, Bishop. Janet, it's the bishop calling you."

"Thank you."

"I understand we're going out to dinner Thursday, Bishop."

"Yes, and the theater."

"That's where I'll catch my rest. Theater puts me to sleep." They heard Alexander hang up.

"Janet, how are you getting along?"

"Okay. I'm sort of worn out. Evelyn and I were out all day yesterday shopping and seeing things, and we were up half the night with some friends of hers. Today we're just lying around."

"Janet, I'm calling about Miss McGee. Have you been in touch with her today?"

"No. Why?"

"She's checked out of the hotel and gone to stay at a guest-house."

"Really? What's going on?"

"I have no idea. I'm looking for clues."

"Do you suppose it was something with—" She caught herself.

"With what, Janet?"

A pause. "I can't say. It's not something she wants people to know."

"Janet, I don't want to be a snoop, but isn't it up to you and me to find out if there's trouble?"

The tourists formed a circle around the bishop, waiting to greet him. They were chattering loudly. Lillian Kite tugged at his sleeve. He cupped his mouth to the phone so Lillian wouldn't hear:

"The man here at the hotel says she seemed upset."

"You want me to talk to her?"

"Would you?"

"Yes. Where's she at?"

He gave her Rosella Coyle's phone number. "Now, go easy on her, Janet. If she's safe and sound and seems to know what she's doing, don't press her."

"She always knows what she's doing."

"Yes, of course, but I mean if she needs help—that's what you've got to find out."

"I will."

"And you'll call me back?"

"Sure."

"The Gresham Hotel."

"I've got the number."

"Ask for Room four-oh-two."

"Okay."

"Thanks, Janet."

"Sure."

"I'm sorry, I hope the room will do for the night, it's tiny," Rosella Coyle apologized to Agatha, leading her up two and a half flights of stairs: "My lodger from Longford will be gone

tomorrow and then you can move into his room." Rosella Coyle
was tall and gaunt. She had a trace of auburn in her white hair,
the vestiges of beauty in her dark eyes. There were loops of
tiny glass beads sewn to the flat bosom of her pink Sunday dress.
Following her up the stairs, Agatha saw that she wore threadbare slippers and dark brown stockings slipping down her legs
in rings.

"Here it is," Rosella said, pushing at a heavy door stuck in
its frame. "Not a palace by any means but it's clean." She kicked
and the door flew open.

The room was higher than it was wide. The walls and ceiling were pale gray and unadorned except for a mirror over
the sink. The pattern was worn off the blue linoleum covering
the floor.

"This will be fine," said Agatha, setting her suitcases down
at the foot of the narrow bed, which looked deep and soft, warm
and inviting. With the bishop and the tour group converging
on the Gresham this afternoon, what could be better than this
hideaway? She foresaw days alone, moving about Dublin at her
own pace, thinking long thoughts on park benches and in coffee shops, thinking farther ahead into her retirement now that
James wasn't looming in the way.

"As a rule I'm not this crowded in May, but I've six girls from
branch banks in the West come into the city for training, a gig-
gling passel and not a pretty face among them, you'll see for
yourself at breakfast." She handed Agatha a key the size of a
table fork and much heavier. "Come down to the sitting room
for tea if you've a mind to. We'll have a biscuit and a chat."

"Yes, tea would be just the thing."

"Half an hour then?"

"Yes."

"Right."

Rosella Coyle pulled the door shut and went down the
creaking stairs.

Agatha sat on the bed and looked out the narrow window.
The day had turned cloudy. Leaves lifted and fell lazily in the
breeze. She took off her shoes and lay on her back and thought
about liars. Ordinarily she never passed up a chance to confront a liar with his lie, but this one she would have to let go.

She never wanted to see James again. Had he perpetrated four years of lie upon lie, she wondered, or had he told only one foundation lie that caused everything built upon it to topple and crash? The letters of these four years couldn't have been all lies, she decided; they had the solid ring of truth, as did James's voice. One foundation lie, then: his claim to be a teacher, not a priest.

Agatha dozed for a few minutes, then awoke to the sound of footsteps on the stairs. She felt groggy.

"Miss McGee," said Rosella Coyle knocking on the door.

"Come in, it's unlocked."

She put her head in. "It's a woman on the phone asking for you."

Lillian Kite came to mind. "Oh, dear," she said, sitting up. She didn't want to link up with Lillian and her impulsive, headlong touring style. She didn't want Lillian drumming her ears with witless talk when she needed to think what to do with the rest of her life.

Following Rosella Coyle down to the phone in the front entryway, she felt groggier with each step, and under the grogginess she felt the beginning of a headache. She never had headaches. She was never groggy. Was this residual jet lag? Love lag?

Rosella Coyle handed her the phone. "Tea when you're finished," she said, descending another half flight to the sitting room.

"Miss McGee, are you all right?" It was Janet.

"Yes, of course I'm all right."

"I called the hotel just to see how things were going for you, and they said you moved. How come?"

"I wanted to avoid the tour group, Janet. I decided to get to know Ireland through my own eyes instead of through the eyes of C. H. Garvey. Doesn't that make sense?"

"But I thought James O'Hannon would be showing you around."

"Oh, well . . ."

"What about him, Miss McGee? Are the two of you having fun?"

"Oh, well . . ." A long silence.

"Miss McGee, are you there?"

"James O'Hannon and I had a very nice time together. He's . . ." Her voice quavered, to her disgust.

"Miss McGee, I was wondering—"

"Wait a minute, let me finish. I was about to say of James O'Hannon . . ." Another silence.

"Yes?"

"He's not my type."

"He's not? You're not seeing him anymore?"

"That's right."

"So what are you doing with your time?"

"I'll be looking into my family tree." It was no longer a fib.

"Will that take you all week?"

"I'll be sightseeing as well. The rhododendrons are blooming in Howth, I'm told. And they say the zoo in Phoenix Park is very good."

"Miss McGee, I was wondering if I could see you tomorrow."

"Where?"

"Wherever you want. Evelyn has exams all day, so I've got nothing going on."

"All right." Better Janet than Lillian any day. Janet was easy to talk to. Or not to talk to. "Shall we meet in the early afternoon?"

"Sure."

"Which would you prefer? The zoo or the seafront?"

"I'll leave it up to you."

"All right, the bus to either place leaves from near the General Post Office on O'Connell Street. I'll meet you there at one-thirty. It's the big, gray building with the tall pillars."

"I'll be there."

"How are you getting along with the Fermoyles?"

"I'll tell you tomorrow, okay?"

Before the bishop's phone call, Janet and Evelyn had reached the giggly part of their empty Sunday. Evelyn, having had less to worry about in the past few years, was a free-form giggler, while Janet was slower to start and quicker to become sober again. Now, soberly, she hung up the phone and flopped back on the soft white sofa and told Evelyn, who was sprawled on the pillows at the other end, that something was fishy with Miss McGee.

Fishy, Francis Raft's word for anything suspicious, set Evelyn off on another spasm of giggles.

"No, I mean it. She doesn't sound like herself."

"Fishy!" said Evelyn with a shriek.

Janet laughed politely, then folded her hands behind her head and looked at the ceiling. "When she's upset her voice sort of fades."

Evelyn's open-mouth laugh emptied into a long yawn. They hadn't gone to sleep until four this morning. The evening had begun with a movie, a James Bond, which they had gone to with Evelyn's boyfriend, Willie Hughes. He was a quiet fellow who followed directions well, Evelyn being bossy. He was tall and pale. To conceal his baldness he combed his sparse blond hair across the top of his head. Looking at it, Janet thought of Randy's thick curls and how much she enjoyed gripping them. After the movie they went to Ryan's Pub on Westmoreland Street and drank beer in the noisy cellar, which was packed with young people. Their party expanded to include a young couple named Milt and Faye, who were studying law with Willie Hughes and whose talk was full of litigation. Then along came a friend of Evelyn's named Rita Slade, who wore a fresh rose over her ear, drank twice as much as the others and told dozens of jokes about God and sex and the IRA. Rita Slade's looks were marred by one severely drooping eyelid.

It was nearly midnight when Jack Scully joined them, coming in from the Peacock Theater, where he was appearing seven times a week in *Buried Child*. He was taller and better looking than Willie Hughes and had more hair. It was plastered down in a ducktail, and his sideburns extended far below his ears, a necessity, he explained to Janet, for his role as an American kid of some years ago who considers himself quite a hotshot. Jack Scully hovered around Janet, smiling at her a great deal, telling her stories. She saw traces of makeup around his eyes and felt something electric in her spine when he bent close to speak in her ear. She hadn't reacted to anyone this way since Randy first began paying attention to her in the Brass Fox.

From Ryan's Pub they went to a small pub on Duke Street, where a four-piece band and a tenor performed the same country and western songs Janet had been hearing at the Brass Fox. Even the Oklahoma drawl was the same. When the pub closed they went to Jack Scully's apartment in a dark part of the city Janet could never have found again if she tried. The apartment was small and cluttered and smelled of pot. Milt and Faye smoked and continued their discussion of litigation. Evelyn and Willie Hughes smooched in a dark corner. Rita Slade fell asleep on the floor, crushing the rose in her hair. Janet and Jack Scully listened to recordings of Broadway musicals. By the time the party broke up, Janet knew the plot lines of *Sweeney Todd, A Chorus Line* and *Forty-second Street.*

"Fishy?" Evelyn repeated, her yawn dying away.

Janet said, "Something went wrong between her and that man I told you about. I could tell the way she said his name. Before she met him she said his name like she was in love."

"Jeez, unbelievable in a person that age."

"Well, maybe not love, but something like it. Real strong friendship."

"Unbelievable."

"When she said his name just now her voice sounded dead."

Evelyn stood up, tucked her shirt into her jeans. "Want a beer?"

Janet nodded. "Thanks."

Returning with two bottles, Evelyn said, "So what will you and she do tomorrow?"

"Go to the zoo maybe. Is there a good zoo?"

"Good enough, if you're a child. What else?"

"Probably go someplace and look at the sea. She's crazy about the sea."

They drank. They gazed out the window at the light and dark clouds layered over the Wicklow Hills.

"What were you telling Jack last night on his doorstep, that you'd see him again?"

"That I might," said Janet.

"When?"

"Wednesday."

"And do what?"

"Maybe take a train trip. Maybe go to Belfast."

"Oh, Jack's a cad. What would Randy say?"

"What's wrong with that? He said we'd all be going."

"How can we all go? We've got exams on Wednesday."

"You have? Well, there's Rita. She said she'd go."

"Rita will go if she remembers that long. You can't depend on Rita."

"Well, if it's just Jack I won't go."

They sat in silence watching the light change over the hills. It brightened, then darkened. Janet nearly fell asleep.

Evelyn said, "What's Randy doing this minute, do you suppose?"

Janet calculated the time. "Sleeping. He sleeps late on Sunday."

"Let's wake him up."

Randy picked up the phone on the seventh ring. "Hello," he said sleepily, then, "Janet! Is that you? Where are you?"

"In Dublin."

"What's wrong?"

"Nothing's wrong, I'm just calling."

"God, across the ocean?"

"How are you, Randy? How's Stephen?"

"Fine. Hey, Janet, wait till you see what I got you." He stretched the cord around to the living room, where the Spooner Mark IV stood in the middle of the floor surrounded by its eleven attachments. The six bottles of blue shampoo sparkled in the morning sunlight; the tubes of chrome gleamed like silver.

"You mean a present?" she asked.

"For your homecoming."

"Really? What is it?"

"Surprise. You'll love it." Saying this, his heart fell. Saying it didn't help him believe it.

"You didn't spend too much, did you, Randy?"

"Naw." Six hundred twenty-five dollars. He felt terrible.

"How's Stephen. Is he there?"

"He went to church with Mother."

"So how is he?"

"Fine."

"Really? Is he fine? Did his sniffles clear up? Was it a cold?"

"No, just the sniffles, he's fine. So, Janet, how's the trip?"

"It's fine. You should have come."

"No, I'd of missed a big sale. Get this, Janet—I sold a top-of-the-line Spring-Flo the day you left."

"Oh, that's wonderful, Randy. Who to?"

"Her name's Ecklund. The new pharmacist in town."

"Oh, her. Watch yourself with her, Randy. I hear she's on the make."

"Yeah?"

"That's what they say."

"Well, she'll have an easier time of it now with the softener. Her face'll clear up."

"Oh, Randy!" yelled Evelyn, who had been pressing her ear to the phone. "You're still as tough on girls as you used to be."

"Hey, who's that? Is that you, Evelyn?"

"Hi, Randy, you've got a great wife, you know that? It turns out we're the best of friends."

"Hi, Evelyn. How are you and your folks?"

"Just fine. How come you stayed home, Randy? Aren't you afraid of hurting a person's feelings?"

"Business reasons. It's a good time for selling. I sold a top-of-the-line water softener the other day, and tomorrow there's a chance I might sell a house."

"A house?" Janet took back the phone.

"I'm showing two houses for Dad tomorrow. He's out of town playing in a golf tournament that was delayed because of rain, and he's letting me show two houses to four different parties, and I've got a hunch I'll sell one. See, I've got this promotional idea."

"That's great, Randy, but don't get your hopes up too high, you know what I mean."

"Yeah, well, this one house, the Vaughn place, it's listed for over a hundred thousand. Think of my commission on that."

"Super, Randy." A pause. "So tell me about Stephen."

"He's doing fine. He's upstairs all the time. Mother's having people in a lot. I guess she took him around last night to visit some friends."

"What did you do last night?"

"I went out to the Brass Fox for a beer. Saw Karen and Sally out there. Karen broke up with Bob. Brian Johnson took her home."

"She's always breaking up with Bob. So what did you do out there? Like, did you dance?"

"Just with Karen and Sally is all."

"Nobody else?"

"Naw, I thought I might, but I didn't feel like it."

"It's all right, you know, as long as it's just dancing."

"Yeah, but I didn't feel like it. I talked mostly to Eugene Westerman. Remember him?"

"Eugene Westerman? He sold my dad a used pickup that never ran right. He's crooked."

"I don't know, Janet, there's a lot he can teach a guy."

"You'd be better off dancing, Randy."

Evelyn broke in. "Randy, what time is it there?"

"Ten, a little after."

Janet said, "If I call again at twelve, will Stephen be home?"

"No, she's taking him to the country club after church."

"Are you going along?"

"You know I'm not crazy about the country club."

"How about if I call around two?"

"Yeah, they'll probably be back by two. Hey, Janet, you don't sound very excited about the house. It's the old Vaughn place on River Street."

"I am, Randy, and I'll be even more excited when it happens."

"No faith, huh?"

"Of course I've got faith, and I think it's wonderful about the water softener."

"Janet, how about if I drive to Minneapolis and meet your plane Saturday? What time you coming in?"

"Five o'clock. But there's a good bus connection."

"I know, but I can't wait for the bus, Janet. It takes three hours."

"Why? What's wrong?"

"Nothing's wrong. I just want to see you when you land."

"Yeah? That's great. Randy, is something wrong?"

"Nothing except I'm lonesome for you."

At this Janet was speechless. So, for a moment, was Randy.

"We could go out to eat on the way home," he said. "We hardly ever go out to eat, except hamburgers at the Brass Fox."

"That's a great idea, Randy, but there's Miss McGee and Mrs. Kite to think about."

"That's okay, they'll fit in the backseat."

"You'll bring Stephen?"

Damn—to be married a year and still feel yourself playing second fiddle to a four-year-old. That was the whole point of driving to the airport, to see her before Stephen swallowed up all her attention. "I don't know, Janet, it's a long drive and he gets restless."

She knew better than to press him. "Whatever you decide, Randy."

"I'll be there when you land."

"Good. And Randy?"

"Yeah?"

"I'm lonesome, too."

"Yeah?"

"For you."

"Yeah? Hey."

"And I'm excited about the house."

Lillian Kite sent the bellman off with her coat, suitcases and shopping bags. She did not follow him to her room. Instead, she followed the bishop to his, telling him how frightfully high the prices on Irish menus were, how narrow the Irish roads were, how cute the Irish children and goats were. In the lobby she had begun this recitation the moment Dick Baker hung up the phone, reviewing for him every mile and meal between Shannon and Dublin.

Stepping off the elevator on the fourth floor, she said, "In Cork I bought the cutest wall plaque that says May the Wind Be Ever at Your Back, and at the Cork hotel they gave us a breakfast that would choke a moose, all of it delicious except

180 · Jon Hassler

the sausage, which didn't hold a candle to Jimmy Dean Pork
Links. All over Ireland the sausage is too mealy, don't you find?"

"Actually, I hadn't noticed," said Dick Baker, unlocking his
door.

She darted in. "Well, you notice next time and see if you don't
think they put a lot of meal in with the meat. Eat four or five
links for breakfast and see if you aren't bilious till noon."

Her description alone was enough to make him bilious. He
had a delicate stomach. He carefully watched what he ate, but
he hadn't watched carefully enough at All Hallows. He was eager to take off his shoes and lie down. He remained standing,
hoping this might shorten Lillian's visit, but she went straight
to the only soft chair and settled into it.

"What's become of Agatha? They said at the desk she wasn't
registered."

Dick Baker said, "Off researching her family tree, I suppose. Over here you find your ancestors in parish records,
mostly out in the country."

"Give me the city over the country every time. I've spent my
life looking at country and I don't see why all the fuss about
Ireland. Pretty, yes, I'll admit it's pretty, but come now, Your
Excellency, if you've seen one pasture you've seen them all, and
if you've seen one beach you've seen them all, and as for the
ocean, it's just water, if you ask me. But the cities and towns,
now, that's where this trip is worth the money, the shops and
restaurants and quaint hotels. We were in a place called
Waterford where everybody else went off to some glass factory or other and I went around the town and found the best
little souvenir shop that sold the loveliest little tea sets, and when
we got back on the bus and everybody was showing off what
they'd bought I saw it was all just plain glass with nothing
painted on it, so I handed around my teapot with little sham-
rocks on the one side of it and everybody said they'd sure missed
it by going to the glass factory. Some of them said the glass
factory was interesting, all right, but when you pressed them
for the truth they finally admitted it was noisy and the floor
was wet."

The phone rang.

"Excuse me, Mrs. Kite."

"Go ahead, don't mind me." She reached into her blouse and adjusted some straps.

It was Janet. "I talked to Miss McGee."

"Ah, good for you. What did you find out?"

"She said she moved to avoid the group. She wants to be alone."

"Is she in trouble?"

"No, she didn't sound like it. She was just sort of sad or something. I'm seeing her tomorrow afternoon. We're either going to the zoo or out to look at the ocean."

"Call me afterward, will you, Janet?"

"Sure."

"Give my best to the Fermoyles, and I'll see you Thursday evening."

When he hung up, Lillian said, "Was that Janet Meers?"

"It was."

"Janet's sorry she's not with the group, I bet. It was a great mistake, her and Agatha going off like that on their own. Agatha will be jealous of me for eating lobster Friday night in Cork, she loves lobster, and wait till I tell her I talked to some foreigners. That's something I never expected to see in Ireland, foreigners. I was sitting at a table in the fish restaurant with two women from Holland who didn't know six words of English between them, and it made me realize how limited life is when you don't know English. I tried telling them about Minnesota but I couldn't get through to them because the only words they understood were 'please' and 'thank you' and 'salt' and 'rain.' "

The phone.

"Hey, listen, Dick, have you forgotten it's dinnertime? We're all in the dining room waiting."

"I hadn't planned to eat, C.H. I had a big dinner at the seminary."

"Listen, Dick, Garvey Travel's paying for your dinner so there's no sense letting it go to waste, and besides, the group's been waiting since Thursday for a chance to mingle with you."

"Mingle with me?"

"That's one of the things they paid for, you know."

Dick Baker sighed. "Okay, I'll be down."

"Right, and if you see Mrs. Kite up there tell her it's time to eat."

"She's here with me."

"Oops." Garvey laughed lasciviously and hung up.

18

"REMEMBER THAT NAME, my countrymen, in Ireland's blackest hour the name Benjamin Wakefield is the blackest name we know, for he's the bloody butcher who shot down Paddy Creely and his three children Mickey and Erin and Owen, as well as the heroic lad of the IRA."

Janet stood listening at the edge of the small crowd in front of the General Post Office. The man was standing on a box and speaking into a bullhorn. He wore a flat, tweed cap, a brown suit and an armband of mourning. Below him on his left stood a young woman holding a large black flag on a long pole. The tail of her dark gray shirt hung out over the top of her long black skirt. Two other women, one young and one old, stood behind a table with their backs to the post office wall. The young woman urged passersby to sign their names in the large book of blank pages open on the table. The older woman held out a box for donations. According to the tattered banner on the wall above them, this was the Committee for One Ireland.

"This battered old land will never know peace, my friends, until the British baboons give over their rule of the North."

Janet stood near enough to hear both his natural voice and his amplified voice at the same time. His natural voice was easier to understand; the bullhorn gave it a twangy echo.

"We are the Committee for One Ireland. We need your help for our one goal and one goal only, that the six and twenty-six become thirty-two united counties under God's open blue sky. Now let me hear it from those who agree!"

Only two or three spoke out, and those timidly, near the back of the crowd. It seemed to Janet the wrong time for a political rally, and even though this was the site of the Rising of Sixteen, as Alexander Fermoyle had instructed her, it seemed the wrong place as well. Monday afternoon and the city all business. Cars zipping up and down O'Connell Street. Sidewalks crowded with shoppers, sightseers, derelicts, office workers on lunch break. High green buses pulling up to curbs and disgorging and swallowing crowds.

"Now once more, louder. Let me hear a shout or cry from you who agree that Ireland must be united and free!"

No shout, no cry. Only here and there a murmur of assent.

"Am I among friends or enemies? Tell me, is this the Dublin of Pearse and Connelly, or have I wandered into the enemy camp? All right, if that's what I've done, then let me hear from all who *dis*agree with me."

He listened for disagreement. There was none. His eyes came to rest on Janet.

"Tell me, lass, what do you make of what's happening in Belfast?"

"What's happening?" she asked.

People behind her snickered.

"My God, where have you been, the Hebrides? We're talking about Paddy Creely and his three children wiped out by the RUC. His oldest daughter shot in the head in the street and she no sooner laid to rest than the rest of the family, all but Annie, his wife, gunned down in the basement of their very own home. It's the crime of the decade, my friends, and it's the outrage that will finally arouse this tired old island to action. And here I've brought a man straight from Belfast who'll tell you what action I mean."

The speaker got down off the box, and a younger man took his place, a slim, short man whose beak and hooded eyes reminded Janet of the sparrow hawks that sat on the power lines running past her farm. His eyes darted shiftily over the crowd the way sparrow hawks scanned thickets for prey.

"I live across the street from Paddy Creely's house. For twelve years I worked side by side with Paddy on the assembly line of the Sampson Tractor Factory." This man's voice was nasal and weak; through the bullhorn it was reedy. "For many years at Sunday Mass I knelt across the aisle from Paddy and his wife, Annie, and their kids. Last Friday evening at dinnertime I went over to the Creely house and helped carry four dead bodies out of the basement and helped Annie up out of the basement in a state of shock, home only a short time after the funeral of her twelve-year-old daughter."

Janet saw Agatha coming down the street in her bronze-colored raincoat. She carried her matching umbrella over her arm. There was a moment, drawing close, before Agatha saw her, that Janet noticed a remarkable change in her face. It was older than it had been on Friday, deflated somehow, her eyes less sharp. But the moment Janet said, "Miss McGee, here I am," the eyes came instantly alert and she smiled. She took Janet's hand and drew her away, against the wall of the post office.

"What's going on here, Janet? Why is that girl waving that hideous black flag?"

"It's a demonstration. They're talking about what happened to Paddy Creely and his family."

"Oh, the papers are full of it. It's unspeakable."

"And see that woman over there behind the table? She wants everybody to write their name in that book for Mrs. Creely. The Book of Condolence, she calls it." The woman in charge of the book was stabbing passersby in the shoulder with her ball-point pen, urging them to stop and sign. Hardly anyone did. "And they're asking everybody to go to Belfast tomorrow for the funeral. There's going to be a special train."

Agatha looked at the banner on the wall. "I never heard of the Committee for One Ireland."

"I heard somebody say they're a fund-raising branch of the IRA."

"Then they're terrorists," said Agatha. "In the name of God and country the IRA goes around bombing buses and murdering people in their beds."

"Are you sure? I thought the IRA was Catholic."

"They claim to be Catholic, but there's nothing Christian about them."

A man who had been listening to the speaker turned and glared at Agatha. Wearing wire-rimmed glasses and a clean, cheap suit, he had the look of a junior accountant.

"They're on no one's side but the devil's," she said, as much for the young man's benefit as Janet's. She squinted down the street. "I think . . . yes, that's the bus to Howth. Come, Janet, we can catch it at the corner."

They sat at the front window of the upper deck and were carried through all the gradations of Dublin's poverty and wealth, beginning with the wretched neighborhoods near City Centre and ending with the riches near the sea. Agatha was uncommonly quiet until, near the end of the ride, she made a summarizing statement, as Janet expected she might. "Have you noticed, Janet, there are fewer bus stops among the rich, and no joggers among the poor?"

On the advice of the conductor they got off at the base of a path winding uphill through a wood. They climbed, pausing a few times to catch their breath and to read Agatha's guidebook which instructed them to smell the wild garlic (they did), to stroll the grounds of Howth castle (the gate was locked) and to veer left at the fork in the path (they did) if they wished to see the best of the rhododendrons.

The view from high ground was spectacular—the gardens and lawns of a swank hotel, thousands and thousands of rhododendron blossoms big as cheerleaders' pompons, the manicured green of a golf course sloping down toward the sea. They spent twenty minutes at the crest, Agatha looking out over the water, Janet strolling away and back again, glancing at Agatha to read her remote expression and finding it unreadable. The day was thinly overcast now, the sun blank white, the sea and sky aluminum.

"I can't get enough of the sea, Janet."

Moving close to her, Janet said, "I like the lakes better at home. They're smaller. They don't remind you how big the world is, the way this does."

Agatha's voice was a whisper: "Yes, there's so much more to the world than we realize." After a moment she drew herself out of wherever she was: "Janet, doesn't the sea air make your skin feel soft?"

"It does." Janet put her hands to her cheeks.

They followed a path downhill that turned into a steep, curving street through the town. The street led to the harbor. A fishing fleet was moored on the leeward side of the pier. On the breezeward side a flotilla of gulls bobbed. There were no

whitecaps but the swells were high and they set off explosions
of spray on the rocks. The tide being out, the spray fell short
of the bench where Agatha and Janet sat down.

Agatha took a tablet from her purse and showed Janet the
five sketches she had done since Friday. "You know, I was never
any great shakes as an artist, Janet. I sketched only for school."

"I remember your sketches. Mostly farms." She took the tablet
and studied the pictures. Knob Harbor as seen from the Plunketts' front window. A thatched cottage near where they had
stopped with the bishop for lunch. The General Post Office as
seen from the Gresham. The Ha'penny Bridge. The back of a
high old house with little creatures at the foundation, cats or
rabbits. "What's this?"

"The house where I'm staying."

"These are cats?"

"I'm glad you can tell. I'm an artist by default, really. I got
started in the days before we had an art teacher at St. Isidore's, and we were all expected to teach it. Once a week I
forced myself to find a subject and try to get its likeness down,
but imitation has never been my strong point."

Janet saw what she meant. The tall-masted fishing boats in
Knob Harbor might have been half-shells of walnuts suspended on strings.

"My strong point was always composition."

"I know," said Janet, remembering the period every Friday
afternoon when the sixth grade would return from lunch to
find a chalk drawing on the board, framed in a chalk rectangle, and they would pay attention while Miss McGee pointed
out that each element—this tree, this barn, this road—was
placed where it was for a reason—to lead the viewer's eye into
the scene, perhaps, or to give the picture balance. She went on
and on about balance. Then she would hand out large sheets
of paper, and the students would go to work on pictures of
their own, first sketching in pencil, then shading with watercolors. Though she encouraged them to bring sketches to class,
she seldom allowed them to reproduce exactly what they
brought. It was the artist's job to rearrange nature, she said;
life as you met it needed a great deal of straightening and fixing. Everything in nature had once had its place, she ex-

plained, but some things since the Fall of Man had been *mis*placed, and the artist had to set everything right.

Taking the tablet from Janet, Agatha coiled herself into her sketching posture, crossing her legs and sitting forward over the tablet on her knee. She uncapped her pen and faced off to her right, away from Janet. Her head bobbed, eyes up, eyes down, as she began drawing a rocky headland in the distance. Without pausing, she asked Janet about the Fermoyles and how she liked staying with them.

"It's like you said on the way over, Miss McGee. It's a great opportunity for me to get to know an Irish family. But it's nothing more than that, if you know what I mean. They're very nice to me and everything, but they're so busy I feel like I have to be careful not to be in the way. I see hardly anything of Evelyn's parents. Her mother's gone all the time getting her new boutique ready to open, and her dad when he's home is always reading or typing in his den."

"But you're getting along all right with Evelyn?"

"Sure. I wouldn't say we're the closest friends that ever lived, but we're fine. We see things. We've gone to two movies. But she's busy, too. Today and Wednesday she's got tests all day."

Janet watched her sketch for a while, then said, "Miss McGee, tell me about James O'Hannon."

"What would you like to know?"

"Everything."

Agatha went on drawing. "He's tall and a little overweight. I think he should lose eight or ten pounds. He has a mellifluous voice."

"Mellifluous?"

"Pleasing. It comes from very deep in his chest and partially out through his nose."

Agatha stopped sketching, her eyes falling on an elderly couple leaving the town and walking down toward the pier.

"He dresses the way most Irishmen dress, for warmth rather than style. He took me out to dinner. It was an upstairs restaurant over a fabric shop. I ate cod. He ate steak. We talked nonstop for three hours."

"What about?"

"Everything. The way we do—did—in our letters."

They said no more for a time. Agatha completed her drawing. She held it at arm's length.

"It isn't very good, is it, Janet? The cliffs haven't any depth to them. That was always my problem, I could never achieve the illusion of the third dimension."

"I see what you mean." Janet took the tablet and pen and with an impulsive stroke she put a gliding gull high in the sky over the headland. Suddenly the sketch was better. The bird for some reason gave depth to the scene. She looked at Agatha, who nodded.

"Now answer me this, Janet: Why should that bird make such a difference? It's only a tiny scratch of ink. It draws the eye away from the land, and yet it improves the looks of the land. How can that be?"

Janet handed back the tablet. "I don't know, but it sure helps."

Agatha wondered if there was an artistic principle about providing the viewer with some distraction in order for the core of the work to come into focus. She recalled the tantalizing, elusive image of Judas in the Last Supper painting, drawing the eye away from Christ while heightening the drama that Christ was at the center of. In the night sky didn't you see a dim star better if you looked slightly to one side of it? In the past four years hadn't she come to a fuller understanding of her own life by concentrating on the life of James O'Hannon?

"Things throw light on things," she said.

"And all the stones have wings," Janet replied automatically. It was one of the many scraps of poetry the sixth grade had had to memorize. Though she had long since forgotten the names of the poets, and though some of the verses, like this one, were sheer nonsense, Janet enjoyed keeping the poems in her head.

"Things throw light on things," Agatha repeated, this time more softly and to herself. It was a line she favored not only because it seemed true, but also because the man who wrote it, the son of a nurseryman, had grown up among flowers, as Agatha had.

The elderly couple, their heads bent in rapt conversation, came strolling toward Agatha and Janet. They were talking about a garden. Janet heard the woman say, "I think we ought to cut back on the lilies and give the roses more room." The man said, "I'm thinking we should get someone in to repair the wall." They strolled on, toward the lighthouse. The man was tall, slightly stooped. The woman, much shorter, walked with a graceful swing in her step. Her hands were deep in the pockets of her long coat. Their heads were bent toward one another.

"Miss McGee, do you think Randy and I will look like that someday?"

Agatha gazed after the couple, imagining their long, harmonious marriage. They might have been Agatha's mother and father. If the world had been ordered more perfectly, they might have been herself and James.

"They seem so *used* to each other."

"Yes, I see."

"With Randy and me, it's like we're not that used to each other. It's not that we have fights or anything, it's just that we're a long ways from being like *that*."

"It takes time to be like that." Yet weren't she and James like that on the pier at Dun Laoghaire?

"I think the biggest problem is he resents Stephen. I wish he wouldn't feel that way. Stephen likes him just fine."

The man and wife paused to look down at the water breaking on the rocks. The man took the woman's hand.

Agatha pulled her eyes away from them. She folded away her sketch of the headland and began another.

Janet opened her purse and took out her pocket map. She studied the east coast. She found Howth. She found Belfast. She put the map away.

"So what's he like, Miss McGee? I mean, besides his voice and his ten extra pounds."

"He carries himself with a certain bearing. Remember Father McGuire when he was at St. Isidore's? He reminds me of Father McGuire, his way of walking. Not with a swagger exactly, but with his chest puffed out a bit. And like Father McGuire he neglects to polish his shoes."

Janet saw that the lines of her sketch were going nowhere. She was doodling.

"What does he teach?"

"Well, his teaching . . . it's a special kind of teaching . . . it's done from the pulpit at Mass."

Janet frowned. "He's a priest?"

Agatha turned to her with a smile.

"I didn't know that, Miss McGee." She saw that Agatha's smile was actually a grimace fixed tightly on her face. "Oh, Miss McGee, you didn't know either, did you?"

She put her arm around Agatha's sharp, bony shoulders and felt her tremble.

Agatha allowed this embrace to go on for half a minute, then she patted Janet's arm and said, "I know a place downtown that has the best coffee and rolls."

On the bus Janet asked, "Are you and James O'Hannon meeting again?"

"No."

The bus sped beside a bay of flat mud.

"Do you wish you were?"

"No . . ."

It was slow going near the center of the city; traffic was heavy.

"But we were kindred spirits, Janet. James said it himself. He said our hearts were alike in so many ways, and he wasn't surprised, because we were Irish. There's always a bond between Irish hearts, he said."

The bus halted in a long line, waiting for a stoplight. The light changed twice before the bus could proceed. Janet weighed this a long time before she said it:

"I'm part Irish, you know."

Agatha patted her arm. "I know."

19

RANDY'S FATHER, delayed by his golf game in Berrington, bestowed four of his Monday appointments on Randy. He charged him with three showings of an unattractive green house on the north end of Main Street in the morning, and with one showing of the stately old Vaughn house on River Street in the afternoon.

At 9:00 A.M. Randy parked in front of the green house and unloaded his Spooner Mark IV from the trunk of his car. It took him three trips to get it all into the house, first the heavy canister and hose, next the kit containing the eleven attachments, and finally the case of blue shampoo. He placed the canister at the center of the empty living room and spread out the eleven attachments on the floor around it—tubes, nozzles, brushes. Behind all this, where they caught the sunlight, he stood the six half-gallon jugs of shampoo. Sell to the buyer's weakness, Eugene Westerman had said. Randy would offer the Spooner free to whoever bought this house.

Waiting for his first family to show up—the Browns—he took out his handkerchief and wiped his fingermarks from the canister. What homeowner could resist it? After standing back and admiring it for a minute or two, he went out and sat on the front step and opened his father's pocket notebook to the page devoted to this house. He scanned the column headed *Plus*, and the column headed *Minus*. Under *Plus* was natural gas heat, new electrical wiring, partially completed family room in basement, new insulation in attic, property tax under four hundred dollars last year, very large closet off one bedroom. Under *Minus* the roof needed shingling, the yard was small and scrubby, sometimes at this end of town sewers backed up into basements.

Randy recalled his mother telling his father that she would eventually prevail and the city council would lay a new sewer line the length of Main Street. "When?" his father demanded in the surly tone he always used when profit or loss was involved. "Eventually," his mother repeated. Randy knew what "eventually" meant. It meant she would get the city council moving on this as soon as her husband consented to some large favor in return. In history courses Randy had never had difficulty understanding the balance of power between nations; all his life he had been eyewitness to the balance of power between parents.

At the bottom of the page Randy saw the selling price: thirty-eight thousand dollars. His father's commission was invariably 7 percent, and though Randy had asked for the full 7, his father told him over the phone last night that he could have only 3, the remaining 4 being needed to cover the overhead at Staggerford Realty.

Fair enough, thought Randy, figuring with his pen on an empty page of the notebook. Three percent of thirty-eight thousand was eleven hundred forty. With that he could pay off the four hundred five dollars remaining on the Spooner, buy Janet a more modest homecoming present (say a set of eight beer glasses from Sears, Roebuck) and still have over seven hundred in cash to show for the ten days he stayed home from Ireland. Put that seven hundred together with the seven hundred he had saved on air fare, and you had fourteen hundred. Life was full of opportunities once you learned to see them.

The Browns arrived in a dust-covered car at nine-thirty. They were a young husband and wife with two toddlers. All four of them wore T-shirts, khaki shorts and scruffy tennis shoes. Mrs. Brown was a nervous blonde who kept her hand to her hair all the time, patting it, scratching it, smoothing it. She explained that they were moving to Staggerford because she had been hired to teach sixth grade at St. Isidore's. She said that both she and her husband had lost their teaching jobs in the city for lack of enrollment and her new job wasn't all that promising either, because the woman who had hired her, Sister Judith, had told her confidentially that St. Isidore's had only two more years to live.

"It's such a comedown moving here after living in the city," said Mrs. Brown, "but beggars can't be choosers, and these days teachers are beggars."

Randy asked, "What city are you from?"

"The city of Fargo," said Mr. Brown. He was carrying the smaller child and pulling the other by the hand. He was a pale man with thick glasses and hairy legs. He wore an unchanging expression that was slightly sour. Did the appearance of this house displease him, Randy wondered, or was he suffering from low self-esteem, being unemployed—a condition familiar to Randy.

"I have just the place for you here." Randy held open the door. "It's one of our less expensive, and yet it's a dream of a home."

"A what?" said Mr. Brown.

"A dream of a home," Randy repeated. This was one of two dozen expressions of the trade his father had taught him. Or was it dreamhouse? Yes, that was it. "A dreamhouse," he said.

Mrs. Brown paused when she came to the Spooner Mark IV in the living room, but Randy urged her on into the kitchen. He would explain the Spooner at the end of the tour when it came time to clinch the deal. They went into the basement and looked through a half-finished wall into the furnace room. They stepped through the wall and looked into the furnace.

They went up to the second floor and looked into the two small bedrooms. Randy pointed out the roomy closet off the front bedroom. "A dreamcloset," he said. They went and stood in the small bathroom. Randy said, "The whole house was re-wired three years ago, and there's new insulation in the attic."

"Can we see the attic?" asked Mrs. Brown.

"Well, I don't see how." Randy looked at the small trapdoor in the ceiling. "We'd need a ladder."

"You mean that's the only way into the attic?"

"Maybe if you stood on the edge of the bathtub . . ."

"Let's go out and look at the yard," she said.

The yard was listed under *Minus* in the book. There were

large sandy patches where grass wouldn't grow; the two shade trees were dying. They circled the house in a hurry, and when they got back to the front door, Randy said, "Now let's go in the living room and talk it over."

"Oh, I guess not," said Mrs. Brown. "What do you think, Joe?"

Something gloomy, by the look of him. The older child was whining and trying to pull Joe toward the car. The younger one, in Joe's arms, was filling its pants. Joe said, "Nope."

"Wait," said Randy, following them to their car. "The Spooner vacuum you saw in the living room, it's part of the deal. It's yours free if you buy this house."

"I've got a vacuum," said Mrs. Brown.

"But not a Spooner Mark Four, I bet."

"No, but my Hoover's plenty good."

They got into the car. Joe started the engine. Through the window Mrs. Brown said, "Thanks, we'll get back to you."

"Here, take this." Randy gave her his card, knowing she didn't want it. *We'll get back to you* was what they always said when they weren't interested.

They drove away. Randy sat on the front steps and waited for the Hogansons.

The Hogansons, Bubba and Violet, arrived late for their appointment. Bubba Hoganson was on coffee break from the grocery store where he worked as assistant manager. He was wearing his green apron. Violet Hoganson, seven months pregnant, was having an attack of asthma.

"Hurry up and show us what you got here, Randy," said Bubba, "I ain't got all day." He was a fat young man with a golden moustache that hid his mouth. Shopping at IGA, you would find Bubba overseeing the cashiers and insisting that you had missed certain weekly specials. Whenever you declined what he offered, Bubba would look incredulous and hurt. It made no sense to Bubba that you should turn down kitty litter at ninety-eight cents a box simply because you had no cat.

Randy said, "This is a dreamhouse for a family starting out. When's your baby due?"

"July," said Violet. She was a small, freckled, sandy-haired woman. She wore a silky-blue maternity sundress. "We're hoping to find a place before the baby comes." She gave herself a little puff of Adrenalin from an atomizer.

His father always said Randy should be more chatty, so he said, "Can't have babies where you live, I suppose."

"Babies, but not dogs," Violet said. "Bubba says no child should be without a dog, so we're getting one." She turned to her large husband. "But please, Bubba, not that Great Dane."

To his wife Bubba said, "Never mind," and to Randy he said, "Let's get this show on the road."

They went through the house in twenty minutes, during which time Bubba smoked three cigarettes. He flicked the ashes into his cupped hand and rubbed them into his apron. The smoldering stubs he flicked out windows.

Returning downstairs and leading them into the living room, Randy said, "And here, this vacuum is worth nearly a thousand dollars and I'm throwing it in on the deal at no cost whatsoever."

Bubba gave him a skeptical look. "And the house is how much?"

Randy opened the notebook and displayed the selling price. "Thirty-eight thousand—see, I'm not charging you a penny for the vacuum."

"Hey, what's this?" Bubba's eye was caught by the *Minus* column. "What's this about the sewer backing up?"

Randy snapped the book shut. "It's just a matter of laying a new main. The city's going to do it. It's going to come up at a council meeting pretty soon."

Bubba snatched the book from him and found the page. "What's this about the roof?"

Violet's wheezing was worse. She stood bent over, her hair falling forward around her face.

"The roof'll just need shingling someday, it's no big deal. Every place needs upkeep."

"And what's this about the yard?"

"There's nothing wrong with the yard. It's just little, is all. And the trees in front are just sort of dying."

"Both of them?"

"Yeah, elms, you know. I guess a beetle of some kind."

"So what shades my kid's dog?"

"The house. Put your dog on the north side of the house."

Bubba went out to look at the yard.

"I've got to sit down," said Violet, gasping. She was bent farther over, her hands on her knees.

Randy helped her across the room to the Spooner and eased
her down on the flat-topped canister. She sprayed her throat
but her pipes were closing faster than she could atomize them.
Her cheeks were flushed, her lips blue. He knelt beside her
and watched as she sprayed her throat again. After a time, when
she could spare enough oxygen, she said, "I'm sorry, Randy."

"No, it's all right."

"I usually get better"—she inhaled—"in about fifteen minutes."

Randy sat back on his heels.

Bubba poked his head in at the door. "I'm going back to work,
Violet. You can walk home, okay?"

She nodded.

"Hey, she's sick," said Randy. "You can't leave her here
strangling."

"She'll be all right." Bubba withdrew.

"I'll be all right," Violet whispered.

Randy hurried to the front door. "Hey, Bubba, what about
the house?"

Bubba was getting into his car. "I'll get back to you."

Randy looked at his watch. His next clients, an old couple
retiring from a farm, were due in a few minutes. He waited
outside for a while and then returned to Violet. She was strug-
gling to breathe.

"You're not better, Violet. You can't walk home."

"No. Would you call Bubba at the store?"

"The phone's not connected. Come on, I'll give you a ride."

He helped her out to his car and drove her the nine blocks
to Meadowview Apartments. She showed him which entrance
to park near, but she made no move to get out. Her eyes were
shut tight. She seemed to be suffocating. He drove her to the
hospital and helped her into the emergency room, where she
was given an injection. At the admissions desk he asked to use
the phone and dialed the IGA.

"Hi, Bubba, this is Randy."

"Randy, the yard's too small. We've got to have room for a dog to run. And don't call me at work, I'm busy."

"It's Violet, Bubba. I've brought her to the hospital. She can't breathe."

"Yeah? Well, she'll be okay, she gets like that."

"They gave her a shot and said she could go home in half an hour."

"Good, tell her to walk home and I'll check in with her at noon."

"Bubba, for God's sake, she's your wife. Come and give her a ride."

"She can walk, it's only about four blocks."

"Bubba, she's seven months pregnant and she can't breathe. You've got to give her a ride."

"Hell I do. You can't be soft on a wife when you're breaking her in. Now, good-bye, I'm busy."

"Good-bye, you heartless bastard."

He returned to the emergency room, where Violet was sitting behind a curtain. She smiled at him. "Sorry to be such a bother, Randy." She was breathing easier.

"No bother at all. You seem better."

"Yes."

"I'll be in the waiting room when you're ready to go."

"No, I'll call Bubba for a ride."

"No, it's okay, I'll take you."

"No, you've got work to do."

"No, I'm free." The farm couple had been due at the house twenty minutes ago. They were probably gone by now. "I'll see you in the waiting room."

Half an hour later, after delivering Violet home ("Thanks a million, Randy, we'll get back to you on the house"), he drove to the north end of Main Street to pick up the vacuum and lock the door. There was no sign of the farm couple.

Driving from the green house to the Vaughn house on River Street, he wondered if, instead of sales, he ought to go into human services—social work, nursing, counseling, stuff like that. Passing up a house-showing in order to help Violet Hoganson had made him feel virtuous. There was a lot to be said for charity. It was a great feeling. Maybe in trying to be a salesman he had been going against his nature. Maybe it was his nature to be a saint.

But by the time he had transfered the Spooner into the Vaughn house, he felt like a salesman again. It was impossible not to love this house. Like most of those on River Street, like Agatha McGee's just three doors to the south, the Vaughn house was stately. It had rooms nobody bothered to build into homes anymore—a foyer, a sun-room, a pantry. It had seven bedrooms if you counted the two under the eaves on the third floor.

The old, odd widow Vaughn, who had been found dead three years ago in her pantry, had left no children (her only son was killed in Korea), and so her considerable property emerged from probate belonging to distant, lucky relatives. The house had gone to a grandniece named Eunice Noznick, who together with her husband, Norman, owned and operated the Noznick Entertainment Group, which consisted of two drive-in theaters on the outskirts of Minneapolis and the Paramount Popcorn Supply in St. Paul. The house had been for sale for nearly a year, listed at a hundred five thousand dollars. Randy was calculating his potential commission (thirty-one hundred fifty dollars) when Otto Kessler pulled up in a white Cadillac.

"This is a home you'll love," said Randy, shaking Otto Kessler's hand on the veranda. "It's luxury living with all the charm of yesteryear."

"Yeah, yeah, let's see what you got here, kid." Otto Kessler crossed the veranda and let himself into the house. He was a short, wide man who waddled when he walked. He was chewing an unlit cigar. He carried a pocket notebook much like Randy's.

"It's a classic beauty in a prime location," said Randy, hurrying to keep up. "Look at this beautiful formal dining room. Notice the built-in buffet and mirror."

"Yeah, yeah," said Otto Kessler, pausing to write something in his book, then dashing through to the kitchen.

"Double sink and drainboard," said Randy. "Dishwasher."

"Yeah, don't waste your time telling me the obvious. Let's have the inside dope. What's the square footage upstairs and down? How big is the furnace? How many inches of insulation in the walls and roof? What's the tax rate in this neighborhood? How much will the owner come down?"

Randy, on the run, read from his notebook. He had never shown a house to such an expert. Otto Kessler put his ear to the walls and rapped. He opened and closed all faucets and flushed all three toilets. He switched circuit breakers on and off. He turned up the thermostats and went around listening at heat registers. It was in the basement, gazing up at the floor joists the thickness of railroad ties, that Otto Kessler let his admiration slip out: "God, ain't them some beams."

The sun-room was the last stop on the tour. Randy pulled open the doors and stood aside proudly.

Otto Kessler frowned at the Spooner display. "What's all this crap?"

Randy said it went with the house, free.

"Listen, kid, you take me for a sucker? What would I want with an industrial vacuum?"

"Industrial?"

"What's it cost, all them gadgets?"

"Over nine hundred dollars retail. What do you mean, industrial?"

"That's an industrial vacuum. You think a house vacuum costs nine hundred dollars? Now, what I want you to do is multiply that nine hundred dollars by ten and subtract it from the price of the house and I might be interested. I'm looking at this place as a duplex, see. Get down in the middle nineties and we'll talk. But before we talk I got to know if a duplex on this street goes against zoning. Your old man said on the phone there might be a zoning problem."

"There is, come to think of it. No multiple-family dwellings on River Street." He'd heard his parents argue about this. His mother insisted on keeping River Street classy.

"Is it hard to get a variance from the zoning board?"

"Depends. The city council's the zoning board. Sometimes they'll grant a variance, sometimes they won't." Randy followed Otto Kessler outside. "Here's my card, Mr. Kessler."

"And here's mine. I'm going down to city hall and snoop

around, talk to the city clerk. If I'm not back here in an hour you've lost yourself a sale because of zoning." On the way to his Cadillac he spat tobacco shreds into the grass.

Standing on the veranda, Randy read the card. It said *Superior Realty, Duluth.* Otto Kessler's title was *Investment Property Specialist.*

Monday evening. Dinner for three in the Meers dining room: meatballs and gravy, creamed corn, raisin cream pie.

"Eat your corn, Stephen dear," said Mrs. Meers.

Stephen, nibbling sadly, asked, "When's Mom coming home?"

"Saturday," said Randy, helping himself to more meatballs.

"How many days is Saturday?" Stephen wore a new white shirt with a stiff collar that scratched his neck, and stiff new shoes that made his feet ache.

"Five," said Randy. He didn't blame Stephen for his melancholy. He was lonely for Janet himself.

"How else will you grow big and strong if you don't eat your corn?" Mrs. Meers wanted to know. She was dressed for Monday night study club, where this week she was giving the book report. She wore a dark blue suit, a white blouse and a polka-dot necktie.

Stephen put down his fork. Tears welled in his eyes. His mother had been gone forever, it seemed, and it would be yet another day before he was taken out to the farm. How could he endure another day with Grandmother Meers? She took him along when she shopped for dresses. She combed his hair all day long. She made him lie down between three and four. Evenings weren't so bad, when Grandfather Meers came home and took him out for rides and bought him ice cream and read to him before bed, but tonight Grandfather Meers was away.

"What's the matter, Stephen dear, aren't you feeling well?"

"I want Mom to come home."

"Yes, I know, but just think of all the other people who love you. Here's your very nice daddy and your very nice grandmother, and after a while your very nice grandfather will come home. What more could you want?"

"My very nice mom."

The phone rang. Randy went to answer it. His father was

calling from the Berrington Country Club to say he hadn't finished in the money but his game was pretty smooth for this
early in the season and he was especially happy about his woods.
He'd be staying for the banquet and be home late. "What about
the houses, Randy?"

"The guy from Duluth seemed interested in the Vaughn
place, but he went and checked into zoning and never got back
to me."

"Yeah, River Street's zoned against what he wants."

"Maybe he could get a variance. How about asking Mother?"

"Can't talk now, Randy, we're sitting down to eat. Tell your
mother I'll be home late."

When he returned to the table, his mother said, "What's this
about zoning?"

"The guy I showed the Vaughn house to, he wants to make
a duplex out of it."

"Oh, Lord, can you imagine? That lovely place a duplex?"

"I told Dad he ought to ask you to try for a variance."

"No way, not on River Street. Nothing brings a nice street
down faster than multiple-family dwellings."

"Not even gas stations?"

His mother laughed loudly. "Oh, Randy, don't bring that up."
She sipped her wine and laughed some more, behind her
napkin.

Many years ago, B. Winston Quimby, a man of property (and
the father of the witless invalid who first introduced Agatha to
chaos), had died and left a small parcel of land to the town of
Staggerford on the condition that it be used as a park for travelers. It was ideally situated for this, lying between Highway
Four and the Badbattle River at the edge of town. But it was
also ideally situated for a gas station, and after decades as a
wayside park the city council sold it to an oil company for an
irresistible amount of money. Homeowners adjacent to the park,
together with a few environmentalists, protested, but with
Councilwoman Meers spearheading the project, the sale was
accomplished and the city treasury enriched. So, secretly, was
Staggerford Realty, in its role as the oil company's agent. Thus
the Quimby Wayside Rest was now the Jiffystop Stationstore
with eight gas pumps and an all-night lunch counter (where

Janet's sister was night shift fry cook). This was only one of several deals of questionable ethics, Randy knew, on which his parents had collaborated.

"Your father knows better than to ask me for any more favors, Randy."

"Why? Have you lost your clout on the council?"

She shook her finger. "Listen, nobody on the council out-clouts your mother."

He knew this, but he teased, "You're sure?"

"Look it up in the minutes. Nine times out of ten I cast the swing vote."

"Well, don't be surprised if Dad asks you to use your clout again."

"Fat lot of good it will do him!" There was anger in this.

"Oh, yeah? What is it this time?"

"Remember last fall when I got sewer and water out to the west end, where your father sold those five lots? He said for that we'd go to Hawaii after Christmas, but we never did."

"You'll go. He always comes through, eventually."

"Well, he's taking his sweet time. And don't forget I got Mrs. Albrecht and her animal shelter declared a public nuisance so your father could get more for that property across the alley from her, and he said we'd use the commission to carpet the house. Do you see any new carpet in this house? Look how it's worn over there by the door."

Randy looked.

"So from now on when your father wants me to do him favors, I'm taking my sweet time." She looked at her watch. "Good-bye, boys, I've got to run." She kissed them both on the forehead and hurried away. "Stephen, when you've finished your corn and pie, help your daddy clear the table."

Waiting for Stephen, Randy took his father's notebook from his pocket and browsed through it. The sales diary at the back indicated a severe drop in business.

Stephen said, "Randy, when's Mom coming home?" He was poking holes in his raisin cream pie.

"Saturday, I told you. And call me Daddy, will you?"

Lots of fork holes, then a few finger holes. "Randy, how many days is Saturday?"

"Five, I told you. And when are you going to start calling me Daddy, the way your mother wants you to?"

Stephen put a raisin in his mouth and chewed it for a minute. "Tomorrow, maybe."

"Why not today?"

Stephen gave him a sly squint. "I'm taking my sweet time."

They cleared the table and settled down to watch television. Before long, Stephen fell asleep. Randy's thoughts went roaming back over his day's work, all of it to no avail. To sell to a buyer's weakness you had to know the buyer well enough to know his weakness. Who did Randy know? Who displayed weakness? Ms. Ecklund, that's who. She was lonesome. She had made eyes at Randy.

It was late in the evening when Randy thought of this. He tightened his necktie. He carried Stephen outside and laid him on the front seat of the car. He stood for a minute at the trunk, looking over the Spooner, counting the eleven attachments. He slammed the lid and drove the dark streets to Ms. Ecklund's house.

He knocked on the heavy storm door and heard her call, "Come in." He stepped through the inner doorway and into the front room and heard her say, "Who is it?"

"Randy Meers."

"Oh, yeah? Super. I'm in the kitchen."

He went into the small kitchen, where she sat at a small enameled table doing her nails.

"Hi. Could I talk to you for a minute?"

"Why not? Sit down. God, isn't it hot?" She sat with one of her shapely legs curled under her. She wore blue shorts, a white T-shirt and obviously no bra.

"Yeah," said Randy. "Real hot."

"My house is so stuffy. I've got screens in the basement, but who knows which ones go where? Guess I'll have to hire myself some help." She raised her eyes seductively to his and smiled. "Who do you know that might like to help me with my screens, Randy?"

"Let's see," he said, and looked away. Her smile and the prospect of helping her put screens on all her rooms, ending with the bedroom, excited him. However, the prospect of betraying Janet saddened him. "I don't know."

"What did you want to talk about, Randy? You mind if I go ahead with my nails?"

"No, go ahead."

Again the alluring smile. "Some things you get started, you just can't stop, you know?"

"Yeah." He sat down at the table. It was exotic watching her do her nails. Janet never colored hers. Janet clipped them short and neat and let it go at that. Watermelon Red, said the label on the tiny bottle.

"Ms. Ecklund, I was wondering."

"Call me Connie, would you?" She was bent close over her thumb.

"I was wondering, Connie, if you . . ." No, Eugene Westerman would hold off for a while with the vacuum pitch. He'd start with small talk.

"Go ahead and say it, Randy, it's probably nothing I haven't been asked before." She looked up. "God, you're a doll."

"Well, what I was wondering . . . I see you've got nice carpet in your front room. I suppose you've got it in your bedroom, too."

A throaty laugh: "It's more athletic on the floor, I know what you mean."

"No, I don't mean that. I mean I wonder if you need a really good vacuum cleaner."

"A what?"

"See, I've got this great Spooner below cost."

"What? Are you serious? You come here at ten at night to sell me a vacuum cleaner?"

"It's got eleven attachments and six bottles of rug shampoo."

"Randy, you're too much." She blew on her fingers.

"I'd like to show it to you, it's out in the car."

"God, you're a doll."

She followed him outside, holding her fingers stiffly apart. Approaching the car, which was parked under a streetlight, she laid her hand across the small of his back, arresting him for a moment, but only for a moment. He went to the trunk and opened it. She looked in the front window and jumped back, startled.

"What's that?"

"What?"

"On the seat. A little boy?"

"Oh, that's my kid."

"You've got a kid?"

"A stepkid. My wife's kid."

"You've got a wife?"

"Yeah. She's in Ireland." He lifted the canister out of the trunk. "Now, here without doubt is the greatest vacuum on the market."

She backed away. "Randy, I don't fool around with married men."

"Who says we're fooling around? Now, this isn't your ordinary Spooner, it's the Mark Four."

"What's she doing in Ireland?"

"Well, it's our honeymoon, actually." He lifted out the kit of attachments.

"Your honeymoon!"

"Well, see, we were both going, and then I decided—"

"Randy, I really don't need a vacuum, okay?"

"At least wait till you see it. I can give you a three-hundred-dollar discount."

"That's okay, Randy." She returned to the house. "My vacuum's plenty good." She went inside.

Standing at the trunk, he heard her latch the storm door and the inner door.

20

TUESDAY WAS market day in Ballybegs. At six in the evening
the central street was still jammed with cars and cattle and tables of fruit and fish. Bishop Baker inched along in his yellow
Mazda until he could drive no farther, then parked in front of
the post office. He left his car atilt, the left wheels up on the
sidewalk. He made his way on foot toward the steeple pointed
out to him by a red-nosed woman behind a table of apples and
oranges. "St. Brigid's, it's called, Father." Her "Father" rhymed
with "lather."

He wished he weren't wearing his clerical suit. It was caus-
ing a stir as he proceeded down the street, men lifting their
caps to him, women bowing and smiling. Three or four people, catching sight of the episcopal gold chain across his vest,
actually blessed themselves.

He had spent the day at St. Patrick's Seminary in Maynooth,
and it was for the edification of the seminarians and their con-
servative professors that he had dressed this way. Leaving
Dublin this morning, he had considered throwing his civvies
into the car and changing before he got to Ballybegs, but if
James O'Hannon was truly the scoundrel he seemed to be, a
bishop might need to pull rank.

James O'Hannon. He had gotten the name from Janet over
the phone. Last night, home from Howth, she had called the
hotel as promised and reported that Agatha was sad because
of a falling-out with an Irish friend, a secret pen pal she had
never met before. No, she wasn't desperate, just sad. This was
as much as Janet wanted to reveal, and Dick Baker had had to
extract the rest piece by piece. It was the word *secret* that had
made him suspicious. He had a nose for secrets, an irresistible
need to know the story behind a cover-up. This he had inher-

ited from his mother, the probing postmistress. Why secrecy in a person as straightforward and self-assured as Agatha? What could she possibly have to hide? Something that undermined her assurance, evidently. In a spinster pushing seventy, could it be romance?

"Janet, was this pen pal a man?" he had asked on the phone.

"Yes."

"How long have they been writing to each other?"

"I guess four or five years."

"Was she getting serious about him?"

"You mean was she in love?"

"Yes."

"I don't know. I accused her of it the other night, but I was sort of joking."

"Janet, who is this man?"

"I don't think I should say."

"Why? Did she tell you in confidence?"

"Not exactly, but she wasn't talking to anybody about it, not even Lillian."

"Janet, I have to be sure she isn't being taken advantage of. There are men who prey on elderly women for their money."

"It's nothing like that."

"How do you know?"

She was silent and he had to press her. He reminded her that Agatha had not sworn her to secrecy. He said that as tour leader he was responsible for her welfare. He promised that he'd never let Agatha know he knew.

Janet was persuaded less by his pleading than by his position. She remembered Agatha preaching the primacy of bishops in grade six.

"She got over here and found out he was a priest."

"A priest! A Catholic priest?"

"Yes, in a little town outside Dublin."

"What town?"

"I don't know."

"What's his name?"

Silence.

"Janet, I'll never let on that I know."

"Promise?"

"Promise."

"Okay, then. James O'Hannon."

Dick Baker came to a circle of men in the street. They surrounded a handsome brown horse on a lead and were listening raptly to the haggling of the buyer and seller. He stopped
for a minute. The seller was making much of the horse's an-
cestry, while the buyer insisted the creature was too old to be
worth the asking price. The buyer and seller spoke not to each
other but to the crowd, and the crowd responded affirmatively
to everything. Yes, indeed, this mare's father was sired by a
famous racer. But yes, there was no denying she was over the
hill, you could tell by her teeth. The horse meanwhile gazed
placidly out over the men's heads, ignoring the clamor, imagining perhaps a sunny pasture.

Dick Baker moved along. He flattened himself against a storefront to make room for a pack of running boys, followed by a
pack of running dogs. He turned down a side street leading
toward the Gothic steeple and the sea. He crossed a grassy park
that separated the church from the village. He was struck by
the curious way the great, gray church stood at a distance from
the village and faced away from it. St. Brigid's put him in mind
of a dark giant brooding inwardly, and ignoring, except for a
few hours every Sunday, the villagers whose lives it controlled.

He left the park, crossed a road and opened the gate in the
high iron fence surrounding the compound of gray Catholicism—school, church, convent, rectory, cemetery. No signs of
life anywhere, no movement except for the boughs of the trees
caught in the wind blowing in from the sea. On the wind were
a few drops of rain.

In his study, the pastor of St. Brigid's sat at his desk with a
bottle of whiskey before him and a glass in his hand. Watching
through the window as the man in black came through the gate
and approached his house, the pastor regretted the bad luck
of living only twenty miles from Maynooth. Too often St. Patrick's Seminary found themselves hosting more visitors than
they could put up overnight and farmed them out to the
neighboring rectories. Last week he had had to take in a priest
from Antrim, a tiresome old man who stayed up late, snored
through the night and wanted breakfast at seven.

As the man in black got closer, the pastor squinted and sat forward. A bishop, by God. Why hadn't St. Patrick's the decency to call ahead? He stood up and smoothed his white hair. He folded under the waist of his gray sweater so the tattered edges wouldn't show. He went to the front door.

"You're Father O'Hannon?"

"I am, Bishop, I am. Come in." He looked for a car. Bishops never used public transport. "You came by bus?"

"No, my car's in the town." Stepping into the foyer and shaking the man's hand, Dick Baker smelled whiskey.

"You're from America—the Midwest, I should think, with that flat way of saying 'car.' You're needing a bed for the night?"

"No, no, I'm here only for a short talk, if you can spare me the time. Dick Baker's the name. Diocese of Berrington, Minnesota."

James O'Hannon flinched, then froze, then recovered and said, "Come into my study." He turned and led the way.

Dick Baker smelled meat cooking. "I've come at your dinnertime. I can come back later."

"No, I can eat anytime. *Do,* in fact, eat anytime. Thought I'd have myself a little tea, then decided to cook myself a beefsteak to go with it." In the study the two men stood facing each other uneasily. "Not much of an eater, I'm not, but after three, four days of picking and nibbling I like to sit down to a beefsteak."

"You do your own cooking, then."

"Such as it is. And my own housekeeping, as you see very plainly."

So he saw. The room was strewn with old newspapers. There were clothes draped over the backs of chairs. Three black socks lay on the floor. The room's only ornamentation was a large print of the Grotto at Lourdes hanging high on the wall above a filing cabinet. On the large desk was an untidy pile of letters, books and candy wrappers. The bottle of whiskey and glass stood on the front page of *The Fortress.*

"Sit down, Bishop, I'll get you a drink."

"No, please, I don't believe I care for a drink." The bishop's stomach was acting up. Seminary grub again, besides the stress of this visit. He sat on the edge of the sofa, avoiding the end where the cat hair was thickest.

"A drop together before we get down to business." James went to the kitchen, ignoring the bishop's refusal.

Waiting, Dick Baker glanced at the *Times* lying at his feet. When he realized it was six weeks old, he felt sad. He had a few men like this in his own diocese, priests who despite their lack of domestic talent refused to hire help, and he always felt this same twinge of sorrow upon entering their houses. Never mind if the men themselves were comparatively happy, the messy house and the haphazard diet stood in the bishop's mind for the absence of a companion in the life of every priest. Two people living together never seemed to tolerate quite so much squalor as a man might live in by himself. All priests are pathetically alone, he thought, myself included.

James handed him a full tumbler of straight whiskey, then went to his desk and sat down. "Agatha's told you about me, then."

"No, actually she hasn't. She's told a young woman who's traveling with us."

"That would be Janet."

Dick Baker nodded. "I have it secondhand through Janet. You might think it's none of my business and you might be right, but on the other hand we're fellow priests and Agatha McGee is a friend of ours and I must tell you she's quite upset."

"Yes, well." James O'Hannon looked at his hands, front and back. "I saw Agatha in my church Sunday. Saw her rushing out the door as I came out on the altar." He folded his hands. He unfolded them. The wind rattled the window. The room darkened. The priest reached behind him and switched on the overhead light, which was harsh; it deepened his wrinkles, heightened his age. "Yes, well, we became the best of friends, Agatha and I, through letters, it goes back a number of years."

Dick Baker sipped only enough whiskey to wet his lips. "I understand that, but the point is—"

"I know what the point is. I didn't tell her I was a priest." James fastened his eyes on the bishop's and kept them there, unblinking. His voice was strong and firm. "Haven't you ever wanted to know a woman, Bishop, not as a priest but as a man?"

"Surely, it's natural enough. But we decide against it, do we not, when we're ordained?"

"Only insofar as a thing like that can be decided. With some of us the urge is always there."

"Of course, but always to be suppressed."

"The urge I'm talking about is not the urge of the flesh, Bishop. I'm talking about the urge of the spirit. The urge to understand a woman, to share one's soul with her. Purely a meeting of hearts and minds, I'm saying. Isn't that innocent enough?"

"Why not? Why shouldn't we have women friends? I encourage it in my priests. But then why would we hide the fact that we're priests, unless our intentions are not honorable?"

James O'Hannon took a long drink from his glass. He turned his head to the side and laughed softly. Gazing out the window, he gradually replaced his laugh with a serious look. "The only indiscretion of my life, and in less than two days here's a bishop come to reprimand me." He was speaking to the window. "It's no more than right, of course, justice is served. Some folks fill their lives with indiscretions and no comeuppance, but no sooner do Agatha and I have our little jaunt around Dublin than I'm caught like the timid mouse I am."

Dick Baker sat back on the couch, set his glass on the dusty end table. "It was more than a jaunt around Dublin, Father. It was years of letters beforehand, without her knowing your identity."

James turned to him. "It was that."

The bishop was about to say more, but James silenced him with a raised hand.

"And yet it wasn't that at all. Never in my life have I revealed so much of my identity as I did to Agatha. I told her a thousand things I never told anyone else."

"Except that you were a priest."

"One fact withheld out of a thousand."

"The most pertinent part."

"Perhaps, perhaps not. Look at it from my side, if you will,

Bishop. I wonder how well you know Ireland."

"This is my fourth visit."

"I wonder how well you understand the priest's role in the Irish village. Except for a few Church of Ireland families, who think me an oddity, I have the respect of nearly everyone in Ballybegs. I go into O'Donovan's pub and all the men lift their caps and mumble something subservient as I pass along the bar. There's even one old man who genuflects, I swear to God. Out on the street—you saw it yourself if you came through the town—the priest gets nothing but worshipful smiles and esteem."

"Yes, that's how I see it."

"And how does it compare to your towns in Minnesota? Is your town a princedom and your clergyman a prince?"

"No, we're not so Catholic as all that."

"Then you're lucky, by God. I'm sixty-six, Bishop. Since the day of my ordination I've been that sort of prince. Now, your average Irish priest, it's to his liking." James O'Hannon's words grew thicker on his tongue, his voice louder. "It's grand with him, being a prince. It nourishes him. It makes him strut, if you catch my meaning, and I'm not saying he's a bad priest because of it. I'm only saying I'm not your average Irish priest. I've lived a lifetime as prince and I'm not finding it a pleasant thing to look back on. It's kept me separate from my people, it has, my eminence has. Prevented me from being close to anyone."

Was this man maudlin by nature, Dick Baker wondered, or was it the whiskey speaking? How far gone was he in booze?

James O'Hannon caught the analytical look in the bishop's eye. "I know what you're thinking, Bishop. You're thinking I'm a whiskey priest, but you're wrong. I can go six weeks without touching a drop. Do, every Lent. But there's the odd day now and then—market day usually—when it's borne in upon me how few friends I've had in my life, true friends, and so I come home to this warm, amber friend in the glass. You must know what I mean, Bishop. I've never known a bishop who had a true friend, they're generally so stuffy, bishops. Pardon me a minute, I have to tend to my cooking."

"I can come some other time. Later, after your meal."

"Not at all, you'll join me is what you'll do. I'll put another steak on the cooker."

"No, thank you." The bishop, a borderline vegetarian, had little appetite for beefsteak.

"You'll stay and eat." James O'Hannon went to the kitchen.

The bishop sat forward on the couch and brushed gray cat hair off the sleeves and tails of his black suitcoat. He sat back and closed his eyes, rubbed his forehead. It had been a tiring day. At Maynooth he had been passed politely among the faculty, who surrounded him like bodyguards and spoke vigorously about nothing important, guarding their student body. He hadn't been permitted more than a hello and a handshake with a single seminarian.

From the kitchen came the rattle of utensils and the renewed sizzle of cooking. Then James O'Hannon returned to his desk with a fresh bottle of whiskey. He sat and poured himself a brimming dose. He raised his glass.

"To your tour of Ireland, Bishop. A happy one over all, I trust. I'm sorry I snarled it up for you."

"Thank you." The bishop held up his water tumbler. "I'm here on business as well as pleasure. I'm visiting All Hallows and St. Patrick's, looking for priests."

"You've been to St. Patrick's?"

"I have. Today."

"And you met Colman Connor and John Horgan?"

"Let's see, yes, Monsignor Connor and Dr. Horgan."

"A couple of classmates of mine. Bruiser Connor and Johnnie Horgan. They're lost in their books and theories, are they not? Bruiser was a champion hurler in his day. You'd never believe it to look at him now, would you?"

"He's out of shape, all right."

"Fat as a sow. And Johnnie Horgan, who was always raising hell in the residence hall, now he's dean of theology. What did you think of him?"

"I had very little time with him."

"Just as well, he's a stuffed shirt. I liked him better when he was raising hell in the residence hall. Who else?"

"Father McMahon."

"Mick the Runt. I must say you certainly went out of your way to meet the tiresome ones."

"It was Father McMahon who showed me around." And told him where to find James O'Hannon.

"A year or two behind me in the sem. Puts you to sleep with his talk, Mick the Runt does." He drank, grimaced, rubbed his eyes. "But I was telling you my life story, Bishop. Twenty-six years I've been in Ballybegs. My life poured out into this village, and what life of my own do I have? It's mingle with the farmers on market day and it's chat with a few lonely souls along the strand in the evening when the weather's fair enough for a walk, and it's grow pampered and fat on the cooking of the parish women. They'd bring me in three meals a day if I'd let them, but I restrict their charity to weekends, and then I don't eat half of what they show up with. Don't take my meaning wrong, Bishop, I'm not complaining. I'm not feeling sorry for myself. I haven't got it bad, for a priest. Today was market day, as you may have noticed, and just as I've done on every other market day over the past twenty-six years I spent hours on High Street talking with the men and looking over their livestock and having a few drinks in O'Donovan's pub. I'm not complaining, I happen to like talking to men. I grew up talking to men in the family pub. I have a knowledge of crops and cattle and cars and all the things men talk about, and fishing as well—as a boy I fished one summer in a boat that went out from Skerries. Betting? I can talk betting with the best of them because, don't you see, while I denounce betting from the pulpit, which in Ireland is about as useful as denouncing porter, I'm fond of the races myself, with their sleek horseflesh and their crowds of humanity in a holiday mood."

He drank. He looked puzzled for a moment. "What did you say your name was? Bishop what?"

"Baker. Dick Baker."

"Well, allow me to say this, Bishop Dick Baker, my flock is a lovable flock. I tell them that from the pulpit. At Christmas I come right out and say it. 'You're a lovable gang of God's people,' I tell them, and I mean it with all my heart. So don't get the idea I'm complaining, Bishop. I'm only explaining why I wrote the sort of letters I did to Agatha McGee. Because even though I have everything a priest would want, there's more to life than a priest would want, never mind what they teach you in the sem. You know it as well as I—we're men apart. I'm standing up there at Christmas saying I love my people, and I'm wishing I had a friend among them. I'm held in esteem by them all, but what's esteem worth in the end? Esteem is fine for the likes of Johnnie Horgan and Bruiser Connor and Mick the Runt—talk to them two minutes and you see they've become grand boys for esteem—but I'd exchange all the esteem in the world for a single friend. Will I grill a few mushrooms with your steak, Bishop? I'm fond of mushrooms with mine."

"Really, I'm not very hungry. I was given a lot to eat in Maynooth."

"Eat what you can and leave the rest. Come with me, we'll see to the meat." James rose, gripped the bottle by the neck and gestured for Dick Baker to follow him into the kitchen.

Wearily, the bishop did so. He could have left, gone out the front door and back to his car. He had what he came for, which was the assurance that James O'Hannon was not a perverted priest preying on spinsters but a lonely man without malice. He followed him into the kitchen not because he needed to hear more but because James so obviously needed a listener.

21

MEANWHILE, it was noon in Staggerford, and Randy was driving along a dirt road north of town, delivering Stephen to the farm. It was a day of great beauty, aspens and birches unfurling leaves the color of celery, oaks weighed down with marble-sized buds, pine bark glistening with pitch. When he drove up in front of the farmhouse two of Janet's mahogany-haired sisters came flying out the doorway and attacked Stephen with kisses. Stephen laughed and batted them away.

Karen, nineteen, was short and stout and overly made up. Sally, sixteen, was pretty and silly and overly freckled. There was fondness and respect in the smiles they gave Randy. He was their only brother-in-law. Their sister LeeAnn wasn't married to the man she was living with in Sioux Falls, a mere truck driver not half so handsome or clean or neatly dressed as Randy. But there was also a trace of bewilderment in their smiles, Randy being such a puzzle to them. Why was it so hard to think of him as Janet's husband? Harder still to think of him as Stephen's stepfather? And what did Randy's silences mean? And who picked out his classy shirts, his mother or Janet? And what was he selling this month?

Karen asked him, "Got time to stay for lunch?"

"Sure," said Randy, basking in their admiration. "One thing about being a salesman, my time is my own."

"Patty melt or BLT?" At the Jiffystop Lunchroom Karen had mastered thirteen different sandwiches, but these two were her favorites.

"Either one, I'm easy."

"If your time is your own," asked Sally, squinting up at him in the sun, "how come you didn't go to Ireland with Janet?"

"I got a big deal pending."

219

"A water softener?" asked Karen.

"No, a house."

Both girls said, "Really?"

Not really, but he said "Yes." He had dreamed about the Vaughn house last night. He saw his signature, as realtor, on a purchase agreement.

"Gee, selling houses, Randy. You must be rich."

"Getting there."

"Come on in."

The front porch was cluttered with hens. The sisters kicked them away from the door and led Randy and Stephen inside. Randy sat at the table in the small kitchen. Karen went to work at her sandwich board. Stephen helped Sally set the table with plates and Coke and ketchup.

Randy said, "Janet called me up Sunday."

"All the way from Ireland? What did she say?"

"She was just seeing how everybody was. She's doing stuff with my cousin Evelyn."

"What stuff?"

"They went out and drank beer Saturday night."

"Same as here, huh?"

"Pretty much, I guess."

"Can you eat two BLTs, Randy?"

"Sure."

Francis Raft came in through the back door, beaming at his guests. Stephen leaped up and hung from his neck.

Sally said, "Daddy, Janet called Randy from Ireland, so the plane landed okay."

"Good, we were wondering," he said. "She like flying, does she?"

"Guess so," said Randy. "She didn't say."

"She like Ireland?"

"Guess so. She's going around with my cousin Evelyn."

Francis Raft sat down with Stephen on his lap. "We'll sure as the dickens be glad to see her when she gets home, won't we, Slugger?"

"Sure as the dickens," said Stephen.

During lunch, sporadic eruptions of wit and chuckling broke out and Randy marveled at the cheer pervading this ramshackle house. He sat across from the girls and was charmed by the way their longish hair fell to the side whenever they laughed and tilted their heads in their father's direction, acknowledging his little jokes.

"What's BLT mean?" asked Stephen.

"Depends," said his grandfather. "With Karen cooking, it means Burns a Lot of Toast."

Randy drove home with a high heart. The Raft place always did that for him, made him happy, which was why he seldom went there. It was always such a disappointment coming down from being happy, realizing that he didn't fit into his place in life the way the Rafts fit into theirs. Take Janet—adapting better than Randy to life in the basement of the Meers house, never missing a day of work all year. Take her sister LeeAnn—riding coast to coast with that trucker; he had bad teeth and a pot belly, yet she rode in the cab like a queen. Take the chickens—on the Raft place even the chickens made self-satisfied noises.

Why can't I fit into my place in life? Randy wondered. Or, more to the point, what *is* my place? Will I ever fit into sales the way Eugene Westerman does? Will I ever learn to recognize buyers' weaknesses?

Entering Staggerford, Randy drove to River Street and stopped in front of the Vaughn property. He switched off the engine and sat concentrating on the empty windows of the enormous house. He thought of the gleaming eyes of Otto Kessler when he stood in the basement yesterday and gazed up at the enormous timbers. There was property lust in those eyes.

22

JAMES STOOD OVER THE STOVE, jabbing the meat with a fork. "Imagine building a house this size for a single man to live in. Look around you. I could feed a tribe of tinkers at my kitchen table, and there's a separate room besides for eating in. Look in through there—see?—a dining table I can set ten places at."

Dick Baker stood beyond the range of spattering fat, holding his tumbler of warm whisky. He had already sipped his limit and was feeling slightly dizzy.

"And you ought to see the library at the back of the house, or what was intended as the library. I use it for a guestroom because it has a fireplace and the bedrooms do not. It's enough house for royalty. Well, leave it to the Irish to confuse their priest with a king." He laughed. His face turned bright and happy. "Now for the mushrooms."

From the refrigerator he drew a jar of mushrooms and spooned them over the thick meat sizzling in the skillet. "I picked these last autumn in the forest up the coast. There's a ravine that's a grand place for mushrooms in the autumn."

"No, really," Dick Baker protested. "I'll skip the mushrooms."

James turned to him, laughing. "Admit it now, you don't have faith in my ability to pick the good ones and leave the poisonous ones alone."

"I'm sorry to be so finicky. It makes me a difficult guest, I'm afraid."

James spooned out mushrooms and held them dripping over the jar, or nearly over. "These are delicious. I picked them in September and froze them immediately and thawed them out yesterday and mixed them with a lot of butter and salt and let

223

them stand overnight, so they're prime." He came at the bishop with the spoon.

The bishop ducked. "No, thanks."

"See here. You've got to give them a taste." James O'Hannon ate the spoonful, swallowing, licking his lips, beaming. "Like so." Juice ran down his chin. He spooned out more and came at the bishop again.

The bishop shook his head, his mouth tightly shut.

"But you *will* have them cooked on your meat, will you not? I'll be hurt otherwise."

"No, you see—"

"Look here now, I'm going to make a mushroom-eater out of you, Bishop. Look here now." James kicked a small dish out from under the table. He got down on his knees and spooned mushrooms into it. "Lady Wellington, where are you?" He rang the dish with the spoon.

A fat gray-green cat came slowly out from behind a dust mop standing against the wall.

"Here's the proof, Bishop, we feed mushrooms to Lady Wellington and see if she dies." James handed the jar to the bishop and sat on his heels, waiting. "This isn't the first time I've had to do this for skeptical dinner guests."

The cat sniffed the mushrooms, then backed up and stared at them. She was a long-haired, short-legged cat whose coat matched the hairs on Dick Baker's suit.

"Here, I know what to do," said James, picking up the dish and getting drunkenly to his feet. He went to the stove and spooned meat juice over the mushrooms. He went to the refrigerator and added milk. He stirred it all together and set it on the floor. The cat came forward, sniffed, licked and ate. The men stood watching. She ate it all, then licked the dish.

"See?" said James as the cat walked heavily away.

"Let's give her a few minutes."

"Right. The meat will be another few minutes." James forked up the two steaks and flipped them over, flinching from the flying grease. "I call her Lady Wellington because when she's wet her coat's the color of Wellington boots. Help yourself to the whiskey."

"I'm fine, James. No more."

The cat stopped in front of the dust mop and stood looking at it thoughtfully.

James set the table in the dining room. He put on butter, jelly and a loaf of bread in its wrapper. Dick Baker carried in a tray of silverware, napkins, teacups and steak sauce.

"Let me show you the palace." James took him into the room beyond, and into the room beyond that. Upstairs he took him out onto a balcony and showed him the sea. The sky was spitting a small, cold rain.

They returned to the kitchen, where the cat was sitting on its haunches looking alert and healthy. They each carried a plate-size steak into the dining room. Dick Baker was hungrier than he thought. The meat being tender and delicious, he ate nearly half of his portion, more beef than he'd had in a year. The mushrooms, too, were delicious; after the first timid nibble he ate quite a few. They talked about politics and the Pope. James, solidly plastered by this time, ate fast and carelessly and forgot to make tea. The moment he finished eating, he fell asleep in his chair, breathing wheezily, his chin on his chest.

Dick Baker got up to go. He stood looking down at his host. Clearly this man had the intelligence and self-awareness to be an interesting friend—no wonder Agatha McGee had been won over. How sad for her to lose him. How sad for James to be the esteemed priest of Ballybegs, the heavyhearted prince in his gray, stone palace.

"James," he said gently. One thing remained to ask him. Would he go into Dublin and see Miss McGee once more before she left for home, and apologize? "James."

The priest made a throaty sound in his sleep.

Dick Baker decided to say it in writing. He would leave a note on the desk in the study. Going through the kitchen, he saw Lady Wellington stretched out on the floor with one hind leg in the air.

"The cat!" he shrieked. He bent over and touched Lady Wellington. She was stiff. She was bug-eyed. He felt no heartbeat, no breath.

"James, the cat is dead!" He went in and shook James awake. "We've been poisoned!"

It took half a minute to get James on his feet and into the

kitchen. He stood swaying and looking down at Lady Wellington, whose whiskers were moving slightly. "Dead?" he asked.
"Could it be?"

"James, we need a doctor."

"Could it be?" He rubbed his nose with the palm of
his hand.

"Where's the nearest hospital?"

"Hospital?" He rubbed his forehead, trying to unclog his
thinking.

Dick Baker guided him down the hallway to the front door.
He took a black coat from the hallstand and threw it over his
shoulders. "Answer me, now: Is there a hospital in Ballybegs?"

"No." James blinked slowly. "No, the nearest one's at the edge
of Dublin. St. Finian's Fever Hospital."

"That's where we're going. I can feel the poison working here
in my duodenum." Dick Baker rubbed himself low on
the left.

"I don't feel anything," said James.

"You will. Hurry. Our lives can be saved." He led James
outside. "Where's your car? I'll drive."

"Car? I have no car." His coat fell off.

"No car?" Dick Baker closed his eyes. Please God, a few more
years. Not death in Ballybegs at the hands of a whiskey priest.
Death when it comes by some other means, please God, not
poison.

He helped James on with his coat. The wet wind from the
ocean whipped their coattails as they crossed the street and the
grassy park. Daylight was dying.

James's steps were unsteady. He halted to say, "I'm sure those
mushrooms were good. I've picked in that ravine for over
twenty years."

Dick Baker pulled him along. They came to the town. "Which
way to the post office? My car's in front of the post office."

James pointed.

They were the only ones out. The debris of market day lay
in the street, scraps of paper, orange peels, manure. Please God,
a few more years. The see of Berrington needs me, there's so
much hanging fire. Two ordinations next month, the biennial

budget and, let's face it, Lord, the Chancery doesn't have the most efficient staff.

He leaned James against the Mazda as he unlocked the door for him.

"How are you feeling, James?"

"Me?" James raised his face to the spitting rain. "Fine, thank you."

"There's time to save our lives."

James's uplifted face was wet. He closed his eyes. "It looks like rain."

Dick Baker lowered him into the bucket seat, then ran around and hopped in behind the wheel.

"How do I get out of town?"

James stuck his thumb back over his shoulder, his eyes still shut.

The bishop made a U-turn. "And the hospital? How will I find the hospital?"

"Off the main Dublin road on your left. Mind the signs when you get past the airport." James dropped his head and slept.

Dick Baker drove jerkily through the rain. Please God, it's inconvenient to die overseas. C. H. Garvey will blow his cork— the cost of shipping a body home.

Leaving Ballybegs, he speeded up, careening around curves. Dear God, have I ever been this close to death? Yes, one time as a boy, swimming with my friend Howie. Our first swim of the year, the lake very cold. We dared each other to swim to a point of land a quarter mile from the beach. The lifeguard would have ordered us back behind the rope, but it was early in June, before lifeguards came on duty, before the ropes were up. The wonderful feeling of having the whole lake to ourselves. The horror of that cramp in my side, halfway across. Calling to Howie, far in the lead. Howie swimming back and saving my life, helping me paddle to the point. Walking back to the beach on gravel roads, barefoot. Dick Baker, recalling this, was somewhat comforted. If his life had been spared once, why not twice? And tonight, by helping to save the life of James O'Hannon, wasn't he somehow paying off his old debt to

Howie? He drove through Carrington. He drove through Skerries. He drove past Dublin Airport. The hospital stood gray and dour in the gloaming. Lights shone out from its tall windows.

The twenty-five-minute snooze had sobered James a little. He lurched without help from the car to the door of the emergency room. "Where are we going?" he said.

"The hospital. Hurry!"

"Who are we seeing?"

"A doctor. Our lives are in danger."

"They are?"

Dick Baker pressed the emergency buzzer and entered a dark corridor. A nurse came to meet them. She wore the white veil of a nun. She recognized the chain of gold across the breast of the short stranger. She recognized Father O'Hannon teetering beside him.

"What is it, Your Excellency?"

It was a moment before Dick Baker got control of his voice. "We ate poisoned mushrooms." His voice was high-pitched, just short of panic.

"I don't see how it's possible," said James. The nurse was surprised to see him inebriated.

"We fed them to the cat, and the cat died," said the bishop.

The nurse looked to James for verification. "I'd like to sit down," said James.

She took them into a small, brightly lit room containing a high, hard bed like a table and a high, padded chair like a dentist's. Behind a standing divider was a toilet and sink. James climbed into the chair and began immediately to snore.

"They were picked last September," said Dick Baker, "and frozen over the winter. Isn't it bad to freeze mushrooms?"

"What are you feeling at the moment?" The nurse had a large, strong chin and large glasses tinted blue. "Cramps?"

"Not quite cramps, but nearly. I mean, something's very wrong here." He flattened his hand over his belt buckle.

She gave him one decisive nod. "All right, there's nothing for it but empty you out. Come along, please."

She led him across the hall to the admitting office, where a young woman at a typewriter asked him questions. He recited the required facts about himself and as many about James as he knew. The young woman wore a dark, baggy sweater over a heavy wool dress. Seeing this, the bishop realized that the hospital was very chilly.

The nurse said to the typist, "Please call Dr. O'Neill." She said to the bishop, "This procedure doesn't require a doctor, but as long as he's in the building . . . and as long as Father O'Hannon's in a problematical condition . . ."

The typist picked up a microphone.

"Tell him to hurry," said Dick Baker. He was feeling a shifting of gases. He loosened his belt.

After she put out the call, the typist said, "Please sign here and here and here." He signed and thanked her and hurried across the hall and found Dr. O'Neill, a thin-faced, stoop-shouldered man in his middle age, standing before James and watching him sleep.

"We're poisoned," Dick Baker told him, taking off his suit-coat.

"Mmmmmm," said the doctor. Holding his stethoscope in one hand and his chin in the other, he might have been posing for a portrait: *Doctor Meditating*.

"It was mushrooms." The bishop unsnapped his collar.

The doctor bent over and sniffed at James. "Is he drunk?"

"He's had a great deal of whiskey."

The nun stepped up to James and shook him gently. He opened and closed his eyes. He opened and closed his mouth. He fell back to sleep with a little smile, leaning left, his ear against the nun's breast.

Dr. O'Neill turned to Dick Baker. "How long ago did you eat the mushrooms?"

"Nearly an hour. I feel the poison working." He looked down at his protruding stomach, held it in both hands.

"Mmmmmmmm. There's something not quite right about this. I've known Jim O'Hannon all my life and he's not a great drinker."

"We fed the mushrooms to the cat."

"Now and then you might see him with the one drink too many at the races, but you never see him like this."

"The cat died."

"And he knows his mushrooms."

"Please." Dick Baker squeezed the doctor's elbow.

Dr. O'Neill said to the nurse, "Ipecac, thirty cc's."

She reached into a cupboard and took out a small bottle of brown liquid. She slit the seal and twisted off the cap.

The doctor held it out to Dick Baker. "Drink this down."

Dick Baker snatched it.

"Best to drink it over there." The doctor pointed to the sink and stool.

The bishop rushed to the standing divider, tipping his head back and swallowing as he went. The results were instantaneous. He spouted vomit as he ran. The sound of his retching grew louder and louder. It echoed in the hallway. It went on for several minutes. In rooms down the hall visitors abandoned their loved ones and hurried home. Two or three ambulatory patients left their beds and stole in their nightgowns to other parts of the hospital. Two of the bedridden began vomiting themselves.

Meanwhile, the nurse and the doctor helped James O'Hannon up onto the padded table, rolled him onto his left side and inserted a pink tube into his right nostril. This had a very sobering effect on him, for in order to bend it down his esophagus they had to do a lot of backing out and poking in. His eyes were wide open now. The nurse held his flailing arms. The doctor said, "Sorry to have to do it this way, Jim, but the other way's no good if you're drunk. You could choke on your vomit."

Until now the typist across the hall had stayed at her station despite Dick Baker's retching, but with the addition of James O'Hannon's gagging she went outside and stood under a broad tree, sheltering from the rain. The phone in her office rang unanswered.

Dick Baker, exhausted, at the point of collapse, began to gain control of himself. He sat on the lid of the stool with his chin on the edge of the sink. Then he turned and looked around the divider and saw the doctor attach a large plastic syringe to the end of the pink tube and extract a pint of the contents of James's stomach. Dick Baker turned back to the sink, retching again and asking God to credit this to his account of temporal

punishment due to sin. His empty stomach began to cramp severely. His face, a light green, dripped sweat.

Later, washed up, their lives spared, James O'Hannon and
Dick Baker rested for a time in a lounge down the hall. The
nurse looked in on them every ten minutes. The bishop lay on
the couch. James O'Hannon sat with his elbows on his knees,
shaking. Earlier he hadn't believed he was going to die, but
now he thought he might. His insides burned. There was an
awful rawness from his nostril to his breastbone where the pink
tube went down.

Much later, driving home, Dick Baker was jubilant with relief. He felt magnanimous toward James. He felt, in fact, hungry. He said, "Don't blame yourself, James. It could have
happened to anyone."

James shook his head, afraid that if he spoke he'd rupture
something in his throat. The doctor had assured him he'd be
fine, but how could the doctor tell whether his voice box was
permanently damaged?

"I have a favor to ask of you, James. A favor to Agatha.
Would you call on her once more before she leaves Dublin and
tell her what you've told me? I'm sure it would mean a great
deal to her."

James moved his head slightly in what may have been a nod
of assent.

They drove through patches of rain and patches of moonlight. In Ballybegs, Dick Baker pulled up in front of the iron
gate and took a slip of paper from his pocket. James opened
the door and the light went on.

"Here's Miss McGee's address, James. You can say you got
it from the clerk at the hotel. I'd rather she didn't know I was
involved."

James looked at the paper and nodded. He knew the street,
the block. He could almost place the house. Not far from St.
Stephen's Green. He decided to risk four syllables. "Good night,
Bishop," he whispered.

Dick Baker shook his hand. He couldn't think what to say.
Thanks for the meal? Thanks for doing your duty to Miss
McGee? He said good night, and James got quickly out and
shut the door. Dick Baker sped away.

James went directly to his study and lay on the couch. The thought of the tube made him gag again. He stood up and took off his coat. He kicked off his shoes and found his slippers under his desk. He'd do the dishes. No, first he'd tend to the dead cat.

He switched on the kitchen light and went around the table to the spot where Lady Wellington had lain in her last agony. She wasn't there. He picked up the mop. There she was, against the wall, licking the afterbirth off a kitten while three other kittens nuzzled her belly, nursing.

23

"COME IN. I knew you were the bishop the moment I saw your car. Miss McGee said it would be the color of butter."

"Thank you so much." Dick Baker stepped gingerly into Rosella Coyle's dark front hallway, wiping his wet head with the palm of his hand.

"Have you no umbrella, Bishop? I have dozens to lend you. My guests leave them behind."

"I have one in the car, thank you."

"Miss McGee's on her way down." Overhead the steps were creaking. "I'm wondering why the pair of you are setting out in this weather at all. Go to the pictures when it rains and leave your sightseeing for fair days, I always advise my guests. What can be more depressing than the bogs of Ireland in the rain?"

"Not the bogs, we're going to the Wicklow Hills."

"Hills, bogs, the lot. I've never seen the charm in all those up-and-down roads running between fields with nothing in them but thorns and dirty sheep. Paul Newman's playing at the Odeon."

Agatha, coming quickly downstairs wearing her raincoat and rubbers and carrying her umbrella, noticed how short the bishop looked from above, particularly with Rosella Coyle bent over him like a stork. He looked peaked as well. "You can see Burt Reynolds at the Crown or Jane Fonda at the Strand," Rosella was telling him.

Agatha said, "Don't give in to her, Bishop. She tried that on me at breakfast, but I resisted."

"Don't worry, Miss McGee." He took her hand at the foot of the stairs. "It's Glendalough no matter what."

He had phoned this morning, suggesting lunch in the Wicklows. Her first impulse had been to turn him down because she had wanted to go there with James. Her second impulse had been to accept, for the same reason. Not to go would be to admit that James still exerted control over her.

"You'll catch your death in the hills." Rosella Coyle let them out the door and made them promise to return for tea. She watched them go down the steps and out to the iron gate on the street. She thought what a pair they looked under the tawny umbrella, he a short, chunky man with a rollicking walk and she a short, slim woman with a lively step.

"Sorry to be so late," said the bishop as they came to the car. "I kept having to stop and get my bearings."

"Give me the map and I'll point the way," said Agatha. She opened a door and closed it. "Once I figure out which is the passenger side."

Enclosed in the car with him, Agatha felt antagonism rising in her. If this was a recurrence of their old religious rivalry, she wondered, how could they have been so friendly crossing the Midlands last Friday? Had Janet been their buffer? Maybe this wasn't a renewal of their old rivalry at all; perhaps she was bristling at Bishop Baker because she had been wronged by James, one man no better than any other when it came to dealing with women, all of them frauds.

Dick Baker sensed her mood. At best he was not a good driver, and now as he turned cautiously onto Morehampton Road with his concentration divided between the heavy traffic and Agatha's iciness, he went jerking along, playing the brake and clutch like organ pedals. When he got to the relative safety of the inside lane, he said, to break the unpleasant silence, "My official business is behind me, I'm glad to say." He was clenching the steering wheel with both hands, his eyes darting suspiciously at the drivers passing him on the right. "Two days and nights at All Hallows and yesterday afternoon at Maynooth, and all the while I thought how curious it is that after a hundred years of peace and prosperity in the Midwest we're still coming back to this little island of war and poverty to beg for our priests."

"The reason is we've never had to be spiritually tough in

America," said Agatha. "That's why the Church in America is declining so horribly."

"Well, I wouldn't go so far as to say it's declining."

"Then you're blind."

"Now, Miss McGee—"

"Look at your churches. Who goes to church anymore when they don't have to, but old ladies like myself? Drop into St. Isidore's for daily Mass and you see nothing but blue-rinsed hair."

"But that's only one aspect of the faith."

"The Mass? It's the main aspect, is it not?"

Dick Baker shrugged. "Yes, I suppose. Until now. It may become less important with time."

"What?" Outrage.

"I see changes ahead."

"Ahead, behind, you bishops give us no rest. You're all at sea."

"Exactly. The pilgrim Church."

They waited at a stoplight. The rain beat hard on the windshield.

"If the Church is truly alive, Miss McGee, it can never be completely at rest. Better rough water than the doldrums."

"Nonsense. Better the doldrums than gales and typhoons. Better the doldrums than capsizing and sinking. How many parochial schools have closed in the past year?"

"I guess hundreds, nationwide."

"I don't mean nationwide. How many have you yourself destroyed?"

He turned to her, irritated. "'Destroyed' is hardly the word."

"It's my word." She gave him a withering glare and he, not easily perturbed, felt anger rising up the back of his neck. Had he misread this woman entirely? Was there no heart in her? Nothing under her crust but bitterness?

The light changed. He raced the engine, let out the clutch and shot ahead. He shifted deliberately through five gears, then said calmly, "Six schools of the diocese have closed, to answer your question."

"And what does that signify but decline?"

"Decline of the school system, not the Church as a whole."

"My God. It's the parochial schools, don't forget, that have produced all these priests you're trying to pilfer from Ireland."

He glanced at her again, wondering if he should let up, change the subject. But anyone as dead honest as Agatha McGee deserved an honest adversary. He said, "These Irish priests themselves are outmoded, Miss McGee, a good many of them."

"Ordained priests of God? Outmoded?"

"Many of these Irish priests are stodgy and pompous and not nearly so close to the people as they like to think. They'd be next to useless in my diocese."

"The difference between your diocese and Ireland is that the faith is thriving in Ireland."

"The Irish brand of faith, you mean. It's not right for America."

She folded her arms and showed him the back of her head, her eyes on the blank side of a truck in the next lane.

"I have this sense of Christianity evolving rather fast in the years ahead, Miss McGee, evolving faster in America than elsewhere, turning into something you and I wouldn't recognize. I don't believe, for instance, that parochial schools will go on forever as the instrument for handing down the faith."

"Oh, my." This was a groan. "I've devoted my life to a lost cause."

"No, your life at St. Isidore's has been very precious to the Church, Miss McGee. Your career spanned the years when parochial schools were the glory of Catholicism in America. The school system thrived only because of people like you supplementing—indeed, improving upon—the work of the priests and sisters. But where is the teacher to replace you? And more to the point, where are the priests and sisters?"

"I'm nothing but a relic."

He heard in this remark the cry of a wounded ego. His voice softened. "You're irreplaceable. You've met Mrs. Brown from Fargo. She'll never fill your shoes, and all of us know it."

"Mrs. Brown from Fargo, God help us, she used to be a Lutheran and now she isn't anything. How could you permit Sister Judith to hire her?"

"She's a physical-education specialist. In addition to teaching sixth grade she can organize an athletic program, which the state department of education is requiring of us this year."

"If it's athletics over religion, why do we bother with the school at all?"

"We won't much longer." There. He'd said it.

She turned to him. "St. Isidore's?"

He nodded.

"Next on your hit list?"

"In two years."

The highway grew broader. They picked up speed.

"Surely you're the most depressing man I've ever met."

"Yes." He chuckled, not happily. "I knew you were thinking that."

"How can you function as bishop when you see your churches and schools emptying out? I couldn't live from one day to the next with a view so dark."

"Not so dark if you keep in mind the ongoing quality of the Church, Miss McGee. One way darkens and another lights up. Schools close, other things open."

"What things?"

"I don't know for sure. The Holy Spirit knows."

"Don't you ask Him?"

"Constantly. But He's not one to tip His hand." The bishop drove along thoughtfully. "But I have a sense of the faith returning to the way it was with the early Christians. Groups of families, I mean. Clans, you might say, living their faith together. Instructing one another. Praying together. Formal religion no longer the force it used to be. The faith trusted more and more to families."

"Families? With marriages crumbling like fruitcakes?"

"That will bottom out, as the sociologists say. It's a cycle. The family will be strong again."

She shook her head. "Your problem is your youth, Bishop. Your idealism needs tempering."

"Perhaps." He was driving very fast now, the city falling behind, the Wicklows straight ahead.

"I'll tell you what, Miss McGee: I'll let you temper my idealism if you let me temper yours."

Janet arrived early at Connelly Station. She had ridden the bus with Evelyn as far as Trinity College and walked from there. Connelly Station smelled like the shed her father kept his tractor in—oily, with a faint overlay of smoke. Waiting for Jack Scully and Rita Slade, she stood at the newsstand paging through magazines and listening to the place names drop out of the speaker overhead, magical names—Tipperary, Limerick, Tralee—spoken in a bored, recorded voice.

She waited twenty minutes and the voice was announcing last call to Belfast when Jack Scully came rushing up and thrust out to her a ticket and a carnation. Her heart pumped hard; her face got hot. "Put it in your hair," he said, laughing, "but not yet, we've got to hurry." He was wearing three layers of shirts, a green T-shirt under a yellow sport shirt buttoned at the navel under a long-tailed pink dress shirt hanging open. On his head was a broad-brimmed fedora, surely a relic from a prop room. The flower was wire and nylon.

"Where's Rita?" she called, running at his side along the pier between trains.

"Hurry," he said. Their train was beginning to move.

"Is she already on?"

"Here—in you go!" He flung open a door and steered her into a crowded compartment. He hopped in behind her, slamming the door, and led her out the opposite door and down the corridor.

They came to the club car. Jack bought biscuits in small cellophane packages and two bottles of beer. They sat at a tiny table that jiggled between them as the train sidled eastward and ran along the sea. Malahide, Skerries, Balbriggan. Beaches, grassy dunes, showers of rain. Jack ate hungrily, drank thirstily. Janet nibbled. She had a knot in her stomach. Rita had obviously stayed home.

Winding through the Wicklow Hills, the car moved in and out of clouds so thick that the center line was visible only ten feet ahead.

The vistas must be spectacular, thought Agatha, judging by

the tilt of the car and the number of gears the bishop was shifting.

"What a shame," he said, steering around a tight curve shrouded in boiling gray mist. "Can you see anything at all?"

Out her side window she watched an updraft of cloud rise out of an invisible chasm. "I see rain falling up instead of down," she said, tightening her seatbelt.

At a sign—OVERLOOK—they pulled over to look. Or rather to listen. Somewhere a brook bubbled and sheep were bleating. At the brink of a precipice they stood close to one another, silently, for a long minute. Their antagonism was gone. The difficult road had taken their minds off their argument. Sensing the hidden beauty around them, they felt like two pilgrims entering the unknown.

They got back in the car and descended through a series of switchbacks to the valley of Glendalough.

"At last," the bishop said with a sigh, stopping in front of a hotel. "A snack, Agatha? All this blind, wrong-sided driving makes me hungry."

"I've been starved ever since our plane touched down," she said.

The dining room was unoccupied. A waitress in a black wool suit seated them next to a window overlooking a stream. Across the stream stood the rocky ruins of St. Kevin's Monastery. They lunched on smoked salmon and brown bread. A couple of bites satisfied Dick Baker, who after last night's mushrooms in Ballybegs would be days working his way back to a full meal. He was determined to avoid further talk of religion. He probed and hit on a topic nearly as dear to Agatha as the Church— her family.

Her father read the law in St. Paul and passed the Minnesota bar in 1898, she told him. He set up practice in Staggerford the following year. "It was there he met my mother. They were married on the second day of the twentieth century. My father was ten years in the state senate, one term as minority leader. He was a died-in-the-wool Republican until Roosevelt came along, and then overnight he was converted to the New Deal. He was a big man, good-natured. The best-liked man in town, I think. I loved him devoutly but saw very little of him. He was so often away. He was always busy."

"And your mother?"

"Small like me," she said. "Always busy like my father. Busy at home. If careers for women hadn't been so limited, I'm sure she would have been a horticulturist. Every morning from sunrise till noon she spent in the garden. It sprawled across our entire backyard. She harvested vegetables like a truck farmer. She grew flowers nobody else knew the names of. She founded the Berrington County Garden Club. As a girl I was sent all over town with gifts of bouquets. But I didn't inherit her talent. I have only a border of ferns in front of my house and a small plot of vegetables in back. What was garden to her is mostly lawn now."

The waitress came and took their plates and brought more tea. The sun came out for a minute and flashed in the stream moving swiftly under the window.

"They died within a year of one another. Heart attacks."

"You had brothers and sisters?"

"A brother, but I scarcely knew him. He died in the flu of eighteen."

"You were raised alone then, like me."

They compared their brotherless, sisterless lives. They compared mothers. Agatha felt herself softening. Bishop Baker's cordiality was not forced, as she had once assumed it to be; his amiable smile was not a façade. He was a warm, smart, honest man. Despite the heresies he was tangled in, she found it impossible to go on disliking him. When had she last run on so about her family?

Across the stream she saw a magpie flap up out of the tall grass and into a grove of beeches. The grass, she noticed, was flecked with yellow clover and some small red blossom she didn't recognize.

She said to Dick Baker, "Ever since my mother died, I've felt the lack of flowers in my life."

Word for word, it was the same statement she had written in an early letter to James.

* * *

Approaching Drogheda, the train slowed nearly to a stop and then crept out over the high trestle spanning the Boyne.

"I spent a month in this town last winter playing Biff in *Death of a Salesman*." Jack Scully pointed out the club-car window to the north bank of the river, where the wharfs, warehouses and steeples of Drogheda were slowly materializing out of the gray mist. "It's funny, Janet, but the older I get in real life the younger I get on the stage. I'm becoming an All-American boy, and why should that be? I've never been to America. I'm in *Buried Child* through Saturday week, and I'm in rehearsal as the young druggie in *American Buffalo*." He sat up straight and took off his hat. "Tell me, how authentic do I seem to you, Janet? Quite the American boy, would you say?"

He didn't look at all like a boy to Janet. Though he claimed to be only twenty-three, the creases beside his mouth were very deep, like those of an older man. Maybe onstage he looked younger, but up close Janet was struck by the jaded look that kept returning to his small, brown eyes. "You'd never see that haircut in America," she told him, "except on television reruns."

He smoothed his ducktail, replaced his hat and mugged a merry smile. "Did you know I grew up on a farm, Janet, just like you? I milked cows until I was sixteen and then I ran away to Dublin and never laid eyes on the farm again. I was born for the city—you know? I never saw the city until my train pulled into Dublin the day after I turned sixteen, yet even as a tiny lad I knew I was destined for the city. It can happen like that, a person never belonging where he's lived his whole life."

Janet adjusted the flower in her hair. In her spine she felt the same tingle she had felt on Saturday night when she and Jack lay on the floor listening to records and he had kissed her. Maybe today, away from Evelyn, there would be more of that. She was glad to be away from Evelyn, who was becoming tiresome. After being out late with Evelyn Monday night, Janet had spent yesterday morning waiting for Evelyn to get out of bed. Janet had read magazines, played solitaire on the broad glass coffee table and gazed out the window at the Wicklow Hills. At noon, when Evelyn finally emerged bleary-eyed from her bedroom, Janet realized that her morning had been more enjoyable than her afternoon would probably be, for Evelyn's giggles and gossip were wearing thin.

"It was very dishonest of you not to tell me Rita was staying home, Jack."

His smile remained merry. "What's the matter—I'm not interesting enough for you all by myself?"

"You know what's the matter. The way it looks, the two of us on a trip together." She was half serious.

"The way it looks to who?" He pulled a serious look.

"To Evelyn, and Evelyn will tell her folks, and her mother will tell Randy's mother and she'll think bad of me. Worse than she already does."

"Because of one lousy train ride?"

"Because of the way it looks, the two of us gone on a trip."

"Listen, there's trains returning from Belfast all day long. One leaves about an hour after this one gets in, and if you want to take it we can be back in Dublin before anybody knows we're gone. Another one leaves in the late afternoon, which'll give you time to see the city. Then there's one in the early morning if you want to stay overnight. There's friends of mine in Belfast with extra room in their flat."

"I'm not staying overnight, that's for sure."

"Suit yourself. And relax, would you? It's only a jaunt." Jack Scully considered his chances of seducing Janet. Fifty-fifty, he decided. A shame if he didn't, she being so pretty. She had the farm look, robust and earnest. The moment he met her in Ryan's Pub on Saturday night he had been struck by her eyes and the way her dark hair swayed and fell to the side when she tilted her head. Here in the club car her eyes were dark brown when she looked at him, light brown when she turned to the window.

He stepped to the bar and came back with their second beer. The train slid into Drogheda, stopped at the station. "Well so," he said. "We both of us left the farm for the city."

"No, I don't live in a city," she said, "just a small town. It's only about five miles from the farm. My dad's on the farm yet, with two of my sisters. I've got a little boy, Stephen. He's four. He's crazy about the farm. There's goats and ducks and a cow.

Sometimes a calf. My dad lets Stephen steer the tractor when he's cutting hay."

"We never had a tractor on our place, only a team of horses. And enough cows to make you sick for life of milking. When I was twelve or thirteen I set a goal for myself. I said to myself there's nothing for it but I get on a train to Dublin or I get on a freighter to America by the time I'm sixteen, and that's what I did. The train, not the freighter. The train was easier, it stopped six times a week in Kilconnell."

"You never told your folks?"

"I sent them a card from Dublin. A picture postcard of the procathedral to ease their minds, they're very religious, my family." Jack Scully shifted in his chair, sinking low, folding his arms, resting his chin on his chest, gazing out the rain-streaked window at the empty station platform. "It wasn't letting them down, if that's what you're asking. I've a younger brother, Liam, who's very good about the farm. Mum's favorite, he is. Dad's too, I guess. He'll milk cows till the day he dies and I'll never be missed."

"Don't you keep in touch?" She thought of her father's farm and imagined the sadness of cutting family ties. She thought of Mr. and Mrs. Meers and imagined the pleasure of it.

"Oh, I'll get a letter at Christmas and sometimes before a bank holiday saying, 'Come home, we'll have a family gathering like old times,' but I never go. And wouldn't they turn *me* down if *I* invited *them* to come to Dublin and see a play I'm in? They've never been east of the River Suck."

He asked to know more about Janet, and she obliged. She was intrigued by his expressive eyes, by the number of reactions she could elicit from him. When she spoke of Stephen he grew warm and fatherly-looking. She told him about her mother-in-law, and he seemed to understand. She described life on the farm, and he looked as if he might vomit. Though not nearly so handsome as Randy, he was more amusing. However, it was no fun having to keep guessing which of his facial expressions were real and which were stagecraft. She suspected that the one she didn't care for—the jaded look—was real.

"So tell me about your randy husband, Janet."

"He's a salesman."

"Yes, I can see him. Carries a tiny calculator in his breast pocket, doesn't he, along with about twelve ballpoint pens."

"No, not Randy."

"Not the business type?"

She shook her head. "He really hasn't got the heart for business."

"So what's he got the heart for then?"

"Singing." She laughed.

"A singer, by God." Jack Scully's eyes lit up. "A folksinger is he? Strumming a guitar all the time? A regular busker, that Randy."

"No, he just sings for the fun of it. He'd've loved being at your place Saturday night, singing. He'd've sung some country and then some rock and finished off with some blues. He's got this deep, easy voice, it's great."

"Tell me, Janet: Do you like a man more being married to him, or does it get tiresome?"

"It's only been one year, not quite."

Jack Scully made his eyes round. "He's not your kid's father?"

"No."

"Who is?"

How crude. Who in Berrington County would be so bold as to ask? "A boy I knew." She steadied her beer bottle as the train jerked into motion.

Jack waited to hear more, but she fell silent, her eyes on the wet streets going by. The memory of Eddie Lofgren caused her cheeks to color slightly. Jack Scully found this color very attractive. It seemed to indicate there was a chance. If not overnight, he would at least persuade her to stay until the late-afternoon train. His friends Charlie and Tom, being lovers themselves, would be happy to lend him their flat for a couple of hours.

"Miss McGee, do you mind if I ask about the lodger you had one time? I've heard stories. There was a shooting."

"An atrocity." Agatha shook her head vigorously and looked out the window. She felt edgy from too much tea. She saw the magpie swoop down out of the beeches, then return to its perch in the thick leaves. "Miles Pruitt was his name. He taught in the high school. The mildest of men, a saint I believe, though he had not been to church for some years. The shock of his death was like—" *Like the shock of seeing James on the altar,* she kept herself from saying. Both men taken from her irrevocably. It was odd sitting here telling the story of Miles to the bishop only days after telling it to James. When she finished, she lifted her eyes to the bishop. Her hands lay limp on the table. He knew that the emotion in her voice was too fresh to be traced all the way back to Miles Pruitt. It was the pain of a newer wound. She smiled, unconvincingly. He reached across and squeezed her hands, powerfully.

The rain had stopped in Belfast. The streets were wet. The train pulled into a shed where the wind was cold. Letting Jack Scully take her hand in the crowd flowing through the station, Janet looked for the welcoming sign she had come to expect of cities on this tour. Posted beside the highway into Minneapolis she had seen, "Enjoy the City of Lakes." At JFK, "The Big Apple, Take a Bite." At Shannon, "Welcome to Eire." They stepped out of the station and were faced with gigantic white letters painted on a brick wall across the street, "Screw the Pope."

Jack pointed at a small armored truck passing by. "That's the Royal Ulster Constabulary," he said. "They keep the peace." The truck held five men in gray uniforms, two in the cab and three peering out the back. One of the men in back, seeing Jack pointing at him, pointed at Jack with his rifle. Janet covered her face, screaming. Jack shouted, "You buggers!" The three soldiers laughed, receding down the street.

"Come on, it's a hike to City Centre," said Jack. They followed a narrow, twisting street through a bombed-out neighborhood. Houses gaped open, their walls gone, their plumbing exposed, their curtains flapping and shredding in the wind. They kept to the middle of the road, for the sidewalks were covered with rubble. They came to a house more impressive than the rest, the stonework ornate. Janet went up to a glassless window and looked in. Staring back at her from between the bars of a crib was a cat with a red string hanging from its mouth. At the head of the crib was a grimy pillow, and on the pillow lay a half-eaten rat.

"God!" Janet said.

Jack peered in, then recoiled as if struck. "Christ, I can't stand rats." At this moment he felt his chances with Janet drop below fifty-fifty, Belfast being so absolutely counterseductive.

They walked on. A three-legged dog limped out from between two houses and followed them for a time, a German shepherd with a broken spirit, its head hanging, its coat lusterless, its tongue lolling.

At City Centre they were frisked for weapons and then allowed through a turnstile. Here was clean, quiet commerce. Instead of slogans scrawled across buildings, there were shop windows with attractive displays and well-dressed shoppers stopping to admire them. This might be the center of a city at peace with itself, thought Janet, but then she noticed that among the vehicles allowed inside the portals—buses and taxis mostly—were armored trucks on patrol, and every few hundred yards she came upon an RUC man in battle dress, his automatic rifle in hand, moving among the shoppers as casually as partridge hunters moved through the brush behind her father's farmhouse. The sight of these soldiers brought back the knot in her stomach. She was much farther from home than she wanted to be.

Seeing discouragement in her eyes, Jack Scully tried to divert her attention with a display of books in a window. "A lot better selection of books here than in Dublin, Janet. The English aren't so fussy as the Irish, not so inclined to censor." They went in and browsed. On a discount table Janet found a story collection with an intriging cover, a shadowy woman partially undressed; behind her, outside her bedroom window, cows. She opened the book to a page of lovers quarreling, to a page of strained talk between father and son, to a page of wisdom spoken by a daughter to her mother. She took the book to the cashier and put two Irish pounds on the counter. The cashier, a young man in a suit of blue checks, lifted one of the bills delicately by a corner and let it flutter to the floor near Janet's feet. "What are these?" he said, sniffing, and dropped the other one. He took the book from her and slipped it under the counter and said, "Next, please." A man with four or five paperbacks came up to the counter, looking down at the bills as if they were garbage.

"I forgot," said Jack, coming up behind her. "We should have exchanged for English money."

Janet picked up her bills and they went outside.

"We'll find a bank," said Jack.

"Let's not bother," said Janet. "I don't want to buy anything in this crummy city." She was looking at Jack and thinking how ridiculous he was in his three mismatched shirts and his black felt hat with the wide brim. She was no longer fascinated by the exaggerated expressions he made with his eyes, nor by the wire and nylon carnation that was scratching her temple. Say what you would about Randy, he was honest and handsome and he knew how to dress. The only trouble with Randy was his boyishness, which he was bound to outgrow. Jack Scully the actor would be forever a child.

Jack Scully straightened a make-believe necktie and shot make-believe cuffs. "Come, we'll see our banker about this."

"No, I don't want English money." Janet looked at her watch. "There's time to catch the early train."

"But you haven't seen the city." Disappointment, not totally make-believe.

"I've seen enough."

"You haven't any souvenir of Belfast."

"I don't want anything."

"Not even a beer? Let's stop in for a beer."

"We just had two beers on the train."

"Really set on going back, are you?"

"You don't have to come with me if you want to stay."

They caught the two-o'clock train and were back in Dublin by the time Evelyn finished her exam.

Because rain was sprinkling down again, Agatha and Dick Baker made short work of St. Kevin's ruins. They walked quickly through the cemetery, circled the round tower, stepped in and out of the oratory and hurried back to the car. The hilltops were no longer shrouded in mist, and when they drove up out of the valley of Glendalough, their view eastward, where the gray-green peaks extended toward the sea, was unobstructed. They went in that direction and came to Wicklow on the coast. They stopped at a gift shop. Agatha bought postcards, and the bishop bought a tin whistle with a mellower tone than his old one. Trying it out in the shop, he piped "The Shoals of Herring" and "Kelly the Boy from Killann." Six or eight shoppers applauded.

Driving the coast road back to the city, Dick Baker said, "Agatha, there are three parishes in our diocese administered by nuns."

"Don't I know it." Was this outing to end the way it began, in religious warfare?

"As you also know, your Father Finn is overworked."

"Don't tell me you're putting a nun in his place. I'd die."

"No, I'm not replacing him. I'm appointing an assistant for him."

"Yes?"

"Sister Judy."

"Sister Judith? I'm having a nightmare."

"She's ideal for the job. She's been in Staggerford for some years. She can take over his counseling duties and visit the sick and take his place on the parish council."

"Then who takes her place as principal?"

"I have a replacement in mind."

"If the school's closing in two years, it's no time to change principals. I've seen principals come and go. It takes a principal two years to learn the ropes well enough not to be in the way of the rest of the staff."

"Not the principal I have in mind. She knows the ropes already, having taught there for forty-six years."

"Me?" She examined his smile for lunacy.

"You needn't decide this minute."

24

WHEN HE HEARD his mother moving around overhead, Randy carried his bowl of Wheaties upstairs and stepped out onto the sunny patio, where she was breakfasting on orange juice and coffee. She was wearing the white terrycloth robe Randy had given her for Christmas. He was wearing the brown wool robe she had given him.

"Oh, Randy, you're late for work again. It's nearly ten."

"It's okay, I called Polly and told her I'd be late." He sat opposite her at the glass-topped table. The sun made him squint.

"It's a bad habit, Randy, skipping work."

"I've been working. Making phone calls." He chewed and chewed. "Mother, how hard would it be to get a variance on River Street?"

"The Vaughn place?"

"Yeah, so it can be a duplex."

"Nothing doing, I told you, till your father comes through with Hawaii and carpet for the dining room."

"Yeah, I know, but that's not my question. My question is, How hard would it be?"

Her smile was sharp. "Really, Randy, can you imagine the council opposing me on anything I set my mind to? I've got all but Emery Pitt in my back pocket, and Emery Pitt's hardly ever there to vote because of his emphysema. We make zoning changes almost every week."

"So how about making one tomorrow night?"

"Hold it, Randy. No more deals for your father."

"But for me?"

Her eyes lit up. "You?" She laughed.

"I called Otto Kessler in Duluth. He said he'd make a firm offer of ninety-six thousand if the Vaughn house came with a

249

zoning variance. Then I called Dad at the office, and it's okay for me to go ahead and handle the deal."

She smiled; she was pleased. Her eyes narrowed; she was scheming. "We'll have to get moving on this. We can't have a hearing without a notice appearing in the paper beforehand. Let's see, the paper comes out tomorrow morning, and the council meets tomorrow night, so that'll work out all right, but the notice can't appear in the paper till the application forms are signed. Are you in touch with the owners, Randy?"

"I can call them. They live in Minneapolis."

"They have to apply as owners."

"Can they do it by phone?"

"No. They have to put their signature to the application, and they have to be at the hearing, too—either themselves or their representative. You could be their representative, I suppose. But you'll have to drive to Minneapolis or meet them halfway to get their signatures, and you'll have to do it right away because the *Weekly* goes to press tonight and the *Weekly* won't print the notice without the signatures on the form. Finish your cereal and hit the road, Randy. I'll call the city clerk and he'll have the forms ready so you can pick them up on the way out of town."

Spooning up the rest of his Wheaties, Randy felt a little dazed. Having fallen in step with him, his mother was now out in front, pulling him forward, pulling him nearly off balance—not an uncommon sensation whenever he dealt with his mother.

He stepped inside and brought the phone out to the patio. From his robe he took the page he had slipped out of his father's notebook, the Vaughn page. Five phone numbers were listed for Norman and Eunice Noznick. He dialed three and got no answer. On the fourth a voice said, "Starburst. Showtime at sunset. Double bill tonight: *Singing in the Rain* and *Raised by Apes*."

"Who is this, please?"

"Starburst Drive-in, Norman Noznick speaking."

"Hi, Mr. Noznick, I'm Randy Meers from Staggerford Realty."

"Staggerford what?" There was hammering on the line, then the scream of a power tool and the sawtooth ripping of wood.

"Realty," Randy raised his voice. "You have a house listed with us."

"Oh, yeah. Hey, Eunice, it's about the house up north! Just a minute, I'll put my wife on the phone. Old lady Vaughn was her aunt, you know."

The power saw stopped, the hammering continued. Eventually a woman said, "Yeah?"

"Hi, I'm Randy Meers from Staggerford Realty. You'll be happy to know I've got a buyer for your house."

"I'll believe it when I see it. You've been trying to unload that place for over a year."

"There's a developer from Duluth who's very interested." Randy explained to her about the duplex plan and the zoning variance. He asked that the Noznicks meet him halfway this afternoon and sign the form. Meeting halfway would cut his round trip from six hours to three.

"No way have we got that kind of time. We're doing over the concession stand and we're running behind. We've got to get the plumbing connected and the carpet laid before tonight's show."

Randy's mother said, "Don't take no for an answer. Make them meet you halfway."

Randy covered the phone. "They're too busy. Their plumbing's not connected."

"They're not too busy to come halfway. Do they want to sell their house, or don't they?"

"Mrs. Noznick," said Randy, "in order to bring up the zoning at tomorrow night's council meeting, we have to announce it in the weekly paper, which goes to press tonight. If you could meet me in St. Cloud, I wouldn't have to drive so far."

"So what's the hurry? Won't the council ever meet again? Won't the *Weekly* come out next week?"

What *was* the hurry? It took Randy a moment to realize that he had unconsciously set himself a deadline for making the first house sale of his life. That deadline was Saturday afternoon, when Janet's plane touched down. As a full-fledged realtor, surely he'd get as much attention from Janet as Stephen did.

Mrs. Noznick continued, "If our plumbing's not connected

by showtime, where do our customers go to the can? Have you thought to ask yourself that?"

Randy looked at his watch. "Where will I find you at two o'clock, Mrs. Noznick?"

"Right here in the concession stand."

"Where is it?"

"Where is it? It's right in the middle of the lot. You can't miss it."

"I mean, where's the drive-in?"

"You don't know where the Starburst is? You never been to a show here?"

"No."

"It's just off I-Ninety-four. Take the Plymouth exit."

"I'll see you there at two, Mrs. Noznick, if you'll agree to sign the zoning papers."

"I'll sign whatever it takes to unload that place. It came to me out of thin air, you know. Victoria Vaughn was a great-aunt I forgot I had."

"You won't have to come down very far on your price. I think I can get the buyer up to ninety-six."

"Not high enough."

"Just think about it, Mrs. Noznick, and I'll see you at two."

After hanging up, Randy said to his mother, "My clients are nine thousand apart."

"Not bad for a house in that price range."

They sat for a minute thinking their separate thoughts as they looked out across the deep backyard. A breeze was moving the birch boughs; the tiny new leaves were casting thin, moving shadows on the lawn. Mrs. Meers was thinking she would teach Stephen croquet. She would find the old wickets and mallets and balls in the garage and get him started this weekend, the minute he got home from the farm. Randy was thinking he'd like to move away from this house; he'd like to take Janet and Stephen and start a new life somewhere.

His mother turned to him. "Randy, there's one more thing you have to do. You have to call your father and tell him you're holding out for at least five percent."

"Hold out from Dad? He'd never go for it."

"He'd have to go for it. There'd be no deal if he didn't."

"Yes, there would. Once I get Otto Kessler and the Noz-nicks together, Dad could just step in and finish the deal."

"But Randy—think!—for your father there'll be no vari-ance. I'll make that very clear to him."

Randy stood and picked up his cereal bowl. He said, "Well."

"Do it. The variance won't do you much good if most of the commission goes to your father."

"It'll do me a lot of good. Three percent is three thou-sand bucks."

"And five percent is five thousand."

"How about four percent? That's over half."

"All right. Ask for five and settle for four. Get a move on you now, and I'll call the city clerk and say you'll be stopping by for the forms."

It was hot for May. Randy drove to Minneapolis with all the windows open, creating a sixty-mile-an-hour wind that swept through the car with a howl and drowned out his singing. Be-tween Staggerford and St. Cloud he sang along with his Willie Nelson and his Linda Ronstadt tapes. Between St. Cloud and Minneapolis he had just enough time to run through his sev-eral tapes by the Go-Gos. Randy arrived at the Starburst Drive-in a little after two and drove across the sandy lot to the concession stand, a long concrete building with a flat roof. He parked between two vans. *Noznick Entertainment Group* was let-tered on the door of one. The other said *Shag Riley, Free-lance Carpet Layer*.

Norman Noznick stepped out into the burning sunshine and shook Randy's hand. Norman wore a soiled white suit over a pink, button-down shirt open at the neck. He was a small man in his forties. He had large ears and large eyes that seemed full of tears. "Glad you got here before we left. We were just about to take off for our theater in Bloomington. Come on, Eunice's inside. God, it's hot."

Norman Noznick's tears weren't tears of sorrow, Randy dis-covered when he stepped into the eye-watering pungence of carpet glue. The concession stand was a vast area of new car-pet the color of lemon peel.

Videogames lined one wall, a snack bar lined another, the

walls were covered with movie posters. Randy saw Gene Kelly's engaging smile, Donald O'Connor's goofy grin and saw that the cast of *Raised by Apes* was Japanese. He saw a man kneeling in a corner, gluing—Shag Riley, no doubt.

Norman Noznick called, "Eunice, it's the guy from Staggerford about the house."

Eunice Noznick came out of the men's room with a wrench in her hand. She was a short, stout woman with a red scarf tied over her head to protect her frizzy gray hair. The yellow of her tight doubleknit pantsuit was less brilliant than the carpet, more like grapefruit peel. She was heavily rouged. "Good thing you got here before we left," she said to Randy without looking at him. "I told Norman either you show up in five minutes or we take off for Bloomington and leave you a note on the door. We're doing over our place in Bloomington, too, same as this, only the carpet there's more of an off-orange. Where do we sign?"

Randy laid the zoning form on the snack counter. She signed and handed the pen to Norman. Norman signed.

"I'm coming down to the city again on Saturday to meet a plane," said Randy. "If everything goes okay I'll have a purchase agreement along. Will you be here, say around three?"

Norman said yes, but his wife said no. "We'll be out in Bloomington, Norman. We're getting in our new pop machines on Saturday, remember?"

"Oh, yeah," said Norman, wiping his eyes.

"The Meteor Drive-in," she told him. "Take the Cedar exit." She wiped her eyes.

"As I said on the phone, I think I can get the buyer up to ninety-six thousand, so you might be thinking about what you'll counter with."

"I've already thought," she said. "We'll drop to a hundred thousand."

Norman said, "I think we should go to ninety-six and get rid of the place. It's just standing empty."

"Victoria Vaughn was my relation, not yours!" growled Eunice.

Norman nodded, appearing to see the logic of it.

Four thousand apart, thought Randy as he gathered up the papers, shook their hands and left. Standing at his car, he wiped his eyes and took off his tie and shirt. He drove home in his T-shirt, singing Johnny Cash and Judy Collins all the way and acquiring a severe sunburn on his left arm.

25

ON THURSDAY MORNING, placing before Agatha her standard breakfast of eggs, toast and too much sausage, Rosella Coyle said, "There was a riot last night on O'Connell Street, Miss McGee. Windows broken in Cleary's Department Store and a number of cars parked along Bachelor's Walk had their windscreens broken. They had Paddy Creely's wife down from Belfast speaking in front of the post office, and the sight of her caused the demonstrators to get out of hand. There were a great many cuts and bruises among them, and a policeman broke his leg. The man on the radio says Paddy Creely's wife looked like a woman in a daze. He says she spoke out in a dull, dreamy voice and had to be led by the hand."

"What cruelty!" said Agatha. "She's being used by the IRA."

"Cruel it is. You'd think once her family was dead and buried the world would leave her alone, but that's not the Irish. The Irish are like dogs when it comes to grudges. I had a dog named Brownie one time who loved all my neighbors but one, and that one he bit in the ankle every chance he got."

Agatha ate hungrily, wondering if this fourth breakfast of Rosella Coyle's might put her off sausage for life. She had come down late for breakfast, having taken a long while to fall asleep last night, pondering the principalship of St. Isidore's. A hundred times she had gone from rejecting the job to accepting it and back to rejecting it again.

Clearing away the dishes at the other tables, Rosella Coyle said, "There was even a fire started in the public toilet on O'Connell Street, the gents', but it proved to be the work of a gang of ten-year-old boys, not the demonstrators. Would you believe ten-year-olds up to something like that? It's the children from the poor neighborhoods up beyond Gardiner

Street—they're always keeping their eye out for adult mischief to cover up their own."

They heard the phone ring in the front hallway. Rosella Coyle went to answer it.

Agatha, eating, looked out the window at the neighborhood cats at the back door, where they waited each morning for their rich scraps. Despite clouds of medium gray, the light this morning was strong and made her squint. It was the same pervasive light that moved into Minnesota on certain snowy days in winter and made you uncomfortable, a discourteous light that fell in through your windows and invaded the darkest recesses of your house, your soul. It cast no light, however, on her dilemma. Again and again as she ate, she weighed the bishop's offer. She had come up with three good reasons for going back to work, as principal.

One, she had the skills. She had spent most of her career feeling overtalented for the sixth-grade classroom. She had been second-guessing principals since 1938.

Two, she needed something to do. The idleness of retirement had looked attractive from a distance—hadn't she always loved her summers off?—but now, particularly with James and his letters gone from her life, it looked barren. What would she do in September when everybody else went back to school and nothing lay ahead but the dull days of winter?

Three, she loved St. Isidore's Elementary. She loved the brick, the windows, the hardwood floors. She loved the cheerily painted lunchroom and the velvet curtain across the stage. She was as fond of the building itself as she was of her own house on River Street. Fonder, even, for it housed her children.

But each of these reasons had its reverse side.

One, she was running low on optimism. Though she had the skills to be principal, she didn't have the hope. How could she inspire her teachers when the worth of her own forty-six years of teaching was proving so difficult to appraise?

Two, though she needed something to occupy herself through the endless, dismal stretch of frost and snow and ice between September and May, wasn't a full-time principalship overambitious for a woman of sixty-eight? Why not something less challenging, like learning, finally, to cook. Or Lillian could teach her to knit.

Three, loving St. Isidore's, how could she bear to oversee its demise? How could she instill vitality in a school condemned to death? Of the six diocesan schools already closed, she had heard tales of teachers' morale hitting bottom long before their time was up, of parents transferring their children to other schools at midterm, teachers feigning sick leave and going off in search of other jobs. And how devastating, on that final day, after two years as a lame-duck principal, to be the last one left in the empty halls, to go from room to room and make sure the lights were switched off and the shades were drawn and then to step out the front doorway and turn the key in the lock for the last time ever.

Rosella Coyle returned. "That was your bishop on the telephone, Miss McGee. He asked if he might park his car in front of my house tonight while he takes you out to dinner and the theater. In view of the rioting, he'll take you downtown in a taxi and leave his car here, out of harm's way. If I didn't know better, I'd think he was courting you."

"He is, in a way. He wants me to be principal of one of his schools." She was surprised at the pleasure it gave her to say this. "But it's a school on the skids." The pleasure vanished.

Rosella Coyle went around brushing crumbs off tables. "I was saying about Paddy Creely's wife, she's going to make one more appearance tonight before going back to Belfast. They're expecting even bigger trouble on O'Connell Street. They're installing a steel screen over Cleary's plate glass windows."

The doorbell sounded. Rosella Coyle left the room again. Agatha picked a *Times* off a nearby table and read as she sipped coffee.

Dear Editor,

Without wishing to defame the memory of Paddy Creely, who's coming in for such praise in the press and who was indeed a man of high integrity, I am obliged to point out that his guiding principle in life was hate, and thus his integrity was wrongheaded. I knew Paddy. I used to live near him in Belfast. While ten years of atrocities on Curston Road caused some of us to quit our jobs and move away, they caused Paddy to dig in his heels and hate the Prods with all his might. He said that was the only way the tyranny of Britain would be overthrown and all of Ireland would live in peace. Exactly how hate might lead to peace he never said. He simply went on to the end, blindly believing in the efficacy of hate. Sorry to break in on the eulogizing, but somebody had better speak the truth if Ireland is ever to know peace.

Rosella Coyle returned, looking amused. "A priest to see you, Miss McGee."

"Oh?" She sat back, her fingertips to her heart.

"If you wish to see him, I'll show him into the sitting room."

"A priest? Not Bishop Baker?"

"No, he's taller and older. He didn't say his name and I thought it uncivil to ask. He has a prominent nose."

Agatha pushed her chair back and looked out at the cats. James? She didn't want to see James.

"You're a great hit with the clergy, I must say."

Agatha ignored her, realizing that if she turned James away she'd wonder forever what he wanted to say. "I'll see him," she said.

She went up to her room and checked herself at the mirror. Why had he come? And dressed as a priest? Was he so obtuse as to expect her to go out with him for another day of sightseeing?

Descending the stairs, she felt something of the same bitterness she had experienced the day before with Bishop Baker, an urge to confront all men on the grounds of their wickedness. She stood for a moment outside the sitting-room door, straightening the bow of her blouse, smoothing the pocket flaps of her gray suit. She opened the door and went in.

James O'Hannon stood up and came forward. "Agatha."

"Father O'Hannon," she said coldly, concealing the shock of seeing him as a priest, Sunday's shock all over again.

He took her hand, nodding. "I've come to apologize." He led her to a chair.

"For being Father O'Hannon?"

"For not telling you."

They both sat rigidly on the edge of their chairs. Holding her hand, he felt how stiff and icy she was, and he began to lose courage. He let her hand drop and sat silent for some time, facing away from her. When he resumed speaking, his voice was husky and he was still facing away. "I have been forty years at my vocation, Agatha. I can't complain. I look around me and see that my life has been happier than some other lives, happier than a good many, in fact, yet not so happy as I had hoped it would be." He cleared his throat. "When your first letter arrived years ago, I had already been in Ballybegs over twenty years, and I was nearly insane with boredom. I had been praying for just the very sort of pleasure your correspondence brought me. No, I take that back. I had been praying for less than it brought me."

Agatha wished he would look at her instead of at the far wall, where a framed photo of Deanna Durbin hung beside an engraving of Pope John XXIII.

He went on slowly. "My bishop is of the opinion that his priests do best in long assignments. 'Get to know your parish the way a father knows his family,' the bishop tells us over and over again, and I'm sick to death of hearing it. I did just that, you know, long ago. I got to know my parish the way a father knows his family, and from there I went on to know my parish the way a prisoner knows his prison."

Hanging his head, he looked at his hands, front and back.

"Then came your letters. I can't tell you what they did for me, Agatha. What knowing you did for me." He coughed into his hand and shifted in his chair, still facing away. There was a sudden, small convulsion in his shoulders. Was he weeping? Yes, she saw a tear trembling and ready to drop from the corner of his chin. A wave of horror ran through her. She had never before seen a man weeping.

"Ignore my tears, Agatha—they stand for self-pity. As a priest, I've learned that people only cry over what they've lost, or missed getting, and I'm surely no exception to that. I'd like to think I'm weeping out of sorrow for having hurt you, and that's what I've come here to say—how sad I am to have hurt you—but I'm weeping mostly because of what I had with you . . . and deserve to have no longer."

He faced her now. His expression was unchanged. It was not contorted by grief; indeed, she saw the hint of a smile, yet his cheeks were wet.

"Can you forgive me?" he asked.

Agatha was mute, transfixed by the tears. Her pain came back to her, undiminished since Sunday. It tore her in half. She felt like getting up and walking out the door. She felt like pressing his head to her breast and saying that she, too, was sorry. She felt like suggesting another visit at a later time; perhaps James would come to the States. She felt like saying she never wanted to see him or hear from him again. She said nothing.

He took her silence for dismissal. Assuming she was finished with him forever and wanting to avoid further awkwardness, he stood and went to the door. There he turned and said, "Once again then, I'm sorry." He stood with his hand raised slightly as though to keep his balance, as though to bless her. Then he went out, closing the door. Agatha wanted to call after him, and she might have done so if the door hadn't immediately swung open again.

"I forgot," he said, drawing a sealed envelope from his pocket. "I have a message for your bishop, if you wouldn't mind giving it to him." He laid it on the table beside the door and withdrew again.

She picked up the envelope, puzzled.

> Bishop Baker
> Diocese of Berrington
> U.S.A.

She heard James ascend the half flight to the front door, heard him open the door and close it. She hurried after him. She opened the front door and called his name. He swung around instantly. He came halfway up the steps, she went halfway down. Standing a step below her, at eye level, he said, "Yes?"

"James." Again his glistening wet eyes tied her tongue. She looked past him to the street, the cars going by, the people walking. "James, about this message. I feel like a girl being sent home with a note from her teacher. Is it about me?"

"No, no, Agatha. It's Church business. You said your bishop was here searching out priests, so I thought he might appreciate a clue."

Church business—how tedious. She looked down the street toward St. Stephen's Green. "I see."

"It's only that," he said.

The street looked inviting, the trees arching over the sidewalk. "James, I was going out shopping on Grafton Street. Would you walk with me as far as St. Stephen's Green?"

He gave her a little bow. "Of course." He peered at her intently. "Thank you for asking."

"Let me get my coat. I won't be a minute."

They moved briskly along the street, Agatha holding his arm. The breeze was cool and fresh. They said very little, the traffic too noisy for easy conversation.

Entering the green, they slowed down. They stopped to look at swimming ducks, at flowers. They found a long, empty bench and sat down. Here Agatha felt less tense than she had in Rosella Coyle's parlor. She spoke slowly, carefully:

"Your life in Ballybegs, James. It's like my life in Staggerford. Happy enough. Happier than most, I suppose. But too much the same from beginning to end. And then, to break the sameness of it all, your letters started coming. No two letters the same. No day quite the same for me when one of your letters arrived. They meant more to me than they should have, I admit it now. I should not have allowed them to mean so much."

"For my part I cannot say that, Agatha. Your letters have been worth the world to me."

"As yours to me, and that's why I'm at such a loss."

"Must it be over? Our writing?"

Was there no end to it? First he wanted forgiveness, now he wanted more letters. She couldn't think what to say.

"I had thought I'd ask you by letter, Agatha, after you'd been home a while, but I ask you now: Will we resume writing?"

She watched a well-dressed man approach the bench and sit down at the far end. He drew from his pocket the timetable book for the Dublin bus system and paged through it.

James waited for her answer, but she said nothing. Her silence made him feel awkward, as before, graceless, a blunderer. Well, he thought, why not blunder back over forgiveness again? Nothing to lose.

"Agatha, was what I did a sin? Not telling you I was a priest?"

She kept her eyes on the man with the bus book. "How can I answer that? Only your conscience knows your sins."

The man's eyes froze on a page of the bus book as he realized he was hearing a heart-to-heart talk.

"But don't you see, Agatha, over the past four years I've come to think of you as my conscience."

She threw her hands in the air. "Lord help you."

"I haven't known a moment's peace since I saw you in church Sunday. Saw you leaving. I've been in turmoil."

"There's your answer, then."

He nodded. "And if it was therefore a sin, can anyone really forgive me but you?"

"God can. He does it all the time."

"I've asked God. Now I'm asking you."

"Oh, dear, must I tell you this minute? Forgiving is not one of my skills."

They fell silent. They watched another man approach the bench. A derelict with a cane. His suit was soiled and threadbare. He had holes in his shoes. He sat between Agatha and the man with the bus book. He stood his cane between his knees, capped it with both hands and peered first at Agatha, then around Agatha at James, then at the man on his left. His whiskers were a week old. He leaned toward the man with the bus book and said, "I see you're reading Irish fairy tales." He turned to Agatha. "No bus in Dublin goes by the book." She saw stubs of brown teeth.

"Father," he said, leaning forward to address James, "at my bus stop in Rathgar someone wrote, 'Where will you spend eternity?' on the wall, and didn't somebody the very next day come along and add a line underneath, 'Right here, waiting for Number Twenty-two.' "

Agatha and James smiled. The man with the bus book laughed. To James the derelict added, "I thought you would see the humor of it, theologically speaking."

They remained sitting in a row for several minutes, the four of them, watching people pass on the walks. Then Agatha put her hand on James's arm and said, "I'm going shopping now, James. Thank you for coming to see me this morning. It will have made a great difference to me, I know, when I am home and thinking back."

"Am I forgiven then?"

"Yes."

"I meant no harm at all. I thought it was safe sharing my life with you across the ocean." He spoke in a rush. "I never thought you would come and see me. We Irish aren't the travelers you Americans are. Why, I've never seen Cork. You can't imagine my panic when you wrote that you were coming over."

"I can." She stood.

He stood. "We'll write?"

"I can't be sure, James. If we do, please let me write first."

Thinking of the thin quality of the years ahead if she didn't write, he looked very sad.

"I'm sorry," she said. "I can't be sure."

They both looked away, Agatha at a flower bed, James at a tree. After a moment he pointed and said, "You'll be wanting to go that way to Grafton Street."

She took the hand he was pointing with and kissed the back of it. "Good-bye, James."

"Good-bye, Agatha." He squeezed her hand, but only for an instant, for she abruptly spun around and went on her way.

26

THE BISHOP CAME for Agatha at seven, and they took a cab to the Camomile Kitchen on Dawson Street. They were the first to arrive. The waiter showed them to a table set for seven. The tablecloth was flowery, the plates heavy pottery, the napkins green linen. The waiter said, "Cider while you wait," and poured from a decanter.

Dick Baker said, "Well, Agatha, Knob tomorrow evening and dinner with the Plunketts."

"Yes, the Plunketts. And the following day, home."

"You're eager to get home?"

She nodded, sipping her cider. It had an alcoholic kick. "I'm eager to see if I unplugged my coffeemaker."

He turned the stem of the glass in his fingers. "Agatha, did you do right, passing up the land portion?"

She nodded. "I've seen it all. More than all." In her mind's eye she saw James pointing to Grafton Street, saw herself—astonishing!—taking his hand and kissing it.

She had gone from St. Stephen's Green to a little church on D'Olier Street for noon Mass, and there she had asked God if the pleasure of knowing James would someday heal the injury of discovering the truth about him, and she was amazed to find that it was already so. The pain of his deception, though lingering, was no longer a chaotic sort of pain, nor was it, she suspected, as strong as the emptiness she would certainly feel if she had never known him. She assured God that her forgiveness of James was complete. However, she didn't go so far as to tell God that she'd resume the correspondence.

The three Fermoyles arrived one at a time from three directions: Nora by car from Dun Laoghaire, having stopped at home to pick up Janet; Alexander by bus from his office; Evelyn, with Willie Hughes, by foot from Trinity.

The first course was mushroom soup. Nora Fermoyle said she didn't see how she and her partner, Phyllis, could possibly have the fixtures and stock in place by opening day. Their carpenter was down with a cold, and the man who was setting up the greeting card display had been called back to London for an emergency sales meeting—something about a strike among artists and versifiers.

Alexander Fermoyle, who had stopped for three gins on the way, said it had never occurred to him that the greeting card industry was as volatile as all that, and he might just send a reporter to London to check it out. Striking versifiers, he said; now, that was catchy. He said the economic state of Ireland worried him a good deal.

Willie Hughes chimed in that his father, too, was worried. His father was in meatpacking and felt that everything had been dandy as long as Ireland was on her own. It was going international that messed things up.

"The Common Market," Evelyn explained.

The next course was fresh fruit salad runny with cream, both liquid and whipped. Wine as well. Dick Baker asked Janet if she was eager to go home, and she replied that she had been homesick ever since yesterday, when she went to Belfast on the train and saw bombed-out neighborhoods and soldiers patrolling with guns. The South was fine, she said, but by going to Belfast she had strung herself out too thin. She was lonesome.

It jolted Agatha to think of her hardscrabble girl in Belfast. "Who did you go with, Janet?"

"Friends of Evelyn's. Rita Slade and Jack Scully."

Evelyn nudged Janet with her elbow.

Alexander Fermoyle said he hadn't finished speaking about the economy. How did things look to the bishop? For his part he believed the nation was stupidly ruled, South as well as North, and nobody knew how to bring the pound up to par and in no time at all Eire would be as socialistic as Sweden.

Dick Baker said yes, he was feeling something he hadn't felt on his previous visits, something ominous. He was wondering how Ireland could possibly survive not only the awful inflation and taxes and unemployment in the South but also the awful civil war in the North. Ominous as well was the sad image he had carried away from the Ballybegs rectory, the lonely priest in his cluttered house, but he didn't mention this. He raised his glass of wine and saluted his expectation that tonight's play would cheer him up.

"Not this play," said Willie Hughes. "It's full of terrible things."

"Infanticide," Evelyn explained.

Next came roast duck in orange sauce—Nora had phoned ahead. Alexander Fermoyle, who had been mixing cider and wine on top of his gin, turned to Dick Baker and stated it was high time the Church got down to earth and fixed things at home instead of sending missionaries around the world preaching pie in the sky to poor folks. Mother Theresa—now, there was a nun for you, he declared, reversing himself. Went to India and worked with the dregs, she did. Went around to the rich and gathered up money and medicine and gave it to those funny-looking sods in Calcutta who worshiped cows. Meanwhile, what possible good was the Church doing in Ireland, worshiping wafers of bread in gloomy old churches and teaching nonsense in gloomy old schools? What possible good had prayers ever done anybody?

Agatha and Dick Baker exchanged a look that said they would like to throttle Alexander Fermoyle, his rapid-fire insistence was such a threat to their pleasure; indeed, in the bishop's case, it was a threat to digestion.

Agatha replied, "There's no telling how much good prayers do, Mr. Fermoyle. The human race is a family, and the prayers of any one of us induce God to look more kindly on all of us."

Alexander Fermoyle regarded her coldly. "I don't buy that."

"The Mystical Body," Evelyn explained.

He turned his cold stare on his daughter. "I don't buy it." He turned to Dick Baker. "Do you buy it, Bishop?"

Agatha held her breath. It was one of the fundamental questions separating agnostics from true believers these days.

"The Mystical Body?" said Dick Baker. "Sure, I buy it."

Agatha wanted to cheer.

* * *

They took two cabs to the theater. O'Connell Street was lined with men and women of the police force, many of them cradling bright blue riot helmets in their arms, some holding transparent bulletproof shields, all of them looking natty in their well-tailored black jackets and pants and skirts. They were chatting happily, leaning against the storefronts, obviously enjoying each other's company and the spotty sunshine. They far outnumbered the ragtag huddle of demonstrators in front of the post office.

"There you see the freedom boys at it again," declared Alexander Fermoyle from the front seat of Agatha's cab. "They say the Committee for One Ireland is planning a march to the British embassy, a bigger do than last night."

Workmen in front of McDonald's and Burger King were installing chain-link shields over the windows.

The cabs turned down Abbey Street and let the party out at the theater. They stood in the lobby, waiting for the house to open. They were joined for a minute by Jack Scully. His was a buffeting sort of presence that put everyone off balance. He hugged Evelyn's mother. He delivered a hard punch to Willie Hughes's stomach. He puzzled Agatha by kissing Janet on the mouth. He stepped up to Agatha, who saw that his face was heavily made up and his eyes were wider, brighter, happier than any sane person's eyes ought to be. He said, "I hope you like what we show you tonight, Miss McGee, it's a play about the shit we carry around with us from the past." He slipped from the room.

She turned to Janet. "What was that all about?"

"He's one of Evelyn's friends. He's in the play."

"Why are his eyes so strange?"

Willie Hughes answered her, "He's always excited before curtain time."

"He's on speed," Evelyn explained.

They were an audience of only twenty-four men and women scattered among two hundred seats. Word spread among them that because of the expected street riot at least one hundred fifty ticketholders had stayed home.

It was a buffeting sort of play, more absurdist and profane than Agatha cared for, and the effect of watching it in a near-empty theater was eerie. As close as Agatha could tell, it was a play about skeletons in a family closet, one generation falling into the ruts of past generations, the stupidity of human nature, the futility of human aspiration. The most broadly satirical figure was a priest. He was fat and effeminate, a total dud.

During intermission Agatha and Dick Baker remained in their seats.

"Well, Agatha?"

"Barely endurable."

"A sad portrait of the Church, wouldn't you say?"

"Dreadful. Is that the world's view these days?"

"The view of many, I'm afraid. A Church without life."

"Tell me why it is, Bishop, that after centuries of bridging the gap between God and man, the Church is having such a hard time of it now?"

"It's not an age of faith."

"The gap is a gulf. I sometimes have the awful feeling that not only is man pulling away from God, but God is giving up and pulling away from man."

Dick Baker cocked his head, intrigued. "That's very interesting."

"And probably heresy."

"Don't worry so much about heresy, Agatha. It's not a sin to think."

Janet came in from the lobby and sat down. They planned their departure in the morning. They would drive to Knob and the Plunketts. They would fly from Shannon the following noon. Dick Baker asked, "Could you be ready at ten, Agatha? I'll leave the car where it is tonight and come by cab again to pick you up."

"Ten will be none too early. I'm eager to get away. You will have discovered by now that I'm not the happiest of traveling companions. It must be my age."

"It's not age, Agatha. I'm more than ready to head home myself."

"It's not age at all," said Janet. "If I weren't leaving tomorrow, I'd break down and cry."

Alexander Fermoyle returned to his seat and announced that

he had gone out to see what was developing on O'Connell Street, and what was developing was quite a lot. The demonstration had enlarged to a thousand people or more. Paddy Creely's wife was nowhere in evidence, but there was a speaker on a platform urging everyone to march to the British embassy. The police were no longer taking their ease. They had put on their blue helmets and raised their bulletproof shields and were watching warily. "A nice little sidelight, I hope our reporters catch it, there was a small group of boys at the edge of the crowd throwing stones at the police and running from them. Little boys about ten." The lights dimmed, and Alexander Fermoyle settled low in his seat to resume the nap he had begun in Act I.

Near the end of the play Agatha heard the high-low blare of an ambulance racing down Abbey Street, a chilling counterpoint to the action on the stage. It pulled her just far enough out of the play to realize that what she was watching summed up what she had been thinking about Ireland. It was a nation trapped in the rutted ways of her past, the old handing down their griefs and grudges to the young. The siren did for the play what the gull had done for her sketch on Howth pier— gave it dimension—and the play, in turn, a scratch of ink, lent dimension to her impressions of Ireland, which were these: Every morning she had been reading in Alexander Fermoyle's newspaper of new killings, new killers, Protestant and Catholic, British loyalist and Irish rebel. She had seen pictures of the Belfast skinheads strutting in packs, hairless boys of about fourteen, with outrageous slogans lettered on their tattered jackets; they were Ulster's dark young hope. She had it straight from Janet that certain neighborhoods in Belfast were reduced to rubble, and soldiers on patrol pointed their guns at people for fun. Ireland excelled at turning grief into art, and for most of her life Agatha had been enthralled by the Troubles. She had been convinced by song and poem that Ireland's centuries of suffering were a great romance, and she had been curious about Ulster, where the Troubles continued. Now she was no longer curious. She was sad. Curiosity, she knew, was aroused by complexity. From a distance she had thought the Ulster problem was complex, a puzzle with a solution. But at close range she saw now that the warfare in the North was as simple as a feud, as insoluble as hate. There was nothing complex about a blood-spilling grudge. What was simpler than slashing open the human spirit and letting out the beast?

The party left the theater with trepidation, expecting violence, but there was no trouble on O'Connell Street. Rain had driven most of the demonstrators away. Only about two hundred of them remained under the pillars of the GPO, where they clustered shoulder to shoulder with the police force, trying to keep dry. A man was standing on a box gesturing, and as the cab passed by, Dick Baker rolled down his window so that he and Agatha could hear him. He was singing. The words were about the slaughter of the Creely family, and the melody was lilting.

"Not a pretty picture, Agatha. They all look so defeated."

"And wet."

"Are you leaving Dublin feeling the way I do, Agatha? Uneasy?"

She nodded. In her head she was hearing all the ballads of former wars blending into this brand-new ballad in front of the GPO, and this one blending into the ballads of wars to come.

The taxi idled at the O'Connell Bridge stoplight. Agatha and Dick Baker turned and looked out the rear window. From this distance the scene at the GPO was ethereal, hazed by rain, all color washed away, everything gray, including the neon lights reflecting off the police helmets. Clouds of mist rolled in from the sea, obscuring the tops of the pillars. At their base, the people seemed frozen in place, a small mass of humanity packed in a tight, immovable knot. The cab moved forward, and Agatha's vision was further obscured. Through the rain running down the glass, the scene became an abstract, colorless etching of a nation enduring—as well as prolonging—its timeless, crippling pain.

27

BUT THOSE WERE CITY IMPRESSIONS.

Refreshment came from the land. All across Ireland next day the golden sun fell like a blessing on mountains, rivers and fields. Its keen, pervasive light lent a fresh aspect to all the faces it touched—faces of little girls in short dresses jumping rope in the road, of mothers bicycling home from market and of wry old men standing in front of pubs. The sun cast deep shadows in the rusty ditches strung crookedly across valleys of peat, while on the hillsides it lit up hedgerows, haystacks, herds and herdsmen, illuminating the gorse all the way from Dublin to the Atlantic coast. When the yellow Mazda came to a stop at the brink of Knob Harbor and the three travelers got out to stretch, they found the ocean pressed perfectly flat—not a ripple or bubble as far as the eye could see.

Carrying their suitcases into the Plunketts' house for their last night abroad, they were welcomed by George, who was minding the place while Percy and Mary were gone to the grocer's to shop for dinner. George told them that whereas he was usually envious of travelers flying home to the States, there was only one place on earth for him when days got as grand as this, and that place was Knob, with the sea out the front door and the rosebush he'd been husbanding for years at the height of its color, and why didn't they go out and look for themselves. In the side yard, they admired the poppy-red roses for a minute or two; then Dick Baker and George Plunkett took up the Paddy Creely affair, and Janet and Agatha drifted away.

They crossed the road. Janet went down to the water's edge to gather seashells for Stephen while Agatha remained standing on the top of the three concrete steps leading down to the pier, thinking that this might very well be heaven, so clear and

275

warm was the air, so windless the ocean, so unlimited her vision. The line of the horizon was blue and clear, and what lay beyond it was equally clear. What lay beyond it was the principalship. She would take it. To be fair, however, she must warn the bishop, next time she had a moment alone with him, that he'd have an easier time closing St. Isidore's with someone else in charge, that as principal she'd be in a strong position to fight for its life. She was amazed that her course should be so clear, when for weeks it had been veiled in haze. Things throw light on things. After her Irish adventure she could hardly slink home to retirement. James in the National Gallery had pointed to Brueghel and said it was life; now she knew why it had excited him so. Once life has washed over you in tides of joy and anguish, how could you choose to be high and dry? Life was crushing as well as uplifting, but it made no sense to call it quits if the alternative was knitting your days away with Lillian.

She looked at Janet, who was following the curve of the beach and heading out along the stony breakwater. There were dazzling white stones among the gray. Shimmering in the sunshine, the white stones seemed lighter in weight than the gray, not so earthbound. Agatha wished she hadn't nearly a day's wait before she boarded her plane. Part of her enchantment with Ireland this afternoon, part of what made it heaven, she realized, was the prospect of leaving it. This evening and night could not pass too quickly. She longed to fly home and unlock her door and go in and see if her coffeemaker was burned out. She could hardly wait to unpack her suitcases and put on her old shoes and take up her old habits. Tomorrow night she would climb into the firm, wide bed she had been born in, a more comfortable bed by far than any she had slept in during the past nine nights, and when she was rested she'd get up and go to school and take charge. First she'd ask Janet to come in for a day and duplicate and send out a summer letter to the faculty, in which she would countermand a number of Sister Judith's ill-advised decrees with the same impunity she expected Sister Judith would soon be countermanding the pastoral decrees of Father Finn, a man too meek for his own good. Next, she'd order copies of the new edition of the "Baltimore

Cathechism," enough for every grade. Then she'd have a conference with her replacement, the agnostic and athletic Mrs. Brown, and arrange to take over the sixth grade each day during religion period.

Agatha left the pier and walked into the town. She strolled along High Street until she came to a shop with fruit and flowers in the window. The flowers, standing in small, water-filled jars, were snapdragons mixed with sprigs of fuchsia. She went in and bought a bunch for Mary Plunkett's table. Returning to the harbor, she saw Janet standing among the white and gray stones at the far point of the breakwater. She watched in amazement as Janet, with a shout and a flap of her arms, turned all the white stones into gulls and sent them flying out over the water.

At Shannon Airport the next day, after Dick Baker had been led away by C. H. Garvey for a drink and while Janet browsed in the duty-free gift shop, Agatha wandered into the restaurant and found Lillian sitting by herself, spreading out before her on the table, like solitaire, the picture postcards she had picked up at each stop.

"Agatha, where have you been all this time? Where were you in Dublin? I won't say I told you so, but you did the wrong thing by not buying the land portion. As a group, we got the best hotels and ate the best food and saw the top twenty sights in Dublin. Here, I'll show you."

Sitting across the table from her, Agatha was warmed by Lillian's windy warmth. She took up the postcards one by one as Lillian handed them to her, reviewing her route through Eire. It took her thirty-five minutes. "There," she said, "that's it. That's what I saw for my fourteen hundred dollars." She stacked the cards and snapped a rubber band around them. She had swallowed Ireland whole. "Now tell me, Agatha, what did you see for your seven hundred?"

Agatha smiled and looked away. She thought of James walking beside her on the Dun Laoghaire pier, pointing out landmarks. Of Dick Baker standing beside her on that foggy height in the Wicklows. Of Janet riding beside her on the upper deck of the bus to Howth. Of James on the Ha'penny Bridge, taming the gulls. She said to Lillian, "I saw the essence of the Emerald Isle."

Lillian nodded skeptically. "I bet you didn't have lobster. I had lobster in Cork."

Later, boarding the plane, Dick Baker came up beside Agatha and said, "I don't mean to push myself on you, Agatha, but don't you suppose Mrs. Kite would enjoy sitting in first class with Garvey?"

"You've had enough of his company, have you?"

"Not enough of yours."

The switch was arranged. Tucked into her window seat, Agatha took from her purse James's letter, and she handed it to Dick Baker. He was puzzled to see his name on the envelope.

She said, "It's from an Irish priest I met."

The 747 lifted them out over the sea and banked so that Agatha looked down on miles and miles of Irish coastline, green in the sunlight and dotted with gulls. Janet said to her from the seat behind, "I think I see Knob," and Agatha was craning her neck to see it herself when she heard a strange noise from Dick Baker, something between a hoot and a cry. She turned and saw that he was shaking with laughter as he folded the letter and slipped it into the envelope. Being too discreet to ask, she would never know what James had written.

> During our absence Lady Wellington
> gave birth to four kittens.

Meanwhile, in first class Lillian Kite removed the rubber band from her deck of postcards and began showing C. H. Garvey where they had been.

Mrs. Meers signed her name to a blank check and handed it to Randy along with a list of cosmetics.

"But, Mother, I'm already going to be late seeing the Noznicks, and the plane comes in at five. I can't go shopping for this stuff."

"Dayton's in Southdale is on your way," she said. "Find the Elizabeth Arden counter and give this list to the salesgirl. It won't take you ten minutes."

"But it's already noon and I've got to go out and pick up Stephen."

"Give me directions to the farm and I'll pick him up."

"No, I'm taking him to the city."

"What for? It's a monotonous drive for a four-year-old. I'll teach him croquet this afternoon."

"Nope, Janet said she wants to see him first thing. Besides, he'll get a kick out of the airport."

"Oh, Janet!" She uttered Janet's name in a manner that meant God's plan for families was seriously flawed when your daughter-in-law could not only take control of your son but could also take control of your grandson.

At the farm Randy was further delayed by a Denver sandwich with pickles and soup. It was nearly one o'clock when he set out for the city with Stephen. Most of the way they sang. Randy taught Stephen the words to "Blue Bayou," and they went over them several times, working out a pleasing harmony. Stephen hit the high notes the way Linda Ronstadt did.

Leaving the freeway on the Bloomington exit, Randy found the Meteor Drive-in, where tonight's double bill was *Born Erect* and *Star Wars*. He drove to the concession stand, turned his car around and backed up to the door, preparing to enter into the final phase of his plan. So far, Randy's hopes had come true with amazing precision. On Thursday morning the zoning notice had appeared in the *Staggerford Weekly,* and on Thursday evening the city council had voted five to one to allow the variance on River Street. On Friday Otto Kessler returned from Duluth for a second look at the Vaughn house, bringing with him a contractor who would oversee the remodeling. When Randy told them that the Noznicks would come down to a hundred thousand but no lower, Otto Kessler took his contractor down to the basement, where they admired the beams overhead and conferred in whispers. Returning to the main floor, Otto Kessler told Randy he'd go as high as ninety-nine five, but that was the absolute limit because he had never in his life paid a hundred thousand for a house, and now was a hell of a time to go against that precedent, what with the economy so shaky. Though Randy pleaded with him to come up with five hundred more dollars and meet the selling price, his pleas lacked conviction. Randy was not a pleader by nature, and furthermore he had an alternative plan in mind. He would induce the Noznicks to sell for ninety-nine five by offering them the Spooner vacuum. All that new yellow carpet.

Stephen followed Randy into the concession stand of the Meteor Drive-in. Except for the carpet color—tomato—it was just like the Starburst: videogames, snack bar, movie posters. Stephen said, "Can I play Pac-Man?" and Randy gave him three quarters. Randy searched for the Noznicks and found Norman in a tiny office behind the popcorn machine. He was wearing his white suit and dark glasses.

"Oh, hi," said Norman. "We still got a buyer?"

Randy showed him the purchase agreement, Otto Kessler's signature. "He's offering ninety-nine five."

"Nifty," said Norman. He stepped out of his office and called, "Eunice, it's the guy about the house."

Eunice emerged from the projection booth carrying a blowtorch. Her head was tied in a bandanna of blue checks. She wore a muscle shirt and pedal pushers. She joined her husband at the snack bar, where Randy spread out the three pages of the purchase agreement. "Ninety-nine five?" said Eunice. "No soap."

Norman said, "Now, Eunice, be reasonable."

"That's what I'm being. A hundred thou or nothing, it's a matter of pride with me."

"How much pride can you lose over a measly five hundred?"

"Listen, Norman, Victoria Vaughn was *my* aunt, not yours."

As before, Norman was silenced by the logic of this.

"I have the solution," said Randy. "Please come with me." He led them out the door, unlocked his trunk and stepped back for them to look in.

They looked in. They looked puzzled. After a few silent moments, Norman said, "These Fords got bigger trunks than I thought."

"What are you showing us?" said Eunice. "What's this big red can?"

"This is the Spooner Mark Four industrial vacuum, Mrs. Noznick. It's worth over nine hundred dollars. I'll give it to you free of charge if you'll come down to ninety-nine five."

"What would I want it for?"

"For your concession stands—all that great carpet."

She turned and went indoors, saying, "We got a cleaning service comes in."

Norman lingered at the trunk. "If I got a Ford, though, I think I'd go for a hatchback."

Stephen used up his quarters while Randy implored the Noznicks to come down five hundred dollars. Randy had to rush back and forth as he pleaded, for while Norman stood politely at the snack bar where the purchase agreement lay, Eunice was in the projection room forming elbows in a length of copper tubing with her blowtorch.

Stephen said, "Randy, let's go get Mom."

Randy wanted to weep. His deal was falling apart. He had scarcely enough time to get to the airport, let alone to reason further with the Noznicks or stop at Dayton's. His mother would fume when he came home with her blank check and no cosmetics. Her blank check! He took the blank check from his billfold and said to Norman, "What if I gave you a check for five hundred dollars, would you and Mrs. Noznick sign?"

"Eunice," Norman called, "what if the kid gives us five hundred dollars, would your pride be all right with that?"

She stepped out of the projection booth, shooting a blue flame. "You got five hundred dollars on you?"

He showed her his mother's blank check, holding it away from the fire.

"Okay," she said, "where do we sign?"

Randy filled out the blank check while they put their names to the purchase agreement.

Speeding to the airport and singing "Blue Bayou" with Stephen, Randy felt like Eugene Westerman, only smarter. Eugene Westerman might be a genius in sales, but what did he know about love? Stephen had not been eager to ride along to the city today, he preferred the farm, but Randy had given him no choice. If Janet wanted to see her son the minute she stepped off the plane, then Randy would arrange it. From now on Randy would sell himself to Janet through her weakness. Not a bad kid, Stephen. His voice was sensational on the high notes.